The Game Is *DEAD*

by
Rhonda Turpin

This book is a work of fiction. Names, characters, places and incidents are products of the author's imagination or are used fictitiously. Any resemblance to actual events or persons, living or dead, is entirely coincidental.

The Game is Dead

Author: Rhonda Turpin
Compiler: Bucks County Secretarial Service/E. Newhart
Editor: Eri-Ka Banks
Cover Design: Reigning Designs Intl.
First Trade Paperback Edition Printing July 2010
Printed in the United States of America

ISBN: 978-0-9821749-3-7

Dedication

This book is dedicated to my children, Cleo Turpin, and Johnetta Turpin, who's unconditional love allows me to venture forward, and to my grand-children, Shardaya, Ricky, Be-Be, and Nani. Know that anything is possible if you believe.

Acknowledgements

Thanks be to GOD, for continuously seeing me through this. To my ride-or-die chicks: my daughters, Tee and Nett. To the younger version of myself with a little more sense; Eri-Ka Banks, thank you. Thanks Due for the title and ongoing support. Trina Parker and Trina Harper, my true fam. And everyone that's caught up in the struggle and still managing to support my work.

"What lies behind us and what lies before us are tiny matters compared to what lies within us."

Oliver Wendell Holmes

BOOK ONE

Chapter One

As John Gray looked out at the water, the flickering reflection of the bouncing waves appeared to merge with the open, dense soft vapor representing the sky. The thermometer on the door of the top deck read eighty-six degrees, and it was only 11 a.m. The day was clearly going to be a scorcher.

John enjoyed the stillness of the moment. The water was a friend. The ocean was his solace. As he reflected backward, as he often did during the silence, he could not remember a time when he did not reap the rich benefits of sailing. It was calming. It was second nature.

John believed in rewarding himself with toys, as his wife Mary labeled them. What she really did not understand is that the things she called toys contributed to his wealth scale the way the size of a man's penis accentuated his manhood. La Fenetre was a big, long compliment. The name came to him while vacationing in Paris with Mary, on a two-week vacation. John knew Spanish fluently, but his French left a lot to be desired.

His wife saw a dress in the window of a shop called Le Chateau. The dress was short, black, and form fitting, with a large eight-inch burgundy piece of material hugging the front in a slanted position, stopping abruptly under the chest. John had to agree with Mary; the dress was different from anything that he'd seen in New York, where he often took her to shop. When Mary stepped to the clerk inside the store, she pointed toward the dress in the window, displayed on the mannequin.

"La Fenetre?" the clerk asked.

"Dress. There. I want dress," Mary said.

"La Fenetre?" the clerk asked again patiently. Her nametag on the upper left hand corner of her suit jacket pocket said "Anne." Anne did not get offended or snappy with an American customer at any time. Her pay was based on commission with a minimum weekly base salary. Commission was her strong point. She was one of the highest-ranking saleswomen in her district. Anne was no fool. Americans spent money.

Anne took Mary's arm lightly to guide her in the direction Mary was pointing.

"La Fenetre?" Anne asked again, mirroring Mary's actions.

"Yes. The dress," Mary said again.

"Qui, Mademoiselle," Anne said, while smoothly maneuvering Mary to a rack at the right end of the store, full of the dress that Mary saw in the window. Anne looked at Mary a full ten seconds with a critical eye, plucked a size ten from the rack, held it against the front of Mary's body and smiled, all in one swift motion.

"John, she even knows my size!" Mary said, pleased with Anne. "I'll take it," Mary said.

Anne was a true saleswoman. She was not about to let the American get away with purchasing only one dress.

"Uno momento," Anne said, while quickly swarming a nearby rack of clothes. With the smooth movement and deftness of a ballerina, she graced Mary with two tops from the same designer, and two pairs of coordinating slacks—one burgundy and one beige—to match the alternative color used in the tops. Anne was good.

"Qui?"

"Qui," Mary replied, giving Anna a big smile.

Seven hundred American dollars later, and one hundred forty dollars richer for Anne due to her twenty percent commission on all sales, Anne walked the couple to the door, carrying Mary's bags. Anne fanned the bags past the beeper detectors, flanking the doors to make sure she hadn't overlooked one.

Anne was happy and had a bigger paycheck coming. Mary was happy, and John was elated that he only had to frequent one store. Mary insisted on more than one occasion that John accompany her while shopping. He was not a fan of shopping for or with anyone, but Mary made such a big fuss whenever he went, and was so happy about it, he did it. Mary dressed him well, and kept his complete wardrobe up to speed.

They decided to have lunch at one of

the corner cafés where John saw the word again. "La Fenetre" was the name of the café. He thought, *Where have I seen that word*? as they entered the café. As they waited for their orders to arrive, he starred at the name of the café on the menus and on the centerpiece holding the napkins. He was curious of the meaning. He liked the ring of it. What could women's clothing shops have in common with a small café? John was about to receive his answer. Their waiter was bilingual. While sitting at the table, John got an eerie feeling like someone was watching him. That was impossible. He had never been to Paris. He knew no one there. He looked around quickly, and then caught himself. John ordered a double of alcohol. He was sure that he needed to relax a little. All work and no play had made him paranoid.

"What does La Fenetre mean?" John asked.

"It means window. The owner felt that the word window meant opening, growth, and opportunity, so she named the café that seventeen years ago. She is now on café number eight," the waiter said proudly.

John liked the sound of the name, and he liked the meaning that the waiter shared even more. He pulled out his cell phone and filed the name away. When he went shopping for his yacht, the waiter's twin assisted him. The salesman said that he had never been to Paris, and only spoke minimal French, but the mere site of him triggered the word and name John had filed in his phone and memory. Thus, the naming of his yacht, La Fenetre.

The vessel was a soft white that bordered between an off-white and ivory color. It had sharp, prow, graceful lines, and fast speed that made him smile, since the first time he took the boat for a tester. It was truly love at first sight. John had the salesman write up the purchase agreement, stating ten percent down, and short term financing. John instructed the salesman to fax the agreement to his personal accountant, Jay Levert, to finalize the deal.

"Jay, I have bought myself a present. The paperwork is on its way as we speak. Make it happen quickly," John said.

"What is the damage this time?" Jay asked.

"Two million, ten percent down, accelerated financing," John explained.

Jay exhaled loudly into the phone receiver. Jay had been referred to John over twenty years ago by the manager at Cleveland Trust Bank, where John did business. The manager spoke highly of Jay.

"He is brilliant, and thinks outside the box. Also you can really trust him. No one has ever lost money over the long haul with Jay," the manager advised.

Everything the manager said about Jay proved to be true. The man was a wizard when it came to making money work for a client, and teaching clients how to master paying themselves. He followed the strategy and principles of Warren Buffet, one of the smartest investors in the world. Jay Levert was also a Jew, and Jay was a black man. Jay was the only black Jew that John knew, which made him even more intriguing as a person. John had heard that Sammy Davis, Jr. was also a Jew, but was not sure if that was rumor or fact.

"I think you can stand it. But no more major purchases for the next ninety days," Jay preached.

John smiled as he hung up the cell phone. Jay managed John's spending as if each dollar was to be deducted from his salary. John liked that. Jay kept him in check and made him like being kept in check with his spending. Jay was priceless on John's team. John was quickly a multi-millionaire, both in assets and large expendable income.

La Fenetre was equipped for John to be able to live at sea for at least thirty days comfortably. Everything was electronically operated. He could set the speed and direction, and place La Fenetre on automatic sail, read a book, work out, or enjoy the company of friends and foe. John tried to avoid the company of foe, but it was not beyond him to hold a business session on La Fenetre. He was a self-made millionaire, with the help of Jay. John Gray became rich in an overnight true story of rags-to-riches that often depicted the American dream. The only difference between John and many other self-made millionaires that achieved success quickly was that his business was non-traditional. John was an import-export engineer. He exported mostly used, small denomination U.S. currency to Ecuador, in exchange for the plentiful, raw, popular product known as powder cocaine. Plenty of it. Kilos. Imported regularly into the U.S. without any cut on it. Yes. John Gray was a master of import and export. He was as crafty in disguising packages as John Travolta and Nicholas Cage were in the movie, *Face Off.*

Cocaine was not his only commodity. John was the supplier of electronic equipment to over twenty third-world countries. In his mind, the cocaine import business was his income subsidy, but in his heart, exporting electronics subsidized his cocaine business. One business washed the other. Electronic export was one hundred percent legitimate, fueled by the concept of supply and demand. John supplied underdeveloped countries like Ecuador, Tunisia, Zanzibar, and Gibraltar with electronics that were in their countries. Only the wealthy had direct and easy access to electronics through family members and friends that lived in the United States. The majority of people living in some of the countries that John serviced did not, except through one of his many distributors. Only a small percentage of citizens had radios, computers, televisions, microwaves, or refrigerators. Generators were also a hot item on John's list. In Ecuador, up to twelve families shared the pleasure of one television or radio. It was a direct contrast to American households, where many families had a few machines in every home. Computers and fax machines were sold at a three hundred to four hundred percent markup, at the least. Often up to ten times the cost of the item in the United States. John had recently sold a shipment of fax machines that had the capacity to copy and act as a telephone in one for one thousand dollars. His cost was eighty-eight dollars.

Exporting electronics as a business was non-competitive. Many businessmen assumed that all countries could order from the Internet, or call the stores directly. Those were the kinds of oversights that made his profession isolated. Americans took for granted the privilege of electronics. None of the large American-based electronic stores shipped out of the United States. John built strong partnerships with Staples, Office Max, Best Buy, and Office Depot, being able to buy large amounts of electronics at a wholesale discount rate. He also received deals and priority shipping on the cost of shipping containers. The large containers were used to ship merchandise by water all over the world.

John Gray built a lucrative, legitimate network of demand for electronics, and he furnished top quality supply. John's legitimate business venture gave him a net salary of more than hundred eighty thousand dollars a year, plus commission. His subsidy business netted more than twelve million annually. John made a nice, comfortable cushion for himself and his family. If he would have put one hundred percent of his energy into his export electronics business, John could have expanded, and easily made over a million dollars net profit within a year or two. What attracted John to the drug game was the fast turnover of cash, with minimal hours.

"Poppie, I need to attend rehab. I love this shit," John told Poppie often over drinks.

"We would share the bunk bed! I am like Amy Whitehouse—no rehab!" Poppie teased.

It had been over a decade ago since Poppie and him started their business venture.

"I'd like to have a talk with you over dinner. Can you come to my house?" Poppie Hernandez asked John one evening. Poppie was his electronics contact for Ecuador, and a small section of Peru, south of Ecuador. Poppie was plugged in. He worked in close proximity with the government. Poppie supplied the government of Ecuador with electronics for their homes, and also sold electronics to other citizens that could afford it. The government and aristocrats of the country of Ecuador and Peru held the wealth, while the other five percent were peasants, farmers, and drug dealers. The drug dealers also had plenty of wealth. Cocaine and its growth, sales, and cultivation were totally legal in Ecuador, as well as Peru. Poppie could sell a wheelchair to a young dancer in perfect health and convince them that it was a dire necessity for their daily lives. He was a master at sales manipulation.

The product that was being exported was the top of the line. The sale of it in America was through the roof, every time. The rich, white powder had small specks of crystal-like quality that appeared to glisten in the sun, like sparkling diamonds. One kilo easily took two full cuts on it, turning one into three, and marking up the profit three hundred percent. If you tasted the product, it had a medicine-like aftertaste. When John tested the quality, using a pharmaceutical tester, it was reading at ninety-nine percent cocaine. That was as pure as it got. Once it hit the United States, the chemists did wonders. They easily mixed the pure cocaine with manitol, B-12, and a few of the new kids on the block even used crystal meth as a form of cut. The game had changed tremendously over the last few decades. Twenty years ago, a supplier would be shot and killed for mixing pure cocaine with all the different substances. In the days that people like Richard Pryor smoked dope, they were smoking a high percentage of pure cocaine, and there were more snorters than smokers. With the increase of crack sales, the principles and morals had diminished to an amateur hustle. It no longer took charisma and a sharp business mind to get ahead and win in the drug game. The new kids on the block did not even know what the original rules were. John did not like it, and neither did Poppie. They were the original entrepreneurs. However, the money kept them chasing the dream.

Both men were firm believers of the cliché that said if it is not broke, don't try to fix it. They were paid. Why stress about the quality once it left their hands? Let the younger set worry about that, or the customer. Both men were not humanitarians, to say the least.

The capital of Ecuador was Quito. Poppie chose to live and do business in Guayaquil. Guayaquil is the largest city, and the commercial center of Ecuador. The city also had the largest chief port. Ecuador's main labor force was agriculture. The farmers believed in using old-fashioned farming equipment and methods. However, lawnmowers, weed whackers, and hedge clippers were at the top of the list of small farming equipment to be sold.

Guayaquil's landscape consisted of miles of coastal plain instead of mountains and forests. The plentiful rich soil made the growth of the coca shrub reach its fullest potential, measuring about twelve feet per plant. The rich green leaves on the small trees registered dollar signs. Poppie was a manager of the cultivation and manufacturing of the drug in its original form. The only persons in between the transaction of Poppie and John were the actual farm workers that were supervised by Poppie. Surprising to John, there were no real problems with drug abuse in Ecuador or Peru. The foreigners were as interested in the drug as Americans were in the art of filling a glass of water out of a faucet. It was common knowledge that the drug was a commodity in America. That was the peak of interest with citizens. They simply did not care. On the other hand, when someone discovered a mule from America, all hell broke loose.

"I want to be in the business!" Uncles, aunts, and even the elderly wanted to be a part of the trade. Cousins and other family members came out of the woodwork to join in, and possibly reap the benefits that came with the business. There was not a clear road out of poverty in the country. When a citizen was assigned a job and class, there were not a lot of avenues to travel to redeem themselves from poverty. The American dream was non-existent in a lot of the South American countries. Many citizens wanted to migrate to America in order to be able to realize the American dream, where a person could escalate their social and economic status with hard work, and other factors. Poppie's sister, Maria Linda, went to grade school to become a librarian. When she graduated, she became the librarian near their home. The pay was two hundred dollars a month. That was considered an extremely well paying job. Maria Linda had to work her way up to two hundred dollars a month, over a ten-year period. Two hundred dollars a month American money was the equivalent of two thousand a month income in Ecuador. That was the incentive to move to America. Many citizens loved their country and their culture. However, a housekeeper could go to America and make up to four hundred dollars a week with overtime and a second part-time job, send home two hundred dollars a month in American money to their family, which was equivalent to sending home two thousand dollars a month by Ecuador standards. That added up to twenty-four thousand dollars a year, and a very comfortable, wealthy family in Ecuador. Many would save and finance a family member's trip to America, pooling in to raise the children and other family members left behind. America was a clear out to poverty.

Ecuador got its name from the word Equator, that meant Ecuador in Spanish. The equator crossed the city that allowed John to serve the large farms that were sparsely flanked by forestland, as well as the coastal plains that had different technology needs.

Poppie worked for the government managing large haciendas that extended over two hundred acres. The practice was common where large farms were owned by the government. The government leased the farms to managers, receiving large monthly payments that included rent as well as a percentage of profit sharing. The government was not interested in the day-to-day events of the farms. Only a large bottom line mattered. Poppie safely cleared a few acres of forest that were connected to the acres that he managed, and cultivated his own coca leaves crop, manifesting his crop into U.S. currency subtly and quickly. The government acres grew potatoes and part sugar cane. Government officials did not visit the farms. That was the purpose of leasing to a manager. It was the same concept of having a landlord in the states. Once you signed your lease, you mailed in your rent in the U.S. In Ecuador, Poppie dropped off the rent payments every few months. The government's only involvement was to collect monies from the properties they owned throughout the country. Poppie was not unique in his actions. Many other managers cleared out forest areas and grew their own crops, to subsidize the small monthly payments that the government provided. Many homes did not have electricity or running water. One of the perks of running one of the government farms was that you were included in the small twenty-five percent of the country that had electricity. You also were provided free housing for yourself and your family. It worked out to be one of the more prominent jobs in the country. There was little or no turnover. Managers usually passed their positions on to other family members, once retirement age or sickness set in, and the family member would compensate by fully supporting the retired manager. Nursing homes and passing along the responsibility of caring for the elderly and the sick was strictly an American custom that was shunned in Ecuador and other South American countries. The purpose for having a large family with lots of children was to secure a citizen's old age and comfort level to premium.

John found that a lot of the customs and culture of foreigners were more agreeable with him than American customs.

Poppie trusted John from the beginning. It was something about him. John was considered an attractive looking man by both American and South American standards. His skin was a dark brown sepia color that appeared to glow as the sun darkened his skin hue regularly. His eyes were large and penetrating, with pupils that often danced and radiated a smile when he spoke. His nose and cheekbones were sharp and well defined, and a neat medium, textured well-groomed mustache accented his lips, like frosting on a cake. His voice was a deep baritone that contrasted with its soft tone. When he spoke, the depth mixed with the softness in his tone caused strangers to instantly follow the sound of this voice and sometimes stare a few seconds too long. His walk was smooth and firm. A warrior and a panther moving as one.

Where John was tall and agile, Poppie was short and stout. Poppie spoke loudly often, and was one of the most animated men John had ever encountered. John dressed conservatively and preppy; Poppie loved loud colors with lots of flowers, animals and scenery on his shirts and shorts. Where John came from, scenery and flowers were for pictures or nature, not on your clothes. In the public eye, Poppie was flirtatious, and even openly friendly. He was a true extrovert by nature. He was always eager to tell a good joke, and laugh heartily. His laugh would provoke a stranger to laugh, and not know what they were laughing about—

laughing purely at the sound of his laughter. John was also an extrovert, but he tended to wear a mask that made him appear unapproachable by strangers. When out of the public eye, John was as animated and silly in his words as actions.

Life was going good for both of the men. Whenever John took inventory of his life, he found himself feeling undeserving. He felt that something was in the making. It was not good. It lingered in the back of his mind, no matter how many times he tried to erase it. Mary and his son were the only two things in his life that remained constant and consistent in his thoughts. He couldn't imagine life without them, and hoped that he would never have to.

Whereas Poppie was the self-proclaimed ladies man, John was devoted to his wife.

"Man, did you see that dude's face when you gave him the price? I thought that he was going to piss on himself!" John said jokingly, while copying a customer's facial expression and actions.

"You are crazy!" Poppie said, laughing so hard he could barely get the words out.

Both men complimented each other in business, and felt the same way on most matters, with the exception being women, spoken or unspoken.

"John, if you ever see me with someone, whether it is my family or not, never talk around them. Why create witnesses, when they are not committing a crime? You set yourself up for trouble," Poppie warned.

The man was always sharing wisdom with

his American friend. However, John did not feel the same way. The money was never traded with the cargo pick-ups. The two men always chose to meet discretely, using both countries as their potential meeting place. Poppie liked to visit the Islands, and vacation at the same time. John would bring Mary along, and had no problem speaking in front of her. When John spoke openly once, in front of Poppie's wife, the man almost had a seizure. They did not agree about the treatment of women. Poppie's culture encouraged Latino women to be treated as second-class citizens, or submissive beings. If divorced or separated, John could not believe that women had no right to the children. That was unheard of in America. John treated Mary as his equal and his friend. Mary was the only person that he trusted whole-heartedly with his life.

After losing both his parents, and being estranged from his sisters and other immediate family members, Mary became his lifeline. Before meeting Mary, John did not believe in all the hype about having a soul mate. Mary made him a believer. As John looked on to the water and its peaceful waves, he remembered the last conversation he'd had with Mary and got an instant hard-on. As he gazed, just below the surface of the water, an image of something appeared. *What the hell?* There was a clear, distinct image of a body. It was a man. His clothes were torn and bloody. Half of the face was missing. The image was vivid in John's eyes, and just as quickly as it appeared, the body faded before his eyes. He blinked. The hairs stood up on his arms and the back of his neck. John was shook. He thought about calling Mary, but what would he say? *I think I just saw a ghost or something like that?* He placed the phone back down.

In Ecuador, the government controlled the telephone system. He was one of the few people that had access to phone service, as a result of Poppie requesting that they have an open, international line with unlimited minutes, and minimal monitoring. John and Poppie preferred that they have no monitoring, but that was unheard of. There was no such thing as a government line for a non-government employee.

Less than an hour ago, Mary called him, telling him explicitly all the things she wanted to do to him, and also added what she wanted him to do to her. As she was explaining every minute detail with clear sound effects that included slurping and moaning, John ejaculated in a towel, filling the small fold in the towel up as he held his penis tightly to keep from messing up his pants. He had a change of clothing on the boat. He kept a full wardrobe in his small bedroom below deck, but he did not wish to change. Instead of the apparition that he'd just seen that had his hand shaking, he tried to focus on Mary. She was at home, in the comfort of their air-conditioned bedroom, with her legs spread eagle, naked as the day she was born, with her trusted companion named "Prince." Prince was a dark brown dildo, made with the texture of real skin, eight inches long, and the same circumference as John's penis. They both agreed that Prince should be as close to the real thing as possible. Still, Prince could not perform all of the tricks that John could, but he worked out in a squeeze. John had been on the road for three weeks. During the last few days, Mary began to miss him. She always sensed when the trip was almost over, although he never talked of his whereabouts or return time over the telephone.

Because of John's extensive travel, phone sex was one of their favorite hobbies. Mary put all of the 1-900 phone sex women to shame. John asked himself many times, *Where in the world did she learn all that from?* Mary's daily contrasts in who she was, and what she could and would transform to at the tip of a hat in the wind was what kept John captivated with her. It was never a boring month with Mary.

Petroleum was the chief export product in Ecuador. Their main trading partner was the United States, therefore whenever La Fenetre pulled into the seaport, shining like a new penny and glistening in the sunlight, the boat blended right in along with its American owner. Ten percent of the population of Ecuador was black in skin color like John, therefore there was no shock to see a black person in any context.

The main route to Ecuador from Miami was via the Atlantic Ocean to where the Caribbean Sea joined, meandering through the Panama Canal to the Pacific Ocean, and hitting the dock at the Bay of Santa Elena. John sometimes stopped at several of the small honey holes near Lopez, that were in route to Ecuador. Poppie liked to mix it up sometimes. Lopez had a small population of a little over twenty thousand people. Poppie had a girlfriend stationed in Lopez that had been with him since her high school years. In fact, he had a separate family in Lopez. Maria had five children by him that were all teenagers. Poppie supported her and their children. Small towns like Lopez were reserved for the well-connected and well-known only. The circle of Americans that were able to dominate the export cocaine trade was extremely small. Many newcomers found out the hard way that if you did not get an invitation, you were going to come out short. The game was extremely territorial. Not much different from the States John realized. Many Americans were lucky if they were able to exit a town like Lopez with their lives. They were often stripped of their bartering cash as well as any other valuables with the robbers receiving the protection and tip-offs from the local police. They were a crew of bandits and gangsters that created their own set of rules. The government did not interfere with the actions of the citizens of cities like Lopez. The local police called the shots.

John was able to learn the culture of the area and surrounding countries from his legal dealings with the electronics business. Poppie also gave him heads up and the inside scoop, as well as a key to the surrounding cities. There were many lessons that only an insider could teach someone. Poppie wanted business to be full of longevity, so he held nothing back in the lessons he gave John.

"Mi Amigo!" So good to see you!" Poppie yelled, walking toward the boat where John appeared to be staring at an object that only he could see out on the horizon. His arrival time was noon. John was savoring the moment of peace and serenity. The port at the Bay of Santa Elena was not a place to daydream, once things got in motion. With the presence of Poppie, John knew things were about to get hectic. It was something about the business that John could never understand. He was not new to the game, however, once the action began to jump off, he started sweating. His heart began to beat fast. His senses became more alert. The men in Poppie's employ got right to the business at hand. Poppie marched to the compartment at the bottom of the boat, and like soldiers, the men began to follow his lead and command. Although he spoke in Spanish, John understood the orders. The men began to scramble around quickly, grabbing the large wooden crate full of electronics, and passing them to their left to the man standing two feet behind them waiting, creating and completing a human assembly line.

The line formed from the container of La Fenetre to the flatbed of a truck in waiting with driver in it and all. A second truck waited to unload Poppie's merchandise onto the boat. Poppie supervised, but traveled in his own vehicle, chaperoning the truck to and from the docking area. As smoothly as the dozen men loaded the cargo onto the truck, they mirrored their own movements when filling John's boat with large crates marked with Sugar and Potato labels. That was the crop that Poppie raised on the farm. No one looked twice at the work team. The workers did not have a clue, and did not care. They only cared about their monthly checks. If they worked extra hard, Poppie believed in bonuses. That was the only thing motivating their minds in the hot sun—a nice fat bonus before Independence Day. Independence Day was August 10th in Ecuador. It was a very big holiday. Poppie vowed bonuses for all men each year that topped last year's production and performance. The crew was due a nice bonus within the month.

The port was extremely busy. The country was preparing for Independence Day, along with the regular import traffic. As the business of switching cargo wound down, John and Poppie exchanged a few words. No matter how many times that John picked up the hot cargo, his mind never seemed to relax. His stomach was doing flip-flops while he watched. In the back of his mind, he always went over the idea of forgetting something. Today the thought of him forgetting something was even more prominent than ever before. He repeatedly went over the day's past events, as well as the transactions that were taking place before his eyes, filling up his boat. Everything appeared to be on point. Still, he couldn't shake the feeling. He concluded that it was the long distance sex he had with Mary that had him a little thrown off. Boy, was his Mary a freak!

John managed to get his mind out of the gutter, and focus on the project at hand. Everything went smooth. Poppie gave him a manly embrace, and within fifteen minutes following the loading of the cargo, John was off to sea. The two men believed in traveling with the flow of traffic. It was three o'clock, and the water traffic was busy, in both directions. John blended in well. La Fenetre was fifty-two feet in length, and twenty feet wide. John decided to shower and work out. He had a fifteen by eighteen foot room built with a full weight lifting machine, sauna, rowing machine, and Jacuzzi. Mary loved the full Jacuzzi. It was built to accommodate a party of six. John did a vigorous workout, and then jumped in the shower, changed clothes, and decided to read the newspaper. He kept up with world events. *USA, Today* and the *Wall Street Journal* kept him abreast of world events. Mary watched CNN every morning, and read *Newsweek* weekly, so if there was anything he missed, she didn't hesitate to tell him in.

The day progressed. The sun set as he passed through the Panama Canal. The canal was an important commercial and military waterway. Although Panama and the United States had a treaty, more than ninety-five percent of the seven thousand employees that governed the canal were Panamanians. The canal had never posed a threat to the businesses John ran. They were on the lookout for terrorists and people that chose to start war. There was a distinct profile that security looked for in the canal. John did not fit the profile. John felt relaxed. He missed his wife. He was gone ten to twenty days of each month during nine months out of the year. The winter was the only time that he cut the number of trips down. South America was not the problem. The United States was. During hurricane season in Miami, he was delayed from being able to enter during one year for more than two weeks. He ended up having to camp out in the Bahamas, and then the ultimate catastrophe happened. The storm moved southward, toward the Bahamas with less than a two-hour notice. John barely got out alive. His boat that he owned before La Fenetre was damaged and destroyed beyond repair. That was the last trip that he made during adverse seasons. Mary loved having him home most of the month during the winter in Cleveland, Ohio. Usually, immediately after hurricane season ended, the two of them would spend the first three weeks of the month of November at their Key West, Florida home. Mary found and decorated the condo herself years ago. It was her favorite home, out of all three that they owned.

As he passed the Islands, John decided to put his boat on automatic sail. Where the best time to travel from Ecuador was during rush hour water traffic, approaching the Florida Bay area posed a problem in broad daylight. The best time to approach the dock in his boat John determined from years of experience was immediately after dark. Too late would pose a security problem, and too early may get one arrested, with the illegal cargo he was carrying. He knew how to space and time his arrival.

As he got closer to the States, thoughts of seeing Mary soon began to cause him some anxiety. Mary had that effect on him, even after all the years they had been together. As the sky turned into a clear dark sheet, with twinkling stars, a beautiful bird perched itself on the side of the rail. John noticed the bird, and at the same time he didn't. The eye contact with the bird was brief. In his mind, he questioned why a bird would be out traveling alone in the dark, and perched on the side of La Fenetre. However, the thought did not last. It was a mere second in his mind. A mere thought. He saw the bird, and then he didn't. He began to focus on getting docked and home. Still, something wasn't right. John knew it, but could not put his finger on it. Also he could not let go of the mental image of whatever that was that he saw in the water.

John decided to wait until around 1 a.m. to make his entrance. He decided to wait until it was closer to the time of arrival before putting together his unloading crew. John did not let anyone ever know his arrival or departure time. That was the quickest way to become a victim. Usually, one of the workers would mention it to his wife or girlfriend, or other family member, they would in turn mention it to someone, and before a person knew it, the arrival time and place was public knowledge, and he was fair game. Game for the crooks, police, and the alphabet boys that included the FBI, DEA, and whoever else wanted to get involved, including the ATF. John never shared that information with Mary. He always gave her an approximate date and time, but warned her that it was subject to change.

It was only 11 p.m. John cut on the 11 o'clock news to see what was going on in the city. While sitting below deck, watching the small thirteen-inch TV, on the security screen he detected movement that was relatively close to his boat. This time of night he was too close for comfort. He quickly went to the screens, enlarged the object, and attempted to make out its owner. It was difficult. The person was using a scrambler. That was not good news. Only advanced operations owned and operated scramblers attached to throw off amateur radar detectors. There was no such thing as an unscrambler. The scrambler represented power. John suddenly began to perspire, remembering his cargo. He sprinted to the deck to look across the horizon of the water, and determine who and what was approaching his boat at a rapid pace. He saw the culprit. It was heading toward him with speed. He was able to make out the words at the same instant that the passengers on the boat made him. It was the U.S. Coastguard. Just as he was about to run downstairs to make sure that his cargo was secure, the Coastguard boat flashed a bright light on him.

"Do not move. We are approaching," someone from the Coastguard boat yelled out of a bullhorn. John heard himself say, "Ah, shit," out loud. He was not a man that usually practiced any type of profanity in a vertical position, but this was an exception.

"Do not exit the deck!" the same voice yelled out over the water, causing a slight echo in the darkness of the night.

Before John knew it, the Coastguard boat was upon him. The crew quickly connected themselves to his boat, and boarded as if they were on land boarding a train. It appeared to be hundreds of them. The number was more like twenty, but at the rate of speed that they were moving around, John was not able to keep up. One man quickly ran to the stern. He was dressed down. His outfit said DEA or other federal police officer. When he felt John looking over at him, he stopped to speak.

"Good evening, Mr. Gray," he said, with a sly grin.

"Do I know you?" John asked. *How did they know his name? Were they coming directly for him?* That is what he wondered at that moment. Two other Coastguard officers began to frisk him to make sure that he did not have any weapons.

"If you could kindly face the water,

and keep your eyes straight," one of his captives told him.

"Am I under arrest?" John asked.

"I am not at liberty to answer that. Just remain quiet, and do as you're told, Sir," the man said. John did.

Most men in his position would be trembling and worried about going to jail and being arrested. He was dirty. Very dirty. As dirty as he'd ever been in his life. He put a new number to the record *Riding Dirty* by Camillionaire and Crazy Bone. He was riding filthy. He had over nine hundred and fifty kilos of pure cocaine in a concealed container and compartment under his boat. The Coastguard went right to it. It was triple locked. Air tight, water tight, and secured by a triple combination. How the hell did they run up to the deck less than two minutes later with a brick? How did they get the combinations and all three locks opened that quick? Instead of worrying about his plight, John's mind was racing. The attack was not an ordinary bust. He had been set up. Who the hell did that? *Was it Poppie?* he thought. No. It could not be. Poppie had as much invested as he did. The officer's words snapped him out of his trance.

"Sir, put your hands behind your back. You are under arrest. You have the right to remain silent..." the DEA officer proffered. John did not pay attention to the words. None of the moves made against him were making any sense.

"You drive the boat in. We are going to

take Mr. gray into custody," the DEA officer that read John his rights said to his partner, who was at the control panel of the boat, seeming as if he were in awe like a video game junkie at a video arcade entrance. It was going to be a long night. It was not until John assumed that position that he hated most—hands clasped behind his back, handcuffs twisting in the opposite direction of his wrists, and two strangers firmly grabbing his arms, flanking him on each side—did he start to think about his plight. Over nine hundred and fifty kilos! Damn. Would any judge grant him a bond? John had been to prison before. He had served eighteen months in state prison for having an eighth of a kilo of powder that weighed up at four-and-one-half ounces. Lucky for him it was soft. Cocaine that was cooked into crack carried a much harder sentence.

When a person is out there stacking one hundred dollar bills, and getting paid, no one plans to get caught. That is the problem.

The Coastguard boat did not pull off right away. John sat in handcuffs and watched the search team destroy his baby. They were ripping out panels, and under the deck below smashing glass. Each time they hit the surface of his boat with their tool, he flinched. He knew that they were below trashing his property. He felt disrespected and defiled. His feeling was the same as if one of them had waved their dirty dicks in his face without notice. They had the dope. The necessity to trash his boat and all of his belongings was fulfilling a deeper urge. Most of the search teams despised drug dealers. They knew that the drug game paid more in a month than they would gross in a few years. It was not a profession that was looked kindly on.

As he stared, he felt part of his life being ripped apart before his eyes. John Gray felt tired. The magnitude of the journey in front of him forced him to remember the pain of being incarcerated that was once behind him. It once seemed a part of his past, now it was under the mask on his face, waiting to surface and merge the past with his future. It was an eerie feeling. Like time standing still.

The feeling of betrayal was stronger than his feelings of being violated. John did not have a clue who had set him up. His mind kept trying to focus on a name and face. John refused to allow it to focus. He was in pure denial. He knew that if he allowed the naked face to surface, he may lose it, and he needed to hold it together. Hold it together. He couldn't give in to his thoughts just yet. Maybe when he was alone, but not now. John was not a crying man, or much of a praying man. However, at the moment, he felt like doing both. His shoulders slumped over in defeat. He was breathless and speechless. Lucky for him the agents did not request him to answer any questions. His voice was locked in his throat.

If John would have been paying attention to the details, he would have noticed the large falcon that was still posted up on the edge of his boat, watching everything like an interested spectator at the World Series. He did not notice. At approximately 1 a.m., instead of John Gray arriving at the dock to unload his shipment and calling his wife Mary to meet him, he was being checked into Miami Federal Detention Center, located in downtown Miami, overlooking Biscayne Bay. The charge was possession of nine hundred and fifty-seven kilos of cocaine, with intention to distribute. He was booked solid.

BOOK TWO

Chapter Two

John starred at the glaze of ice on parts of the window, with the snow forming a perfect frame with the window. There was a tree full of branches barely touching the side of the hotel room. The Marriott Suite was his favorite hotel to spend time at away from home. The room always came with stove, refrigerator, set of cookware, dishware, fireplace and kitchen nook. He liked the idea of taking a date to the suite, being able to cook a gourmet dinner for her, screw her brains out, and not have to expose her to his apartment. His apartment was reserved for his steady. He did not have a steady girlfriend at this time, and there was not one on the horizon. His single state of playerism had been going on for four years.

John's quest for the night was named Becky. Becky was not the type of girl that you took home to Momma. She was the type of girl that would fit perfectly into Hugh Heffner's playboy mansion stable. Becky was tall, fair-skinned, and thin, with natural blonde hair, deep blue eyes, and full sensuous lips. Her nose and mouth displayed aristocracy. Standing 5'9", with Jessica Simpson look-alike legs, it was hard not to look at her when she walked past. Becky believed in flaunting her assets. She never wore pants, and every skirt she owned peaked the imagination to the fullest. She did not mind at all giving someone a peek. Becky gave exhibitionism a new existence.

Becky was a full time graduate student at Case Western Reserve University. On campus, the favorite pastime for male students and secretly for professors was to watch the bottom of Becky's naked butt cheeks. Her thong was invisible and worn for decoration purposes only.

The first time John noticed her was at the Social Sciences Library at the campus of Case Western Reserve University. They both were undergrad students. John attended Cleveland State University, studying Architectural Engineering. As a CSU student, he was openly allowed to use the CWRU library. The library was connected online with CSU. With his student I.D., the librarian would swipe his card, and his student information would appear on the screen at CWRU. Case Western had a vast selection of books, and several libraries in different buildings with many floors for each science taught there.

John was not a flirt. He did not openly

come on to women. However, if they openly came on to him, John obliged their advances, if there was an attraction. He was all man, and enjoyed the variety that college life afforded him.

"Do you mind if I sit here?" Becky asked. Becky had been watching him out of her peripheral vision. The tall dark warrior excited her. She made sure she gave him a full view of her ass. No man could resist her unless he was gay in her mind. She introduced herself. His name was John. John was elated that he was sitting down. The six-foot long, three-foot wide wooden table veiled his enormous, stiff hard-on. The table saved him a lot of embarrassment. It was a library after all. There were families signing out books with their children present, and also elderly.

"Do you attend here?" Becky asked.

"No. I'm at CSU. I like your library better though."

"It is awesome, isn't it?"

"Yep," John answered. He tried to get back to his studies afterward. He was trying to grasp the complex architectural design of the Rockefeller Center that was built between 1929 and 1940. The Center was a group of fourteen skyscrapers that were first criticized, but now used as a model for large urban developments. John's final assignment was to create a smaller, similar blueprint and present it to the class. John was beginning to get engrossed in his studies. The silence and serene atmosphere inspired his thoughts. That is why he chose to study at the library, instead of at home with all of the interruptions, such as the telephone.

"Sluuuuuiiiiiirrrrrrppppp!"

What the hell? he thought.

Becky's nasty butt was slurping on a multi-colored candy sucker, like she had never had a piece of candy in her entire life. John looked at her in disgust. How dense could she be? In a library? For God's sake. With children and elderly people in the building openly walking around. Before he could tell her to cut it out, his eyes were drawn to her lizard-like tongue. The freak was wiggling the tip of her tongue at a rapid speed. John instantly became glued to her tongue. He could not turn his eyes away if he wanted to. He did not. The woman had no shame. John's body betrayed him. His face showed anger. His member wanted to transform into the sucker. He was turned on drastically. He was heated. Becky locked eyes with John, and deep throated the sucker. John was a dark-complexioned man. If he could have turned beet red, he would have. His forehead and upper lip broke out into a sweat as he watched Becky tease him while her lips made love to the sucker.

"Want some?" Becky asked and teased. The question was loaded.

"Come on. Let's go," he ordered.

They never made it to a bed. Before he could start his car, in the parking lot, Becky was on the driver's side of the car, firmly unzipping his pants, and groping at his member at the same time. The woman had moves like an octopus. Her hands were all over him. Between his legs, on his chest, and rubbing him firmly.

"Hold up. Let me unfasten my pants, Shortie," he said. John's large thick penis was swollen with excitement.

"Do you have a condom?" he asked. His question fell on deaf ears. Becky ignored him. She was engrossed in the explicit act that she was committing on his body. John did not want to catch anything, but even more so, he did not want to stain his pants or his car seat. Becky took all eight inches into her mouth without hesitation.

"Ahhhh," he moaned.

She wasted no time getting him off. She gripped him with her jaws the same way she gripped that sucker in the library, like a hungry newborn baby grips their nipple when their feeding is late. John tried to outlast her. It was more than an effort. He tried to concentrate on something else. That usually worked in other instances. When he flashed his mind to the visual of her licking the sucker in the library, he came instantly. He did not have to worry about his pants or the car. Becky did not remove him from inside her mouth until every drop was swallowed and he'd been licked clean.

John began to gain composure. He stuck his penis back in his pants, and zipped them up. After that, the few seconds following their sexual encounter was awkward. He didn't know what to say to her. The awkwardness only lasted for a minute. Becky was in her seat on the passenger's side, hiking her skirt up to her waist. *What is this girl doing now?* John thought, with amusement. Becky was a real number. Without looking at him, she pulled her red-laced thong off and discarded it on the floor of his car, like an empty candy wrapper. Becky swiveled her body around to face him, planting her back firmly against the passenger door. She smoothly placed her right leg against the dashboard, planting her four-inch red and black stiletto on his steering wheel. Her left leg covered the back of the front seat, barely missing the back of his head. When he looked down at her, all he could see was her open, exposed vagina, with her swollen clit sitting at the forefront. Before he could make any type of comment, Becky Freak (that had to be her last name) started rubbing her clit seductively. John was glad. He welcomed her self-serving sexual independence. He did not give head on the first date, although he loved to receive it. She was engrossed in touching and pleasing herself, as if he wasn't there. He got a hard-on all over again. His pants were suddenly confining. He unzipped his crotch, releasing his manhood, again. He was to discover that being around Becky required him to have easy access to his crotch at all times.

John watched her make love to her own body with no inhibition. Her left hand played inside her vagina, while her right hand vigorously rubbed her clit. He wanted to help out. When he reached over to touch her, she managed to stop rubbing her clit long enough to smack his hand. She did not want to be interrupted. She wanted him only to watch. Becky added a new dimension to John's definition of a voyeur. Before meeting Becky, he did not realize that he possessed such a high level of voyeurism. He had never touched himself in front of anyone. He was always alone when he had to tend to those types of needs. It was awkward for the first few seconds, but as he watched Becky, he stroked himself in rhythm with her. It was easy to get into the erotica.

"I want to suck you again. I want to feel you inside my warm mouth," she moaned while making sucking noises and licking her lips. She kept talking dirty to him, while he watched her intently. Within moments, they both came, separately but together. That was John's first introduction to Becky.

* * * * * *

At the time he met Becky he did have a steady girlfriend. Her name was Mary Turpin. Mary was the contrast of Becky. Mary was brown-skinned with a smooth, creamy caramel complexion. Where Becky was model thin, Mary had an hourglass figure. Her hips and butt were full and thick, supported by a tiny waist accenting her large full breasts. She was 5'3", and big-boned all over. She had curves in all the right places.

Janice was John's oldest sister. There was a six-year difference between them. When John's mother died of lung cancer, John was only twelve years old. Janice was eighteen. She volunteered to take full responsibility of him and his other sibling, June, who was fourteen years old at the time. The option that they had was for him and June to be placed in foster care. No one in their family stepped up to the plate once his mother died, although there were distant relatives living around the Cleveland area. His mother had not been close to them. John and his sisters did not really know them. His mother was also named Mary.

During the twelve years of his life that he knew her, she had single-handedly raised her three children. Mary was a proud woman. She worked full time as a domestic worker, cleaning houses of wealthy white families that lived throughout the Cleveland East and West suburbs, for cash payments. She was paid well, considering the era and the fact that she was uneducated and unskilled. Mary was very skilled in the domestic arena. Her week was full. Some of her customers were only half-day jobs. On these days she scheduled the other half day near or on the same bus line of her previous client to lessen travel time. Mary was paid from twenty to fifty dollars for a half-day of work, and extra for laundry, ironing, or cooking. Four to five hundred dollars cash was good pay for a second generation young migrant from the south, when minimum wage was only a dollar and twenty cents an hour. Her clients were doctors, lawyers, and business owners. On Friday, she always came home with some type of gifts for her children. John and his sisters had a rich collection of books, ranging from Louisa May Alcott's *Little Women*, to John Steinbeck's

Of Mice and Men. They also owned a full set of Encyclopedia Britannica that was upgraded yearly. When the children of the families that his mother worked for bought new ones for their children, the Grays would receive upgrades. Atlas, and books feature famous works of art were also a few of the gifts given to her children.

It was at six years old, while studying the intricate Roman designs used at the Vatican and throughout Rome, John decided he wanted to be an architect. He did not know what the job entailed, but was infatuated with building and church designs throughout history.

Because Mary was uneducated, she preached regularly about the importance of education. She pushed all three of her children toward pursing education. Sometimes she even shoved.

"Education is the key out of poverty," she pounded into their heads regularly. She did not have time to pursue an education. She explained to her children that she scrubbed floors and did laundry so that they would not have to.

June was lazy. She hated to read or apply herself. She said she wanted to be a *Solid Gold* dancer when she grew up. Janice complained that their mother gave them hand-me-downs and never bought them anything new. She rebelled against her mother by refusing to touch the books, stereo, or any other gifts they were given. If she could have refused the clothing, she would have, but there was nothing else for her to wear. John felt his sister's complaining was unwarranted. Most of the shoes and clothing were barely worn, or still new with the price tags still attached. He was the one that held on to every word his mother said about getting educated. He read non-stop. No one in his family was surprised when he announced at ten years old that he would be going to college. Mary was very proud of her son.

"He will be our first generation college graduate in our family," she boasted to anyone that would listen. When she died, John was the one who grieved hardest for his mother. Six years later, when he began his freshman year, his mother was his silent inspiration. He knew that wherever she was, she would be pleased if she were looking down on him.

John did not know his father. Whenever he questioned his mother, she was very vague about his name and physical description. In fact, that was one of the few times in their relationship that Mary got sudden selective amnesia. Ordinarily, her memory was sharp.

Janice had met her father, although he was not a part of her life. He was Mary's first love, and the first man to break her heart. June and John had a different father. From picking up bits and pieces from Mary reluctantly, John and June both concluded that their father was a married man. There was a strong void in John's life many times, from not having a male role model. However, he never shared the void with his mother, and always made her feel that it did not matter, and that she was all he ever needed. She bought into it.

Directly out of high school, immediately following their mother's death, Janice landed a job at the University Hospital of Cleveland. She worked with the children, at the Rainbow Babies and Children building that was talked about for its progress in research with children's diseases all over the world. Janice did not have a social life. Her job and raising her siblings was her entire life. She volunteered to work lots of double shifts, and enjoyed living vicariously through the lives of the doctors and nurses that worked the floor with her. When she wasn't working, she was at home cooking, cleaning, or assisting John and June with their homework or other tasks. After abruptly losing his mother, John became extremely protective of both his sisters, although he was younger than them both. He was harboring deep-seated abandonment issues that he had repressed. During the years following his mother's death, he had nightmares of also losing his sisters, and being left in the world alone. He was sure not to give his sister Janice any problems, and be helpful around the house. He was the man of the house. He held down his territory like Mohammad Ali held down the champ title. Janice could not date in peace. Any suitor that had to go through him did not choose to return. Janice was a package deal. Her sister and brother came with the deal. It was too much for men her age. John was glad.

At fourteen years old, he voluntarily took over the responsibility of paying the thirty dollar a month light bill at their house from his regular paper route. Janice was elated. That gave her a few extra dollars to be able to put away, or spend on herself. They were struggling from check to check, but had everything they needed.

On one of her days off, John walked into the living room from a regular trip to the grocery store for Janice, to find her sitting on the couch, talking to a pretty black female. The girl appeared to be more John's age instead of Janice's. John was eighteen. Janice seldom had company. John did not realize he was staring until Janice said something to him.

"Boy. Where is your manners? Mary, this is my brother John. John, this is Mary," Janice introduced them.

"Oh, hi," John said, going straight to the kitchen. The aroma in the place signaled spaghetti or lasagna. Both were one of John's favorites.

"Is the food done yet?" he asked anxiously.

"Yeah. It's lasagna, garlic bread, and tossed salad. Make sure you wash your hands, boy," Janice warned.

His family was no longer in the habit of sitting down at a set time to dinner. His mother had insisted that dinner be served at 6:30 p.m., six days a week, with Sundays being early, and that they ate together. No excuses. John enjoyed eating whenever he pleased. Janice worked double shifts often, but always prepared dinner in advance. June was out of high school, and working at a clothing store called Petries. She did not get off work until 8 p.m. All three of them had blossomed into productive adults. They chose to stay together because the small house was paid for. Mary had a mortgage of four hundred dollars a month, and also mortgage insurance. At her death, the small mortgage amount left was paid off. Her insurance policy was minimal. After the mortgage base paid off the balance part for the funeral, there was ten thousand dollars a piece left to her children. Janice was the executor. Janice took her money and bought her a small Dodge Colt that was nearly new. She placed her siblings' money into a savings account, and had not touched it except for the few times that something broke down in the house. Once she needed to buy a hot water tank and have someone install it, and the second time the washing machine broke, and she had to purchase a new one. Because she washed all of their clothes, she did not feel that June or John would mind once they got of age to collect and spend their own money. If they did care, so be it. The three-bedroom house gave each one of them their privacy and an attachment to the only parent that they had once known.

Mary began to come to visit often. Janice always ordered John to escort Mary home. She lived a ten-minute walk from their house. Mary worked with Janice at the hospital. She shared with John that she had no aspirations to go to college, or have a lot of money. Mary only wanted a simple life. A small piece of the American pie. She wanted what most young girls base their daydreams on—a husband, two children, a small house—she did not say a white picket fence, but John held that image in his head while he listened to her—and regular church attendance from her family, especially on Sundays. Mary's father was the associate pastor at Greater Missionary Baptist Church. Pastor Turpin preached the sermon every third Sunday of the month. Mary was raised in the church. John found himself becoming absorbed in her innocence, and was anxious to teach her about the world. He was also anxious to get into her pants. John gave Mary her first kiss, her first embrace, and used a small bit of trickery to take her virginity. He explained to her that he had a medical problem, and that if he did not ejaculate soon, it would cause other bigger health problems. He even had a friend of his that was in medical school and had a doctor for a father draw up his diagnosis, and also a hint of the cure.

Mary was a true trooper. Her love for him caused her to submit herself fully, going against her beliefs and teachings. She believed that good girls waited until they were married. She also believed in loyalty. How could she allow her man to get the term "blue balls?" That was equally unacceptable. She chose to help him. Mary was as sweet as she looked and acted. John was truly blessed to have found her. To make sure that she would belong to him only, he introduced Mary to the joy of receiving oral sex. The first time he brought her body to orgasm, Mary called his name so loud in the hotel that they were at he was sure that the adjoining room would notify hotel security. After the first time Mary lost her shyness about asking for what she wanted from him.

"Um, John, can you do the thing to me, you know that drives me crazy? I am feeling that way," she purred.

John knew that he was being manipulated by that time. Her request always came with a slip of her hand on his member, or a little too much thigh exposed. Mary was working him. He knew it, and he loved it.

John took her everywhere. The movies, plays, the theatre, the museums, R&B concerts, rock concerts, and even rap concerts to see *Scarface* and *Public Enemy*. Her favor artist was Prince. Of course her parents did not have a clue. Almost everywhere he took her, Mary became part of the entertainment. He licked her on the sink tops in bathrooms that they converted into unisex that wasn't. He sucked her in broom closets at concerts with employees guarding the closets for a small fee, and he tasted her for dessert each time he took her out to dinner. His head was reserved for her. John did not allow her to reciprocate. He had freaks lined up that were professionals, and anxious. His favorite was Becky. She always swallowed every drop like it was the finest drink. She really had skills. In fact, no other woman could touch her in that department. Becky was aware that John was sleeping with Mary. Mary was not aware of Becky or any of the other women whose body John frequented. She would have been devastated.

Mary did not crowd him. She was the perfect lady. She sat at home until he called her. She did not frequent bars or clubs. There was a very slight chance of ever running into her during an outing with one of his quests.

Mary's parents treated him with a cool, polite indifference. When he came into the picture, they were not happy. They felt that he was a nice man, but her parents had already chosen a suitor for Mary from the church. Pastor had promised Mary's hand in marriage to Reverend Henry's son, Henry, Jr. It was an arrangement that the parents talked about often. They had not discussed it with Henry, Jr. or Mary. Now it was too late. They witnessed their daughter slowly fall in love head over heels with John Gray. Both parents realized that they should have persuaded Henry and Mary to date instead of consistently prolonging it, protecting them both from growing up too soon. Now it was too late. Finally, Pastor Turpin could wait no longer.

"What are your intentions concerning my daughter, young man?" Pastor asked.

Mary and John had been dating regularly over a year. John entered his sophomore year of college. He was not thinking about marrying anyone, although he did adore Mary.

"My intentions are to finish college, get a job, and then think about marriage when I can financially support a family, Sir," John answered.

Although the sour look on the pastor's face showed that he wasn't entirely pleased with John's answer, he had to respect it. Mary shared with them John's report card, and Pastor Turpin was secretly proud that the young man was an A student, and second in his class. He had never been to college, nor had anyone in his family. He was the oldest of nine sisters and brothers. They were all hard working, god fearing individuals, although half of them did not attend church. He left his parents in Vicksburg, Mississippi, where they lived on the same farm that he and his siblings were raised on. His father manned the same fruit and vegetable stand that had fed and supported all nine children, sending them north with relatives one by one. His parents chose to stay in the south. He visited at least twice a year with his family, and always worked the farm while he was there. His wife Beatrice sold dinners and catered bar mitzvahs for clients. She did not advertise. By word of mouth, through the years she had established a group of regular customers. She also facilitated the fish fry every Friday, and sold dinners throughout the month as fund-raisers for the church. The couple grew up as neighbors in the south, were childhood friends, migrated to the north together, got married and were friends as well as lovers ever since. The pastor did not believe in unchaperoned dating, but found out he had to let go, and go with the times. Times were drastically changing, right before his eyes.

Pastor thought that John was respectable. That changed overnight. On John's twenty-first birthday, Mary announced to him that she was pregnant. They had sex almost every day. The last few times it was his carelessness that told her he didn't need a rubber, and that he would pull it out before he came. John wanted to feel Mary's softness without a rubber. He loved the way she smelled, and the way she tasted. It cost him, and her.

John knew that her father would demand a shotgun wedding. He was determined that he was not about to be forced into marriage by anyone. Mary's parents felt differently. They felt that the couple should be married immediately, to avoid bringing shame to the family and the church. Mary was torn. However, she did not place any type of pressure on John. If he chose not to marry her, she would not force him.

"I'll get us an apartment. I know you don't believe in abortion," John said.

Mary was crushed, but held her feelings from John and her family. That was not the answer she expected.

John rented a one-bedroom apartment, between Mary's parents' house and his home. It was five minutes travel time to either of the houses. John was not ready to totally settle down, however he wanted to provide for Mary and their child. He had his savings, and had made a few small investments that had tripled his money. They could live comfortably and fall back on his savings as a cushion if his earnings were not enough. Mary also worked and made decent money at the hospital, with full paid benefits. Living together seemed to be the most feasible answer for John.

To his dismay, Mary wanted nothing to do with shacking up together.

"If you own the cow, why ever pay for the milk?" she asked him when he suggested it. Mary chose to live at home with her parents. She did visit the apartment regularly during her pregnancy, but rarely spent the night. The more he tried to press her, the harder she rebelled against the idea.

"I have caused my parents enough embarrassment by becoming pregnant. I won't cause them more," Mary explained. There were no accusations of malice in her voice when she spoke about the topic. Their relationship was at a stalemate! John was not ready for marriage. He still enjoyed sleeping with Becky. He also slept with a classmate named Natasha periodically. Although Mary did not know, whenever he chose to marry he wanted to be sincere about it. John did not bring women to the apartment. Although Mary refused to live with him, he did not wish to complicate his life any more than he already had.

His friendship with both Becky and Mary grew. Becky was a good sounding board for business and career moves. Mary was an excellent listener when it came to a lot of life's struggles and John's day-to-day problems.

To John's surprise and humiliation, Mary broke up with him, and stopped seeing him two weeks after the birth of his son, John Gray, Jr. She didn't offer him an explanation. John felt that it was a pressure play. He did not buy into it. What John did not know was that Natasha had approached Mary in front of the apartment and told her of their affair. Natasha was upset because he had cut off having sex with her. Mary and Becky were a handful. Also he had school, and a job. Natasha was demanding. The other two women were not. It was easy to get rid of her. She wanted more than John had to give, and he expressed it to her. Natasha was a woman scorned.

Mary was not naïve in dealing with the deceitful ways of women. Raised in the church, she got an eyeful. Church women were not to be reckoned with when it came to their men, or a man that they wanted for themselves. Women even came on to her father, right in front of her mother. Shame was not one of church women's strong points, so she knew what to expect out of worldly women. Natasha explained to her the dates and times that she had slept with John. She told Mary when her period was. Natasha had picked up early on that John fit her in during Mary's cycle. He was too caught up in juggling women to realize that it was a pattern of when he chose to sleep with Natasha. There were too many coincidences. Mary had learned that there was no such thing as a string of coincidences in life.

Natasha was sincere. She explained to Mary that John had recently dumped her. The woman said that she had kept an eye on his apartment, and followed him around the campus as well as work, and gave Mary an eyeful, and a few pictures of John and Becky. John accidentally called Mary "Becky" on more than one occasion. He often got nervous whenever she would ask him why that name was in his mind. When the woman Natasha brought all of this up, Mary put the complete picture together of all of the pieces that were missing.

The hotel receipts. The whispered phone calls.

The overnight disappearances where John was neither at his family's house or the apartment. He always gave her a vague answer when she questioned him. Mary went from anger, to extreme pain, to acceptance within a two-week period. Her man was a player. That was the reason why he did not wish to marry her. He was not finished sowing his wild oats yet. That is when Mary decided to dismiss herself and her son out of his life. Because she still loved him, she refused to cut him completely off. She led him to believe that she was still in the dark about all of his extracurricular sexual encounters, however, she refused to have sex with him. Some days she could watch him talk to her and her panties would get wet. She wanted to feel his lips on her clit as bad as a dying man needed life, but she refused to give in to him. Loyalty was important to her as it was to him. Mary was heartbroken.

She would not have another man, but she would not be a fool for John Gray. Mary also felt that she was being punished by God for sleeping around, fornicating with John before marriage. She was determined to get right with God before her son had to suffer for her sins. Mary understood that sins of the parents were often carried down to the children, if not atoned for. Her son, nicknamed J.R., was her life. She was determined to protect him with her life.

John wanted to be a good father, but he was not sure of what to do. Because he never knew his father and did not have a male model in his life, he wasn't sure how to interact with his son. He felt proud that the boy looked just like him. He respected Mary to the utmost for being a very good mother to their son. Other than that, he was not sure what to do, or what not to do. He supported his son financially without Mary asking. John hoped that when J.R. became older, they would be able to establish a bond. He was even nervous about holding him. What if he handled him too rough? Even worse, what if he accidentally dropped him, and something were to happen to him? The thought of that kept him at a physical distance.

John graduated from college, enjoying Mary's friendship. He had come to respect her and even confide in her about most things. They talked daily. She always inspired him to do better, and be the best he could be. Although Mary refused to have sex with him, she had become his security and his sunshine.

* * * * * *

His quest for the night was also his boss' daughter. Becky's father was an executive at Office and Home Outlet. Because Becky received full paid tuition and a healthy allowance, she went on to graduate school, where John became employed for her father's company due to a need to support his family. His job was in the marketing department as a Quality Assurance Manager. His duties did not have anything whatsoever to do with architectural design. John discovered that most of the managers employed by Office and Home Outlet held unrelated college degrees. It was a good job. Mr. Barringer, Becky's father, started John off with the healthy salary of 40K. That was considered a good salary for a twenty-two-year old, out of college.

Having Becky on his team was a perk of the job. For four years she kept their sex life undercover from her family and the company, and also kept it interesting and held John's attention. What many people did not know was that Becky had a secret. She was terribly, drastically bisexual. Her favorite dates were the ones where she brought along a female lover, and facilitated a ménage-a-trois. Becky enjoyed variety. She was the only woman that John knew that enjoyed sharing her man.

Her new lover was built much like the slew of others. A few inches shorter than Becky, large firm breasts that appeared to be the result of a professional, expensive boob job, and submissive in nature. Also, one of the requirements of being with Becky was to be a big freak. Leah fit the profile to a tee. The first time that Becky included a third party on their date, and then to bed with them was very awkward for John. What is a man to do? All men fantasize about having two women at the same time. It is an old fantasy. What men who have never experienced that fantasy don't know is that it is not a lot for the man to do. There are many moments where the two women make one feel like he is not in the room. The first threesome made John feel more of an observer rather than a participant. Oh yes. The women double upped on him, and took care of his needs and wants, but a man can only go so many rounds and so many times. It was an all-night party. John found himself being awakened after falling asleep following four hours of fun, to both women each licking his penis hungrily to bring it back to life. Becky and her friend used him again, wore him out, and then again concentrated on each other. Becky used him, and he used her. She needed him for his penis. He used her to receive a nice variety of lovers that were free, pretty, sexy, and freaky. Becky always footed the bill for the hotel, food, and any other need there were for the night. What more could a man ask for? He got all the girls he wanted, never had to frequent bars or talk to strangers and date or go out to meet women, and it never cost him a dime. He was a lucky fellow. Working for her father was an additional perk. Becky had sold him hard. By the time Dan Barringer did hire him, he was already labeled Becky's closest friend and her academic savior. John mused that it was no telling what kind of lies Becky fed her father to make him feel that way, but knowing Becky as long as he had, he could only imagine.

What Dan Barringer or Becky did not know about John was that he used the company as a learning experience, and that he had no intention of retiring for the Outlets. Mr. Barringer was a smart, experienced businessman, who shrewdly built the company from selling pencils on the corner and in school at the age of eleven, to a multi-state, three-hundred store conglomerate. Office and Home Outlet was John Gray's stepping stone. The best part of the job was the paid traveling his position entailed. If sales were low at one of the stores in a different state, it was John's job to travel to that store, complete a standard company evaluation, and then devise a marketing plan for the store to increase sales. John got a chance to travel the country at no expense to him.

Working for Dan Barringer is how John ended up starting his own business when the time came. Mr. Barringer directed all of the problem calls and customers to John. John was the unspoken conflict resolver, quality assurance manager, and change artist with the company. John considered the challenging assignments part of his job and no big deal. Mr. Barringer had been in business for more than twenty years. How John was able to pull an irate customer back in, or go in and turn around a sinking site was a special skill. Dan thanked his daughter regularly with the initial gift being a candy red, drop top Corvette. Becky was elated. In return, she bought John a Rolex Presidential watch, charging it to her open-ended American Express account that her father paid for monthly.

Daddy never noticed.

John took her out to dinner, then to a plush hotel suite, and fucked her brains out. It was a win-win situation for Becky.

John began to notice that international callers were about ten percent of the calls he received. His reply was the same.

"I'm sorry, but we don't ship out of the United States," was John's reply.

After months of turning customers down, John inquired into the reason why they didn't ship out of the country. Customers called regularly for refrigerators, air conditioners, and generators from their Home Improvement Warehouse. Computers, laptops, and faxes were hot items from their office stores. John began to track the number of potential orders and the amount of their orders. The spending ranged from two hundred thousand to eight hundred thousand a month. He took on the special hobby of finding out how to accommodate the international orders. Some of the countries were Third World countries. Others were more advanced in other areas, but not in technology, such as Gibraltar.

John shipped his first international

order while employed for Mr. Barringer. He drop-shipped ten refrigerators to a port in California that were loaded into a large container used to carry merchandise by water. The additional cost of the container and extra tariffs were filtered into the markup of the items once they reached their destination. The refrigerators were going to Gibraltar. Gibraltar was an island surrounded by water, near the tip of Spain. The population was thirty thousand. The second order was air conditioners, shipped by water. The third order was computers, laptops, fax machines, and small generators. While organizing the third order, John connected with two brothers that were in the shipping business. The Miralji brothers had seven ships. They supplied many of the Third World countries as well as Italy.

Shocking Becky and her father, John quit his marketing job with Office and Home Outlets, beginning his own export business titled Gray Exports, Inc., and never looked back.

Chapter Three
Harry Treason

The closet was dark. The small boy was curled up in a fetal position, covered up by his mother's green satin robe. Although the temperature in the closet was extremely warm, the boy's body periodically shivered. Harry did not cry. He did not yell out. He knew that no one could hear him.

His long, tortuous ten years of life had experienced this type of maternally inflicted terror too many times to allow self-pity to surface. At ten, Harry Treason prayed for death. Suicide often entered his mind, but he always quickly dismissed the thoughts.

His Grandma Sue was the only person in

the world who had shown him unconditional love. She told him that suicide was a big wrong. At ten years old, Harry wanted to go to heaven with Grandma Sue to feel her warm embrace during cold winter nights. In his young mind, during distant dreams, heaven seemed unattainable sometimes. Hungry, pissy, and scared, the boy drifted off into an unwelcomed state of slumber. In his dream, Superman saved him and shared with him a tall glass of chocolate milk.

* * * * * *

Anna woke up out of a drunken stupor. *What day was it? How long had she blacked out, and where was the boy?* Anna thought. Her body was sprawled across the living room couch of the small three-room apartment. It was sparsely decorated with a couch, coffee tables flanking the couch, a twenty-inch TV sitting on a four-wheel TV stand, and a Lazyboy chair. The empty gin bottle was a permanent fixture in all parts of the apartment. There was no dining room. The kitchen area was separated by the living room with a thirty-six inch partition. The kitchen held the bare necessities. A sink, refrigerator, electric stove, and small round table with two matching chairs. The walls were all a dingy ivory throughout the apartment. Matching the Queen of Slob's décor in the living room was the kitchen.

The kitchen stank. Dirty dishes, a dried up pot of boxed macaroni and cheese, and a rancid bowl of spoiled milk with crumbs of cereal floating around the surface of the bowl were the highlight of the living arrangement in the apartment. Anna's senses were numb to the smell or sight of the chaos.

Harry grew up with a void in his young heart. He wanted Anna to like him. Despite how she tried to cover up her disdain for him, he saw it. On good days she was not abusive. That was the best that he could hope for.

From as early as he could remember, he attempted to nurture her. He cleaned up her vomit. Put cool rags on her face during hot summer months when the flies were unbearable. The boy figured that if he showed her kindness, she would extend love. Instead, Anna was disgusting. She refused to be sober. She started the day with a bottle of gin. By lunch time, she was a cursing, babbling fool. Once his Grandmother Sue died, there was no reprieve. Somewhere in all of the dark days of living with her and having to fend for himself, the physical abuse started.

Anna tried to help it. She cried to tell herself that he was just a little boy. Her mother's words echoed in her head long after her mother was dead.

"Shut up!" she screamed often.

Harry thought that the words were directed at him. They were not. They were thrown out at the spirit of Sue Treason. Anna wanted her mother to shut the hell up. *Where did her voice come from anyway?* she asked herself often. When she went to see a doctor about the voices of the dead, he gave her Risperdal in large doses. With the alcohol as a chaser, the voices often intensified. Anna Treason was as crazy as a sailor jumping off the deck of a ship into the ocean to get out of the rain. Anna had passed the point of return. She was all the way out there.

What Harry did not realize was that the relationship that he had with his mother would ultimately shape his opinion of all women. During his formative years, while other children were playing with toys and mocking adults, Harry was cleaning up his mother's body fluids. In order for him to sit on the toilet, he always had to clean off her splattered piss and blood from her monthly. He concluded that women were quite repulsive, filthy creatures. *How could a human being bleed regularly from their butts like that?* The boy had witnessed too much of negative nature, too soon in his life.

There were men in Anna's life. During those times, she cleaned herself up periodically. There were never any of them who noticed Harry. He did not feel left out. They were there to drink and moan with Anna. Whenever one of the frequent men visitors was in the picture, Harry was on a mini-vacation. He did not always know if Anna still needed tending to, but was relieved that if she did, he did not have to be bothered with her. The male visitors meant that he could roam the streets at night, and play with other children during the day. The male visitors also meant that the closet prison where Anna punished him at was off limits. A part of him dreaded male visitors leaving. Whenever they missed more than four days of visiting Anna, Harry assumed that their end was near; he was usually right.

Anna reacted sourly. Usually she locked him in the closet for something as simple as breathing. Whenever Anna looked at Harry's aristocratic nose, bright grey eyes, and dishwater blond hair, she saw the face of his father. There was no one on this earth that she hated more than Harry Kern. Harry Kern was the devil personified.

At sixteen years of age, he began sexually molesting her, with the complete blessings and shield of the church. Harry Kern was the neighborhood preacher. Sue adored him. She tithed him with her weekly ten percent, even before she paid her bills. Harry Kern was a walking hypocrisy. He yelled about hell and brim-fire for the sinner that committed fornication. In contrast, every time he got her alone in his small study at the church, he spread her out on the couch and stuck his private member in every hole she had on her body. Nothing was sacred or exempt. After four years of exploiting and violating her, he left her pregnant, violated and broken. She was unsure of herself, unsure of religion, and unsure of the world around her. Anna Treason did not understand where she fit into the complex equation of life. She was also three months pregnant. To her horror, the boy came out of her womb wearing an identical smirk on his face that his father sported the last time that he violated her. It was hate at first sight.

Anna's drinking started the day she was released from the hospital. She could not cope with motherhood without the assistance of a strong glass of Johnnie Walker Red. No chaser. No sipping. Anna took it straight to her head.

Anna attempted to love her son. She wanted to possess the maternal traits that most of life was based on. Anna witnessed mothers caring for their children in the church, at school when a doting parent came to pick their child up, and at home from her own mother. Sue was ecstatic with the birth of Harry. He was her first grandson. Once she got over the shock of Anna violating one of the Ten Commandments publicly, Sue was not able to tear herself away from the boy for long. Harry was the son that Sue never had. He could do no wrong in her eyes. If her son could have looked a little bit more like her, Anna may have been able to dig deep inside herself, and find love for him.

Anna's drinking started out as a casual venture. She'd discovered that if she took a drink each time Little Harry began screaming, his tone would decrease to a tolerable pitch. Anna soon discovered that a drink after feeding, bathing, and dressing her son made her feel almost normal. Normal was her life before Kern ruined things for her. Anna Treason was not able to get back.

Sue watched the downward, negative transformation with sadness. Although she could not comprehend how motherhood could devastate her daughter, she did understand rejection and the scorn of a woman. Anna was hurt and scorned by young Harry's father. Sue wrongfully attributed scorn as the driving force in Anna's life that was chauffeuring her to hell, express route. Her daughter changed before her eyes. One week Anna was vibrant, full of laughter and alive. The next a babbling, drunk idiot on any day of the month after dark. Anna's hair was dirty and matted most of the time. Her breath was foul enough to cause a public emergency from people holding their breath around her too long. Her skin enveloped her body in a dirty pallor of hull.

Sue was not a regular church attending woman, but she was a praying one. She prayed for her daughter to get right with herself and God.

Six months after her grandson's second birthday, Sue Treason died rather suddenly of a brain aneurysm that burst. Sue left to mourn one grandson. Harry did not understand funerals, but he was already beginning to grasp the concept of loss. Each day following the death of her mother, Anna spiraled down into a deep abyss of alcoholism and mental health deterioration.

When Anna's father died, he'd left Sue with a hefty pension from working for the railroad all of his life. Sue left her inheritance to her daughter and her grandson. The monthly check abetted Anna with her daily drinking and squanderance of time. Her whole life consisted of the soap operas and Jerry Springer. More often than not, the television ended up watching her.

It was not surprising that when Harry

started kindergarten, he was heavily ridiculed by his peers. Children did not like him because he stank. Harry was a responsible boy for his age. He'd learned at a young age how to be self-sufficient. He dressed himself. He prepared his own meals, and fed his mother when he could. He took a bath when he felt like it, and he opened a book periodically. He had not figured out yet the complex financial system of life. How could he generate something to eat from the grocery? Where could he get clothing from that fit? He did not have a clue how the flow of money worked.

After watching an episode of *The Little Rascals*, he attempted to steal a pack of lunchmeat from the store. Although his mission was successful, his anxiety overwhelmed him. He did not enjoy his wares. He decided to try another venture. He would volunteer to work for food as he also had seen on TV. Mimicking the actor, he made up an elementary sign and hung it around his neck. Harry was seven years old, extremely thin for his age, but had the deepest, bluish gray eyes that did not match his age. They were the eyes of an old soul that attested to too much at a young age.

Begging worked for him. It paid better than he thought. Harry would position himself downtown in rush hour traffic after school and extend his tin cup. He never went home with less than three dollars a day in change and an occasional bill. On his way home he'd stop at the market and buy something to eat for himself and his mother.

The usual was a box of cereal and a quart of milk, or a pack of deli meat, a loaf of bread and a candy bar for himself. Anna never questioned where the food came from, and she never saw the money. Harry's instinct told him that she would take the money from him if she got her hands on it. He was right and didn't know it.

At seven, his life was routine. Get up in the morning, get dressed for school. Clean up his mother as best he could. Fix a bowl of cereal. Make her a cup of coffee and hand it to her. Off to school. Downtown to panhandle. To the grocer for food. Watch a little television. Eat whatever he'd acquired for his evening meal. Go to bed when he got tired of watching TV. Harry did not have friends. He did not think that Anna would approve of them if they wanted to come home and play with him. The only company that was ever allowed in their house was one of her man friends.

One day, Anna surprised him. Instead of striking him, she stuck him inside of a closet. The first time she left him in there for more than thirty-six hours. Harry missed school, and he missed panhandling. Lucky for him, there were still a few items left in the house. Every leftover penny was gone.

He found out that the thrift store had clothing items for a low price. Every free penny he saved from his daily spoils went toward purchasing an item from the Salvation Army Thrift Store on Superior. Whenever he left downtown on Friday evening, he would always stay a little longer. On Friday a lot of the businesses downtown got paid. On payday people were more generous. He easily had three dollars left over after spending a dollar on food. Harry purchased his own coat, boots, clothing items, pajamas and toys. He even bought his mother presents from the thrift store. The salespeople thought that he was the cutest customer ever, and he often played on their awe. He simply paid them what he wanted to pay them for the items.

"That's six dollars, Little Man," one of the salesmen would say. Harry proudly laid three dollars on the counter, gathered up his items off the counter in a ball, wishing them a nice day. He never required a bag or a receipt either. If Anna noticed anything he'd done for the both of them, he couldn't tell. Most of the month, she was barely coherent.

The more love Harry tried to show his mother, the more she despised his presence.

He made it through elementary school as a loner and an outcast. He spent his evenings watching the show *Cops*, and other true crime series. While watching one of his favorite reruns of *Cops*, he discovered that he wanted to be a cop. He liked how cops had the power over people. Also, Harry had no interest in attending college. It was not that he was dumb. He knew that he could handle college level assignments. The problem was finances. The quicker he became financially independent, the quicker he would be able to move away from his mother.

His senior year of high school marked

his first tragic moment with a girl. For years, Harry watched girls in school from the sidelines, much like a young boy observes his first major baseball game. He wanted to play. He wanted to be a part of the scenes and circles that girls traveled in. He just didn't know how. Because he did not have any friends, he had no one to shoot the bo-bo with. Even the nerds of the class rejected him because of the crude smell that his clothing carried. Harry did not know how to wash, so he often put his clothing items in the bathtub with him when he needed them. He would use them often to dry off with, and then put them over the back of the kitchen chair, where it was warmest in the house. The problem was him layering the clothing to dry. When they did dry, they smelled mildewed. His nose had become immune to the smell.

Harry thought that he was hallucinating one afternoon. *Was the girl named Patty speaking to him?* He did not want to appear foolish, so the first time she openly spoke to him by name, he ignored her.

"Hey, Treason, what' sup?" Patty said the following day.

Although Harry was the only person with the last name of Treason in the school, he still looked around to confirm that she was speaking to him.

She noticed. "Yeah! You!" she said. That embarrassed him so much he felt like a klutz.

"Um, hi," he replied. She smiled, and walked away.

The following day Patty did the same thing.

"Can you carry my books? We are going the same way," she told him.

"Um, sure."

"Don't look so nervous. I don't bite, Treason," she said.

As they walked home together, she talked nonstop about everything from the political climate of the world to the birds flying around them. She was a walking chatterbox, Harry thought. He had never walked with a girl his age. Walking with your mother or grandmother did not count. While she talked, he stole a look at her. Patty was not pretty, but she was not ugly either. She had an interesting look. Her hair was long and auburn. Her nose and lips a little too full for her thin, long face. To further contrast her looks, her chin was long. After studying her a full three minutes without her taking a break from talking to breath, Harry decided that he liked Patty. He could not say that about any other female in this world, except for his grandmother, who was no longer of this world.

Harry spent his senior year with Patty. They walked to school together, home together, and even got summer jobs together at the neighborhood grocers. Patty asked Harry to go to the prom with her. Although it was supposed to be the other way around, he accepted.

Patty started Harry on acid. A few days before the prom, Harry decided to take a hit of LSD with her. Patty was an A student, and also into abstract thinking. Once Harry went on a trip with her, he knew that he'd found her source of inspiration. Most of the garbled stuff that she talked about, Harry discovered was mumble-jumble. Harry was disappointed. He felt the same disappointment when he found out that the most popular psychoanalyst alive, Sigmund Freud, was a cokehead. They say that it's a thin line between brilliance and insanity.

From working at the grocery store, Harry was able to save and buy his first suit for prom. Although he could not afford a lot of the other luxuries that seniors in his class splurged on, he cleaned up well to a sharp-dressed man, if only for one night.

When they got to the hotel room, Patty was the aggressor once again. Patty felt him up good, with fast roaming hands, touching many places at the same time. Harry felt like he was being seduced by an octopus during certain moments. Patty left nothing to his imagination. Before the night was over, Harry had been laid missionary style, doggie style, by a masochist, then spanked with a belt, while tied up, by Patty the sadist. Patty was a very experienced, freaky girl. What Harry did not like about Patty was her constant comments about his two-inch member. Harry did not like the idea that Patty made him feel cheap and used, while she did everything to him imaginable.

"I can't believe you are still a virgin, Treason. You are a girl's dream," she said.

Harry thought that it should have been the other way around, but he did not complain. It could have been a lot worse. He could have been forced to bring in his eighteenth birthday as a virgin. That would have been a tragedy. Patty was truly a beast in bed.

Harry had to soak in a tub of Epson salt to ease the soreness of his behind and private parts. Despite the pain, when Patty invited him over to her mother's house for another romp in the hay, he obliged her. His reasoning was that once he was trained to take her physical roughness, it would no longer affect him. It was the same principle as a good gym workout. The first and second day following the workout it hurt like hell, but as time went on, the pain subsided.

Parallel with Harry falling in lust with Patty, he also fell in awe. She was also a faithful follower of David Copperfield, the magician. He did not understand how she did most of her magic tricks that she performed before him and associates. It made no sense. However, he watched closely, refusing to bat an eye for fear that he would miss an important component. Patty performed everything from making a bird appear out of a hat to making a frog from the pond disappear before everyone's eyes. Patty was also into levitation. She could make her body levitate, and also some small objects.

"How do you know all those things?" Harry asked constantly.

"Life is mind over matter. That's all

it is," Patty always replied.

One afternoon, while Harry was dosing after one of their many thirty-minute lunchtime workouts, Harry was snapped awake to the feel of a drastic temperature drop in the room. It was the middle of July. Harry sat up just in time to see Patty's physical body change from solid matter, to a light cloud of a reflection of what was just before his eyes, to nothingness. Patty disappeared before him. It was the most frightening thing that Harry had ever experienced. *Where the hell did she go?* At first, Harry was sure that she would return as mysteriously as she disappeared. Four hours later, Harry began to panic. He paced the floor. *Should he call the police? Patty's mom? What should he do?* He contemplated his options. He decided that he would call the police.

"Hello. My girlfriend disappeared right before my eyes four hours ago, and I would like a squad car out here, please," Harry said out loud. He decided that the police would either arrest him for a suspect in the disappearance of Patty, or detain and commit him to the nearest mental institution. Do not pass go. Do not collect two hundred dollars. Harry decided to plead the fifth, and leave the area with speed and indiscretion. He knew that once Patty returned, she might be angry with him for leaving, but she had taken things too far this time. Harry had a funny feeling about this one. The flip flops that were occurring inside his stomach were accurate. Patty never came back. There was an investigation. Patty's mother did not suspect him. When one of the officers accused him of having something to hide, it was Patty's mother that came to his aid.

"Leave the boy alone. He was the only friend that my daughter had. Instead of trying to frame him, go out and catch the criminal who has my daughter," the grief-stricken woman ordered.

Harry was going crazy. His guilt was eating away at him. He could not tell anyone the truth for fear that they would not believe him, and make him a suspect. He wanted to talk to Patty's mother, but could not bring himself to tell her the truth. Because he could not tell her the truth, he avoided her telephone calls for the most part. He could not avoid them totally without causing suspicion. *Why did he feel like a suspect, and why was he acting like one?* He felt responsible for Patty's disappearance, although he had no more control over her than the American citizens being able to bring the troops home from Iraq. Patty did what she wanted to do, when she wanted. That was that.

Eventually things died down. Patty's mother stopped calling. The sensationalism of a missing person that many people knew also died down. The disappearance of Patty became a memory for most. It was an unwanted memory for Harry.

Once Harry got over the loss of Patty, he began to sort his wild oats. He began the police academy a year out of high school.

Because of his critical personality along with his inexperience with dating, he was not considered a prize catch. Women were cruel. Because Harry was not endowed in the manhood department, women who did agree to sleep with him did not hesitate to verbally castrate him. "Little thing" and "undersize" were a few of the words that Harry kept hearing from women he tried to date regularly. After getting his emotions torn apart, Harry decided that he did not like the female gender very much. He made a vow with himself. He would not pacify them. He began to go directly to cathouses, where there was regular, open, fair exchange. He began to crave the uncomplicated sex that he got from hookers. They did not care if he did not talk. They did not care that his manhood was short, and they did not complain. In return, they fulfilled every fantasy that Harry could think of, for a small fee. When he graduated the academy, and started to receive a regular paycheck, hooker fees were part of his regular spending budget. Most men craved the wife and children thing. Harry did not. He became married to his career at a young age.

Chapter 4

After John's sudden unexpected departure from the Barringer Outlets, his relationship with Becky lost its flavor.

"How could you disappoint my father like that?" she asked.

"How could you expect me to build someone else's company instead of my own, and yet say that you have love for me?"

"You are a user, John."

"We used each other. It was fair exchange." And that is how their lustful relationship and friendship ended.

John entered the dating scene. What had changed since his college days was that women made just as many booty calls as men did. He did not like the switch in gender playerism. Whenever he went out and met a girl he was interested in, at the first date she was quizzing him about his financial affairs. Also they asked him to pay their car note, rent, and take them shopping immediately after having sex with him. It became monotonous. *What ever happened to the man asking the woman out?* he wondered.

The final straw that sent him running into the clutches of Mary was a fatal attraction named Dominique. She was tall, thin, a criminal attorney for one of the top ten law firms in the county, and independent. He first spotted Dominique at the gym. He watched her do over two hundred side bends. She gripped the ten pound weights with a carved frown on her face. She was disciplined. As John watched her, he mentally undressed her firm, muscle sculpted body. He decided that she would be his next quest.

She was also observing him watching her, so she put extra drama into her movements and facial expressions, so that the on-looker could get the full effect. She loved the attention of a handsome man. He was good looking and a regular at the gym. She'd noticed him on several occasions.

"Hi, my name is John. Can I buy you a drink?" he said, making sure he gave her his most inviting smile.

"I'm Dominique. I have seen you before here. You have a membership?"

"Yes. A lifetime membership. It is even transferable if I die," he answered with a voice full of humor.

"Yeah, I'd like to take a break and get a drink with you."

They proceeded together to the juice bar. The juice bar had a full health menu. There was fruit, naturally made fruit juices and smoothies, bran muffins, protein drinks and bars, boiled eggs with bran toast, and an imported coffee machine. Many members came to the gym before work, since the doors opened at 4 a.m. for the early risers. Most of the corporate world enjoyed their first cup of java and breakfast at the juice bar.

It was one of the perks of belonging to the club. The club also had a separate shower room, dressing room sauna, steam room, and Jacuzzi, for people that wanted privacy without the wondering eyes of the opposite sex. There was a unisex pool, large Jacuzzi and steam room for the couples that wished to workout together. The annual membership was reasonable. For only ten thousand dollars a year, you could enjoy the benefits of having your own spa, full gym and weight room, with a personal trainer on call. The trainer cost extra to have an assigned time slot, but they were always available to spot you, or make sure that you were using the machines properly, to get the full benefit. While employed for the Barringers, Betsy bought him a lifetime gold membership for Christmas. For one hundred thousand dollars, paid up, a person could have the luxury of owning a lifetime membership, with all of the perks. There was a menial fee of three hundred dollars annually to keep the membership undated.

Betsy also owned a lifetime membership, but no longer used the club. She had decided to join the popular country club in the area with her father, and all of their friends. The membership was one of the many perks that John experienced sleeping with a girl like Becky. He had to admit that he did miss the freaky sex sometimes, but did not believe in backtracking in life. Becky had also moved on, and was engaged to one of her father's flunkies at the company. John wondered if her fiancé knew her secret fetish. Probably not. Too close to Daddy, and she couldn't let Daddy find out that his little angel was a bisexual freak.

The marriage of the only heiress of the Barringer estate was local news. And in all of the social columns. The Barringers were not listed in the Forbes top one hundred richest families in the world, however, they easily had ten billion dollars in assets. Barringer could easily be classified into the non-existent top five hundred richest family list of Forbes. Despite the small tug of longing in his groin that he felt whenever he thought of Becky, John was happy for her.

John did propose to Mary the same year. When he thought back on it a month before his wedding was to take place, he wondered what chain of events prompted him to give up his player status. A part of him wanted to change his mind. Marriage was a big step. Most of the people that he knew that had been married were divorced. Some of his friends and family had been divorced more than one time already. Marriage was the ultimate commitment. John decided that it was Dominique's crazy, stalking, bipolar ways that forced his hand. Dominique tried to force his hand into marrying her. She even feigned pregnancy. That was one of the oldest tricks in the book.

After he started to date Dominique, things began to disappear, and he began to experience a storm of bad luck. The first thing that happened to him was while he was at a motel called The Honeymoon Suites with a short, well-stacked stripper named Erotica, his car was stolen. When the police interviewed everyone, in broad daylight, no one saw a thing. John had never had anything stolen from him in his life. He was careful about who he allowed into his surroundings, even while growing up. He never brought riff-raff to his home, although he knew plenty that fit into that category. He was also careful about bringing girls he slept with to his home. He preferred to pay the extra money to take them to a motel. Many of his friends had made the mistake of taking more than one girlfriend to their apartment. No matter how you drilled in a woman's head they had feelings for, to call on the telephone before making an appearance, they always broke that rule. It was just a matter of time. It was a universal problem; that should have been rule number one in the player's handbook.

The police never found his car. He had full insurance, so he did get a rental, and a replacement. They compensated him for his CD collection, and all his other personal items such as his laptop and briefcase that was also locked in the car. Money could not replace the files on the laptop, or his diverse collection of CDs. John had a wide variety, from Janis Joplin, Jimmy Hendrix, James Taylor, Elton John, George Michael, and Kenny G, to Bone Thugs in Harmony, and everything Luther, Marvin Gaye, and Prince ever made. He downloaded a full selection on his iPod, however, there was nothing like having a backup copy of all his music.

Most of his college friends converted their reading selection to the Kindle. When Amazon.com came out with the Kindle, it made travel a breeze. His friends were able to download their selection of books and magazines on a small, lightweight device that was wonderful to have. It fit well into a briefcase, and made good reading. You could adjust the printing to make the book large print with the push of a button. John was grateful that he had not invested in the Kindle. That would have also been another gadget to reset and download to his comfort ability.

No sooner than he recovered from having his car stolen, someone broke into John's house. The crime was done in the heat of the day. What was even more puzzling was that the thief bypassed his large plasma TV to take the brain of his flat screen computer. The answering machine was confiscated, and his photo albums. Even the few pieces of jewelry that he had were intact. The police officer that came to file the report was also puzzled by the selective thief.

"This looks like someone you know," the officer said.

"But who?" John said more to himself that to the officer.

One incident of terrible luck could be construed as a stroke of bad luck. Two in a row could never be considered coincidental. There was an evil force working against the grain of John's life. After sitting in the stillness of the night, weighing the facts, Dominique's face came to him clearly.

Why would she break into my house or steal my car? John wondered. That was the part that he hadn't figured out yet. Their hot and heavy sexual relationship had cooled. They used to have sex twice a day. Dominique would meet him for lunch wearing nothing but a birthday suit and a trench coat, or she would follow him to the shower of the health club, ignoring the sign reading. "For Men Only." Since they both frequented the health club once a day, she choreographed her workout times to match his. After their workout sessions, John counted on her hitting him off with a good blowjob at the least. Dominique had skills in the head department. What he did not like about her was the fact that she was overbearing. She asked too many questions, pried into his personal business and even opened up his mail over the sun visor of his car without his permission. He caught her when he went to pay for gas and pump it. She did not try to conceal her nosiness.

"What you doing with my mail? Give me that. Ain't nothing in there for you," he said firmly.

He wanted to slap the taste out of her mouth. Dominique gave no excuses, or apologies. He busted her the following week going through his briefcase.

"What the hell?" he said loudly. She wasn't fazed.

"Well, if you would go ahead and ask me to marry you, I would not have to keep searching for my engagement ring, or a proof of purchase from a jewelry store!" she said.

Was this broad serious? No one ever said anything about marrying her crazy self. John decided it was time to cut her off. The more he tried to avoid her, the harder she stalked. He determined that she must have been posted in front of the health club, because no matter what time he went, she was in the parking lot, getting out of her car at the same time he was. What John did not know was hurting him. Dominique had put a tracking device under the rear bumper of his car. She knew where he was at all times by going on her laptop and using the tracking software that monitored the device. That is how she knew where to find his car when she had it stolen and knew when he wasn't home to break into his home. She needed to see who was in his e-mail files, and who he corresponded with. Dominique was determined to have him all to herself, even if it meant having to play detective. John did not know that she had lost her job, for the hundredth time, due to severe mental health problems. Dominique made Glen Close in *Fatal Attraction*, and Mary Morrison's character in *She Ain't the One*, seem like kindergarten students. Dominique was playing for keeps.

It was a turnoff for John. Even the sex was no longer fun. Her breath was bad. Very bad. John did not remember her breath smelling like cow manure when he first started dating her. Her breath was so foul, he had to turn his head when she talked. Also John noticed that her hygiene was careless. He'd noticed dirt stains on her clothing, on more than one occasion. *Had he missed all of that in the beginning, due to the sex being good?* He hoped not. John was no longer attracted to Dominique.

It took him a few more weeks to figure out that she was the main suspect in all of the crimes that were being committed against him, but he could not prove it. Every woman he tried to date also caught drama. She stole their cars, had crooks break into their homes, and lived off illegal bank capers posing as the women and removing their funds from their bank accounts. It was outright identity theft. Although she did not work, with her felonious capers, she had a nice stash of money. John's laptop and CD collection alone made her fifteen hundred dollars cash. The sale of his home computer and other electronics paid her car note, rent and car insurance for the following month. John did not have a clue. All he knew was that he wanted Dominique out of his life, and she would not leave him alone. Being rude did not work. Telling her the truth did not set him free. The final straw was when he received a call from his bank informing him that his August checks had bounced. John was not one to check his balance often. He had automatic withdrawal from his accounts on a few of his bills, and for a few of the others like his American Express and MasterCard, he paid online monthly. John always paid the balance in order to avoid interest charges. He did not use his cards monthly, except when he paid for a hotel or went out on a date.

After the bank called him, he went to

the screen of his new laptop to check his account balances. Someone had wiped out all three of his accounts! John could not believe his eyes. He had a money market account with a hundred thousand plus balance that was empty. His savings account that he used for vacations and major purchases was free of over twenty-five thousand dollars. His checking account was used to pay his bills, and live day to day. It was overdrawn by one hundred thirty-six dollars. John sat in the chair staring at the screen in a daze. He was speechless. He did not know how long that he had sat in the chair staring at the screen, but it was dark outside when he came to. He had zoned out. His intentions were to call the bank and see what was going on, but he was devastated. For the first time in his life, John understood how the people that suffered the stock market crash of 1936 felt. The world was devastated at that time. People lost fortunes. John was hoping that it all was a bad dream. He had budgeted, cut corners, and lived frugally in order to establish a cushion in case of hard times. He decided to sleep on it, and start his investigation with a clear head the following morning.

The disaster continued. The bank was not eager to replace his money. The money market account had been emptied out for more than thirty days. The bank said that he acted neglectfully, due to his not reporting the loss until thirty-eight days after the withdrawal. John filed police reports. They led to dead ends. Whoever took his money had thought it out well. They completed a wire transfer to the state of Texas to a fraudulent account. There was a paper trail that ended at a few of the Western Union counters throughout the Texas area. The perpetrator that took his money had wired it by transfer to a bank in Texas, then moved it by phone to a Western Union, and then picked it up as a money wire, using fake identification. It was a woman. The woman fit Dominique's description. After a thorough investigation, it was determined that it was Dominique. The problem with being reimbursed for most of his money was the time frame had lapsed that made the bank liable. The detectives informed him that he could press criminal charges, but that they had checked her assets and income and found that she did not have anything of any value. That was how John got rid of her. He told her that if he ever saw her face again, he would press charges and put her up under the jail. She loved John, but he was not worth going to prison for. She walked away free and clear, with more than a quarter million dollar lick from John alone. Dominique took the man to the cleaners, without becoming his wife. She felt that it was her due for the way he used her body for sex and then discarded her like a dirty tampon.

After Dominique, John was through with the dating scene. Whenever a woman smiled at him, or came on strong to him, instead of reciprocating her advances and flirting back, he thought of Dominique. Women were smart, and not to be played with. That was the moral to his plight with Dominique.

That is what prompted John's decision to step to Mary. Spending quality time with his son did his soul good. With a few years and time, Mary matured in all of the right places. She was always big-boned. Mary was never thinner than a size eight with curves in all the right places. John noticed that her breasts were a few sizes and cups bigger, her butt wider, and her waist smaller, or maybe the contrast of her body made her waist appear smaller.

Mary was easy to read, and easy to be with. She was predictable for the most part when it came to his visits. She would fix their plates, make sure he and his son were comfortable, and then retire to her bedroom. She never interrupted their playtime. John decided when J.R. went to bed. Even if it was late, she allowed him to parent at his pace. He liked that. As he studied her demeanor without her knowing, John came to realize that he liked a lot of things about Mary. She was never demanding. She did not pry. John wondered if she had experienced a different or new lover since he had her. He wanted to ask, but knew that he would be overstepping his boundaries. He couldn't resist.

"So, Mary, who are you seeing?"

"What do you mean by that?"

"I mean, do you date or have a man?" John held his breath for the answer.

"Of course I have man. He is sitting across the table from you, with your silly self," she answered, shaking her head at him.

"Mary, do you think we can become close again?"

"Are you asking me for sex, John Gray?"

He thought a few seconds about his answer. He would not lie. "Yes," he said, plain and simple. He was. Mary was his. He was blind. What he was looking for in the streets was right in front of him.

"You hurt me once, John. I don't know if I can live through that again," she answered, looking him square in the eye. There were no accusations or demands in her voice.

"I am going to go on to bed. When you are ready, tuck J.R. in, and I will see you tomorrow," she told him.

John wanted to run behind her to her bedroom door and ask her to let him in. His son watched on with curious eyes. He decided to think things out. He did not want to hurt Mary again. Hurting her was hurting his son. Her life and happiness evolved around their son. John tucked J.R. in, watched a little of Spiderman with him before he fell asleep, turned the TV off in his son's room, and quietly exited the apartment.

When he got home, he was restless. He loved Mary, but he was not in love with her. She was a good mother, a good Christian, and a good friend. He tried to think of negative qualities. *Was she boring? Would she be a nag once he committed to her? Could she give good head?* Marriage was it. If he committed to marriage, he would try to be faithful. He contemplated what the full meaning of being monogamous would mean. Sleeping with the same woman, every night and waking up to her, during the good, the bad, and the ugly. John was tired of sleeping alone. He did not allow strange women into his house or bed. He loved Mary's cooking. Since the crazy breakup with Dominique, he visited daily after work during the week, and had started to incorporate weekends into his schedule. His son loved seeing him daily. He could have taken him home with him, but he enjoyed Mary's good food and the attention she gave them both. Each day he watched Mary's fat, plump, full butt waltz past him, his lust and love for her grew. It was both. He did not want to hurt her or bring her any drama. He wanted to be sure when he stepped to her. J.R. helped him make his decision.

"Daddy, can you spend the night with me?" J.R. asked. "You can sleep in my bed with me," he pleaded.

J.R. had a small bed. It was perfect for him, but not built for a grownup. Mary and he had already discussed the upcoming opportunity to buy J.R. a new bedroom set, but had not agreed on when.

"Yes, I will stay. I will sleep on the couch," John told his son.

Mary quietly went to the linen closet and pulled out an extra pillow, comforter, and sheets for him.

"Come and keep me company," he told her after J.R. fell asleep. Mary sat akimbo on the floor in front of him, while he stretched out on the couch. She helped him out of his shoes, and tried not to stare when he unfastened his belt and removed his shirt. She already had on a gown and bathrobe. She smelled delicious. She always wore the Victoria Secret lotions that smelled like fresh fruit. Tonight she had on pear.

John's favorite flavor was vanilla. He could not mention that to Mary. Mary never bought or wore vanilla. He had played the field so hard that he could not remember *who* wore vanilla scents regularly.

Mary pulled the sash to her robe snugly around her. She was trying her best not to entice him. She made sure she did not make eye contact. She had not been with a man in four years. Since her son was born, she had made a vow not to bring anyone around him. Mary was still in love with John. No matter how much she wanted to hate him or dislike him, he held her heart in the palm of his hands. Mary knew that their son would bring them together. John was an excellent father. He was attentive to his son, and everything she wished for. She never had to call and ask him for anything. He knew their son's needs. Somehow, even the day-to-day care like Huggies, wipes and Pedialyte were regular drop offs for him. *How did he know to buy bibs and tee shirts regularly?* She wanted to ask him but kept their conversations platonic. Whenever she did steal a glance at him when he wasn't looking, her stomach somersaulted and her vaginal muscle tightened up. Mary wanted to feel him filling her up, going deep inside of her. In her heart, she knew that he was not ready to settle down. She could not explain it, but she knew. Maybe it was the restlessness she saw in his eyes. He was still searching. She did not mind the waiting. She would wait as long as it took. She had faith in him and knew that he would eventually come around, and do right by her and their son. She would not share her knowledge with anyone but her son, and he was too young to understand. All of her secrets were safe with her son. She told him everything. She talked to him every night, until he dozed off to sleep.

Mary did experience another lover after she stopped sleeping with John. His name was John also. His member was eight-and-a-half inches long, and an inch-and-a-half in diameter, much like his namesake, and he comforted Mary a few times a month. Before and after her monthly cycle, her body went into heat. During those times, John made love to her over and over again, without reprieve. It was during her lovemaking sessions with the other John that she learned her own body, what she liked most, where her spots were, and how to master orgasm. Still, she felt lonely. The other John was a forever-hard, natural skinned, brown vibrator with a clit tickler near the handle. There was no intimacy with her vibrator. It was as good as a replacement as she dared. She did not want another man to touch her. She belonged to John, whether he was ready to stake his claim or not.

Although Mary refused to look at him, John could feel her. They were on the same vibe. He wanted to put her to bed, right there on the rug. He wanted to lay her out, and work some J. Holliday on her. He was glad that she was not looking at him. Most of the time he wore a hard on. It would have revealed his true thoughts about her. Being a respectable guy was hard work.

"I want you, Mary," he spoke softly.

She didn't answer. She did not know what to say, and did not want to say anything stupid. Her body had already betrayed her. If John was able to see through her robe, he would have seen that her nipples were hard enough to use as arsenals. Her panties were saturated with her own body fluids from excitement. Her mind wanted to say "no," but her body wanted to jump in his lap.

"Come here."

She came to him. He pulled her onto his lap, allowing her to feel his full erection. It was sticking out like a weapon. John untied her robe. His eyes feasted over her body.

"You've saved all this for me?" It was more of a statement than a question. The look she gave him said it all. As he removed her robe, then her gown, Mary shivered on his lap, despite the warm temperature of the room.

"I won't hurt you, Mar. Don't be nervous," he said.

John took his time with her. After their first round with her straddling him on the couch, he carried her to the bedroom, and locked the door behind him. His son knew how to turn doorknobs. He did not want him seeing grownup scenes yet, and what he was about to do to Mary was very grownup. John was about to get outright nasty with Mary.

When they separated for work the following morning, it was a little awkward. Mary walked around the apartment like she had been horseback riding on a stallion, taking wide, short steps on the soft carpet.

"Daddy, do you live here now?" J.R. asked his father as they sat across from each other at the breakfast table. John realized that it was the first time in his son's life that he was there for him when his son got out of bed. They shared their first breakfast together.

"I will go ahead and drop him off at your mom's for you. It is on my way," John volunteered.

"Uhhh. No. That's alright, I..." Mary stuttered.

"You don't have to explain. I know that I am a touchy subject with your parents, Mary. I'm going to see you later."

John picked up his son, gave him a big hug, and playfully pulled Mary into his embrace at the same time.

While watching Mary sleep the night before after their lovemaking, John made a decision. He decided to propose to her. He spent the day shopping for her an engagement ring. He found one he liked at Bailey, Banks and Biddle Jewelers. It was a three-karat solitaire. The stone was clear. The price was eighteen thousand dollars. Dominique had broke him, but the bank was able to reimburse him for some of the money after litigation. Also, he had good credit. Mary was worth every penny. He could not have his future wife walking around with some diamond chips on her finger. She needed bling. John did not buy women bling they purchased it for him. Mary was a first.

John dialed her number at work.

"Ask your mom to babysit J.R. I would like to take you out to dinner."

"Alright. Pick me up at the apartment at 6:30. That will give me time to shower and change."

John picked her up promptly at 6:30. He arrived thirty minutes early, but sat in the car contemplating his proposal. He was nervous. He did not want to come across like a buster or a lame. Mary had him lameatized. *Was that a word*? he wondered. Probably not, but it fit the occasion.

John knew that once he became engaged, he was stuck. He would never be able to bring himself to disappoint Mary again by calling off a wedding. Engagements led to weddings. Weddings were one of the prerequisites of lifetime commitments. When Mary got into the car at 6:30, John knew she was the one.

They made small talk on the way to the restaurant. He took her to *Joe's Crab Shack* down in the flats. The flats was a place where most of the eateries flanked the Ohio River. You could also see Lake Erie clearly from the docks. Many of the spots on the west bank of the flats had patios that expanded to the water. It was a nice, cozy atmosphere.

Joe's Crab Shack had some of the best seafood gumbo in the country, second only to a restaurant John frequented when he visited the tri-states and ate in Maryland. John loved seafood. He did not know what Mary liked. He did not take girls on dates, and was not sure if she was a finicky eater. Like their son, she was not. He discovered that she also loved seafood.

While sitting across from her waiting for the waitress to return with the menu, he realized that he did not know a lot of intimate facts about Mary. If they were contestants on *The Newlyweds* television show that he used to watch when he was young, he realized that today he would have lost. He vowed to change that.

"What is your favorite color?" he quizzed.

"Purple for royalty."

"Mine is blue," he said.

"There are many blues. Light blue? Dark blue? Navy blue?" Mary said.

"Navy blue."

After more small talk and getting to know each other, they enjoyed food and drinks. Mary drank a virgin Daiquiri, while his eyes looked at her and got a hard on from thinking of her tight virgin stuff.

"Would you like to dance?" he asked. By his third drink, he was feeling a little frisky.

As they slow danced, barely moving more than their hips on the floor, John loosened up his grip on her waist.

"I have a little something for you," he said. He took her by the hand and led her back to the table.

Even though it seems I have everything, I don't wanna be a lonely fool, all of the women, all the expensive cars... Cicso crooned on time. John removed the small square ring box from his jacket pocket. Mary held her breath.

"Mary, I want to marry you and do right by you and our son," he said. She exhaled.

"Will you marry me, girl?" he asked, as he opened the box and slid the sparkling piece of bling on her ring finger.

"Yes! Yes!" Mary cried. She couldn't help it. Her mascara would be all smeared. Mary dreamed of the day John would propose to her, over and over again. She was shaken with happiness.

"Come here, Mar," he said. She was across the table in milliseconds. He pulled her on his lap, kissing her, and embracing the back of her head.

"Get a room!"

They both snapped around to see a conservative family of four that included two children staring intently at them. The children were staring harder than the adults.

"Sorry," John and Mary both said simultaneously.

She got off his lap and reclaimed her seat at the table.

"I would like to do it soon. I like waking up with J.R. staring at me," he said. "I'll let you decide the details, and you just let me know," he added.

"Can we pick up J.R. now and tell him together?"

John knew that she wanted to announce their engagement to her parents more than to J.R.

"Yeah. Let's roll," he said.

Pastor Turpin shook his hand briskly. His future mother-in-law tried to hug the life out of him.

They set a date for sixty days. John and Mary did not want a large wedding. They had a small intimate wedding ceremony at the church. Their reception was held at a banquet hall near the church. There were one hundred guests. Both of John's sisters insisted on inviting their co-workers, friends and family members that John forgot existed.

Mary and J.R. gave up the apartment and moved in with John. He had a house. It was a small two-bedroom house with a finished basement. Before they moved in, he had the basement decorated into a gym. In order to convert his son's area, he moved his office furniture, desk computer and files to the basement. It fit perfectly. His friends shared horror stories of women moving in taking over their homes, closet space, and individuality. John did not feel any of that. Mary and J.R. brought with them a bright aura to their house, and to his life. He had forgotten how to have fun. His son demanded that he regress to childhood at least once a day, and Mary fit right in. When they played J.R.'s favorite game of cowboys and Indians, Mary was J.R.'s horse. His reigns to hold on was her Chanel silk scarf that she'd bought from Sax's Fifth Avenue. Whenever the *Lone Ranger* was shot and wounded, his horse (Mary) had to fall too. Laughter filled the house whenever J.R. was awake. He was a character. John was fascinated by most of the things he did. For the first time in his life, John felt complete.

Chapter 5

Harry's hard work and dedication to his job paid off. Within the first two years of being on the force, he was promoted. After graduating from the academy, he was assigned to man the desk. The most excitement he received besides processing parking tickets and booking in petty criminals was having to body slam a few of the drunks and dope dealers.

The station at Fourth District was a standard police setup. There were a dozen chairs in the waiting area. The long counter was four feet high. The paint was a faded sky blue, with hints of dull gray. The counter's purpose was two-fold—a barrier from the public to prevent unnecessary physical contact, and to serve and protect.

After a year of deskwork, almost every traffic or arrest scene wielded an air of déjà vu. It was all the same. Different faces, different names, but the same role-plays, over and over again.

The only thing Harry hated more than the drunks he booked in were the two-bit drug dealers. They strutted in with their arms handcuffed behind their backs, pants hanging off their asses, full of an attitude. These guys were shuffled into the station regularly, but acted like a crime had been committed against them. Selling drugs was illegal—helllloooooo! *What part of that didn't those people understand?*

Every chance Harry got, he made sure that he punished them in every way he could think of. If they had money or jewelry on them, he trashed it. He had no desire to spend their filthy money or recycle the gaudy jewelry. It went out with the trash to the dumpster. They all came in with cell phones on them. He would stomp their phones with the heel of his black steel-toed boots. He realized that he may be destroying the dealer's customer list that could be used as evidence to convict them. The detectives always asked for the property before charging the clowns to see if any additional charges could be created. Stomping their cell phones in their faces while they watched set them off, and gave him a reason to beat them down.

"Man, why the fuck did you step on my shit like that?"

Harry had to show them who was boss. He answered by issuing a sharp, powerful punch to their solar plexus, or a balanced kick in the balls. That was his response.

While booking them in, Harry never hit anyone in the face or anywhere that was openly noticeable. Serve and protect. Follow the creed.

When Harry received the promotion he had requested, it was hard to contain his elation. The force placed him on the streets, in the center of all the action. He was also happy that the boss assigned him with a good partner. He joined Fox.

Fox was a white, middle-aged, seasoned and ruthless officer. Harry could not have asked for a better partner. Fox took payoffs, laid hookers in lieu of arresting them, and reallocated drugs, money and guns from the streets to his possession. He was respected and feared by his peers. The fear came from wondering if he ever got busted by Internal Affairs would he become a rat. Fox had purposely gathered dirt on everyone. He collected it like a hobby. He announced it. He teased them with their own secrets. He leveraged favors. The fat lady had not sung, so work call was standard. The force feared Fox turning into Aretha Franklin at any publicized bust or shooting. He was a walking investigation waiting to happen.

"Just storing up my insurance policy." Everyone believed him.

Immediately following his promotion, Harry's mother Anna passed away while in a drunken stupor. The doctor diagnosed her with cirrhosis of the liver. Anna was ordered to cease drinking alcohol. That directive was as useless as telling Michael Jordan in the prime of his career that he should not play basketball. Her life revolved around alcohol.

The funeral was boring. The eulogy was full of misleading information. It portrayed his mother as a respectable caretaker, community member, and model citizen. As they read off characteristics, Harry wondered *who* they were really talking about, and whose obituary they stole the wording from. The only people present were members of his grandmother's church. Anna did not attend church services and neither did Harry, so the people were strangers to him.

Harry was relieved Anna was gone. She laid heavy into his pockets. The small government check she received covered her utilities. There was no mortgage or rent payments, but her day-to-day living along with her quality of life funds were his responsibility. One of the monthly costs was for life insurance. Harry paid through Triple A auto club. Anna received an advertisement in the mail ten years ago. The plan offered medical and term life insurance. She was considered high risk. She drank too much, and smoked too many cigarettes. When the woman came to the house to draw Anna's blood, the company also tested for obvious ailments. She received a clean bill of health. If they would have checked her liver, Harry was sure they would have been able to predict her plight. Anna Treason lived her life as one of the walking dead. She drank around the clock, and had no desire to be coherent or responsible. She rarely ate solid food, and did not consider nutrition. Her regular meals consisted of alcohol. Harry paid a neighbor monthly to buy groceries, clean the house, and clean up his mother. The neighbor performed twice a week. Harry could not stomach his mother most of the time. He preferred not to visit, and when he did, he kept the time to five minutes.

The woman lying in the casket had never embraced him. Anna never spoke a kind word to him. She rarely looked at him directly in his lifetime. As he sat in the front row, he observed her body with no attachment or loss. Onlookers watched him for a reaction. His face was stone. Even in death, Anna gave a sour aura when Harry joined the procession for their final farewells. Yes. Her death was a relief. No loss, no sadness. No what-could-have-beens. As he rode in the limo for that last ride near his mother, he contemplated what he would invest the extra fifteen hundred dollars a month her death cleared up for him. He decided that the first thing he would do is spend a few dollars on a hooker to celebrate Anna's death and his newfound financial emancipation.

Harry cruised the Westside. Detroit Avenue was where the hookers had not been hit hard by the crack and crystal meth epidemic. A few of the old timers knew his face. Although he was not in uniform, he made sure to avoid eye contact with a few of them. He decided to dress down in a pair of Chinos, brown Hush Puppies, and a stripped tan and brown shirt. His windbreaker was dark blue. Although it did not match his outfit, it contributed to his mission. The idea was to look preppy.

As he circled the block the third time, he found his choice. He originally wanted the small framed Asian girl. His second time around he wanted the blonde standing next to her. He decided to pick up both of them for double fun. The blonde was a thin, well-dressed woman with Mia Farrow eyes. She looked young, but not jailbait. The Asian woman was petite in physical stature, and would have appeared much younger if it had not been for her eyes. She had deep, large, serious eyes that appeared to have seen too much during her short life. Her eyes were twice her years in age. The two women appeared to be friends. He checked his windbreaker pocket for his badge. He could not forget his badge during this venture. When he pulled over to the curb, he signaled for one of them to come to the car.

"I want both of you," he told them.

Both of the women jumped in. The blonde jumped in the front seat. The Asian hopped in the back, behind her protégé.

"We have our own hotel room. Make a right at the light," Blondie said.

"No. I don't do this area," he said.

The two women made eye contact. They were nervous.

"Don't be leery of me. It is two of you. I don't want to spend my money in this area," Harry said.

Blondie made eye contact with the Asian again. Ms. Asian shrugged her shoulders up slowly, and relaxed them, giving Blondie the seal of approval.

When they arrived in front of the hotel, Harry sent Blondie inside to pay for the room. He gave her a crisp new one hundred dollar bill. She came back with two magnetized door keys.

"Room 321," she said cheerfully.

Blondie was thinking that there was a lot more Benjamins where the first one came from. The room was ninety-two dollars including tax. She pocketed the change from the bill as part of her tip for the night.

Blondie used the key to open the door for them. Harry locked the door behind him.

"For a menage-a-trois we charge five hundred bucks," Ms. Asian informed him.

"You have to pay in advance. We are a for-profit set, no charity," Blondie said, while snickering at her own joke.

Harry neatly placed his jacket on the back of the desk chair. He sat down in a high back Queen Elizabeth chair in the corner of the room. He was ready to start the entertainment.

"Reach in my jacket pocket on the right side, Blondie. There is something for you both," he said. Blondie reached in his pocket. The pocket was completely empty except for his badge.

"What is this?" Blondie asked.

"It's my payment. Let's get naked girls," Harry ordered.

"You cops are all alike. Want it all for free. Never want to pay," Ms. Asian complained, while undoing her skirt.

"Blondie, help her get undressed before I get bored with you both." She did.

It did not take much for Harry to get turned off. One of the girls smelled like cheap perfume over body odor. When she removed her clothes, she released the funk.

Both of you need to get in the shower, and hurry up."

He swatted Ms. Asian on her ass hard when she walked past him. When they came out of the shower, each girl got on the side of him. One started kissing his chest while he lay in the center of the bed. The other began rubbing his thigh.

"Hey, Big Man, I see you are ready?" the blonde said, with a smirk on her face. She was openly making fun of his manhood. He wanted to snap her neck. Harry was ready and erect. All two-and-a-half inches of him. Sometimes it measured two-and-three-quarter inches. He decided at that moment that he did not want either of them touching him. He removed himself from the middle.

"I'd like a show, and make it good," he said as he sat in the chair with a towel in his right hand.

Blondie eagerly lay on her back. She was anxious to be on the receiving end, or she had done this before and liked the bottom position. Harry wondered for a few seconds which one it was, but quickly let it go. Who cared? Blondie opened her legs wide without preamble, and Ms. Asian got busy.

Once Harry released a burst of semen into the towel, he became bored with the two women. He'd planned to spend a few hours with them, but suddenly he wanted out of the room. It was a wasted one hundred bucks. He could have sat at home, stuck a porn movie in and jerked off without spending a dime for a hotel room. As he exited, he threw the towel full of semen on the bed. The towel hit the blonde in the face, causing her to open her eyes.

"Hey! Where are you going? We need to get back to the block!"

"Are you leaving us out here? We need to get back to the strip!" each woman yelled.

Harry was already out of the door before they could get to him. He slammed the door in their faces as they approached him.

"Hey! What about us!" one of the women yelled out the door down the hall.

He ignored them, and boarded the elevator that was waiting at the end of the hall.

Chapter 6

As time went on, John's export business expanded. The Miralji brothers were import-export masters. They had been featured in main stories of every business magazine in the world. The two brothers worked hand in hand. Vuai Miralji was the front line player in their operation. He was the extrovert who swayed customers to use their company to fulfill all of their electronic needs. He was a clever businessman and salesman who did not take no for an answer. Later, maybe. But never no. Bilan Miralji was the flip side of the game. He was quiet, reserved and laid back. He never said much in public except to his brother. He was the brains behind the business, and Vuai was the muscle. Bilan strategically built a multi-billion dollar empire by studying the business climate, the ins and outs of the export business, and customer needs. His business plan resembled a complex formula for the new life-saving medication, instead of an export business, with all of the complex formulas, charts and graphs. Not many laymen would read it and clearly understand it. Vuai was the executer of the plan. He made it happen. They could not have created a better partnership if they tried.

Luckily for them, they were born into it, eleven months apart. Although they were brothers, they did not look alike. Vuai was tall, stocky, dark and fierce looking. At first glance, Vuai would put the average person on defense. His physical looks did not match his kind demeanor. Once he began to articulate, a person was instantly put at ease.

Bilan was shorter than Vuai by a full foot. His physical features were soft and handsome. His eyelashes were so long, many women asked him if he had on mascara. There were many women in his life. He had a wife, a mistress, a wifey, a girlfriend, and a few jump-offs. Because he traveled the world often, he spread his flock all over. It was not unusual for him to be on the road for a month at a time. Sometimes business expanded his trips to two or three months. His wife lived in Tanzania, raising his two daughters, Kahlaali and Bana. His family was used to him being gone most of the year except for the holiday season. During the Christmas holidays, he spent a month at home without interruption. His wifey lived in Gibraltar. His mistress lived in Italy. There was a woman in waiting for him in every town that his ships docked. Custom allowed a man to have as many wives as he was able to support. Bilan would have been able to add quite a few more, but chose to live a more conservative life, instead of living as an international playboy. He took good care of all of his women. He also had a few children with different women that he also supported fully.

Vuai chose to live a semi-monogamous life. He had a wife in Tanzania and a mistress in the United States. He adored his mistress but would never leave his wife, despite her prodding. His mistress was exciting. She was everything that American women projected. She was a dynamite freak in the bedroom, and the perfect lady, hostess, and business woman in public. If he would have met his mistress before his wife, he would have married her. He did not.

His wife was raised in the same city. Dar es Salaam is the capital of Tanzania. Their roots were traced back ten generations to the city. They married at fifteen. His wife did not make demands, nor did she interfere with his business or his double life. She preferred to engross herself in farm life and social life of the friends and relatives in Dar es Salaam. Her life was full with the raising of their two children, cows, pigs, chickens, and a few hundred acres of land that her family and employees manned. The contrast was what he enjoyed most about the two women in his life. They were very different in all ways.

It was Vusi Miralji that made the first contact with John. The brothers did not have a secure connection in the States. The few people they dealt with did not want to be bothered with drop shipping orders to them, due to the taxes, time frames, and other intricate obstacles that occurred frequently in international exporting. An associate had ordered a computer and fax machine for his travel company in Gibraltar. He passed on John's name to Vuai and Bilan for contact. They were impressed at the quality of the equipment and the short period of time it took to receive the merchandise. Being the negotiator that he was, it did not take long for Vuai to put John on the team as a willing participant. When John researched the business history of the Miralji Brothers, he knew he'd struck gold, literally. The men hit it off like they had been knowing each other all of their lives.

The Miralji Brothers' main headquarters was stationed in Gibraltar. The brothers chose the island as their main port due to the diversity of people and the location. The far western limit of the island was Cape Trafalgar in Spain and Cape Spartel in Tangier at the furthest angle. The eastern boundary was the British overseas and Point Almina in North Africa. The Mediterranean Sea and the Atlantic Ocean flanked the Pillars of Hercules. The large stones gave Gibraltar its fame, also known as the rock of Gibraltar. The port was a masterpiece for easy access to the world. Each direction exiting the island created a meca of countries waiting to be serviced.

Zanzibar and Chile were just a few of the countries the brothers supplied. With the Miralji partnership in place, John shipped all merchandise to them. The brothers marked up the items a few notches, then filled the many international orders. Both men agreed on bank wire transfers as the means of payments. Bilan handled the payments. He transferred half of the order price up front, and then the other half upon receipt of the merchandise.

A few of the new customers insisted on meeting John in person before placing large orders. The brothers did not allow this until a customer had proved themselves worthy. They were good businessmen. Once a customer paid consistently, they qualified for a direct discount on some of the items. One of the potential clients was Poppie Hernandez. He ordered for the government. The Miraljis did not like dealing with the governments of small or large countries, so they were willing to eliminate themselves as the middle man after the first few large orders. The brothers were not greedy, and understood that all money was not easy money. However, after years of doing business with different governments they determined that they would rather not. They had made a small fortune from Ecuador throughout the years. The country was constantly expanding. It was literally a money machine.

"Our customer in Ecuador has changed management. The new manager wants to meet our supplier. He wants to negotiate cheaper rates," Vuai Miralji told John.

"Is the amount of orders he generates worth all that?" John asked.

"Yes, my friend. Ecuador is expanding daily. They are attempting to modernize. One of his complaints is the turnaround time it takes for them to receive merchandise. He feels that if he eliminates us, he can cut down the shipping time, since the orders we receive originate in the United States," Vuai Miralji explained.

"Does he have an order in?" John asked.

"Yes. A very large one," Bilan Miralji said.

It was a very big order. One hundred refrigerators, one hundred microwaves, one hundred fax machines, one hundred generators, and a few computers, answering machines, telephones and car stereo.

"This is just the tip of the iceberg," Vuai Miralji said.

John could not stop himself from calculating his profit margin in his head. Cha-Ching!

That was the beginning of John and Poppie's long friendship and business relationship. It was also the beginning of John's increase in travel. The Miralji Brothers continued to fill orders for the eastern sphere of the world. They had no interest in the southern part of the world. It was just as lucrative. Dealing with other countries and learning their culture made John appreciate being an American.

Before his travels, he'd taken many things for granted. Even in his poorest days, John always enjoyed running water, flushing the toilet, electricity, and many other electronic toys. There was also a wide selection of television programming in the United States, where Ecuador had three government-monitored channels. In many of the countries he serviced, electronics were for the rich or elite. The first amendment granting freedom of speech was non-existent.

Farming was as much an Ecuadorian custom as baseball was to America. Growing coca leaves was legal. What was surprising for John was that there was no problem with drug abuse in Ecuador. Cocaine was legal and plentiful. If you have a big enough plot of land, you were allowed to cultivate coca leaves, but the citizens did not overuse their product. A few of the Ecuadorians chewed the coca leaves to feel the euphoric effect of the drug, but it was not popular.

If a person had a big enough plot of land, they were allowed by the government to cultivate coca leaves, but the citizens did not overuse the privilege either. There was no demand for cocaine in Ecuador. Americans were going out the game in thousands with the abuse and addiction to crack cocaine. Americans were a spoiled race of people. The more John learned about other cultures, the more that fact sank in.

John's decision to add cocaine as one of his import products was a business decision.

"How would you like to make ten thousand dollars more in profit than you make now on trips?" Poppie said.

"Depends on the risk. What is it?"

Poppie explained the profit margin to him. Kilos of cocaine sold for about two thousand American dollars. The price was extremely negotiable. John did not know what the market rate was in the States but he intended to find out. He knew the routes from Ecuador to the States like the back of his hand. He had also built good working relationships with the immigration inspectors and the coastguards.

John knew men that dealt in drugs. He had a cousin and an in-law that was heavy into the game, but he purposely avoided hustling drugs. A part of him did not want to become involved with the business of it all. From what he read in the newspapers and witnessed on TV, it was a messy, violent business. John Gray was a businessman. He was not a thug, and had no intention to be a thug or gangster. However, John saw himself enjoying an early retirement as he totaled up the figures in his head. John wanted what most humans wanted. He wanted to be rich. The wealth was his driving factor. He never considered the consequences or the fact that if caught, he would ultimately end up in federal prison. No one ever does when they begin a risky venture like he was about to get into.

The first thing John did when he decided that he was going to get into mixed shipments of cargo was to contact his cousin Loot. Although the men were only a few years apart in age, Loot had already been to prison twice. John's father and Loot's father were brothers. After John lost his father, his brother William stopped coming around. John reminded him too much of his own brother and his loss, so he chose to think only of himself instead of helping the children of his deceased brother. Loot's birth name was after his father. No one in the streets was allowed to use his birth given name. Even his family called him Loot. He earned the nickname Loot as a small boy when asked what he wanted for Christmas.

"Give me some loot, Ma," he said, shocking everyone into laughter. Where John chose to go to school and follow the rules his sister set for their household, Loot chose the streets and the hustle of the streets.

Loot's father kept distance between himself and his nephew and two nieces. Loot enjoyed spending time with his cousins. Academia was a constant challenge for Loot, so he dropped out at the first possible chance. The streets picked up his education process. Loot envied John. Both of them grew up in the inner city of Cleveland, Ohio. John was able to hang out on the block and blend in, but he could also fit in at a Fortune 500 sales seminar. Loot could not. His street edge was hardened and showed in his eyes. He had witnessed too much death, pain, and suffering for his biological years.

Loot made up for the lack of book knowledge in looks. He was six feet tall, light complexioned, with soft facial features. His hair was what black people often called good hair. All he had to do was put a little bit of water and Vaseline in it to give it a gloss and texturized look. Loot was pretty. His exceptional good looks combined with his piercing eyes and street edge placed him at the top of the "Most Wanted Bad Boy" list. With his gift of gab, and his womanizing way, girls six to eighty had a crush on him once they got to know him. He did not flaunt his looks, nor was he conceited. He accepted his gift, and never gave it much thought coming up. Both John and Loot were charismatic. They made a good team.

John called Loot to find out the street price of a kilo.

"Hey, Cuz. Can you spare about thirty minutes to talk to your family?"

"Yeah! Man, anytime. You alright?" Loot asked.

"I'm good. I just needed your expertise on something. Let's meet at the Best Steak House on Euclid. I am hungry, and I want some breakfast food," John said.

"Yeah, I hope your tight ass is buying," Loot teased.

"It's on."

The Best Steak House was not crowded. John ordered a full breakfast, although it was late afternoon. Loot ordered a slice of baklava and a cup of coffee.

"How is business?" John asked.

"I can't kill nothin', and won't nothin' die. And you?" Loot said.

"It's good. All good."

"So, what's up, Cuz?"

"I may have stumbled up on something that may interest you. What is the selling price of a kilo of coke?"

"Twenty to twenty-six, depending on who is buying."

"What if I told you I could get them all day long for twelve?" John asked.

"I'd say that we rack um up, drop them

for eighteen, split the six, and get rich. Well, Cuz, let's do what it do!" Loot said excitedly.

"I need you to scout potential buyers. I don't want to meet anyone. I don't need to know about your end. I am playing deep third. I am about to make a pick-up, so when I call you and tell you let's rock-n-roll, you know it's on," John said.

"Alight. Good lookin', Cuz."

The men parted with plans to meet soon. Watching the men exit, they looked as if they came from two different backgrounds. John wore an expensive pair of imported black slacks from Italy with a pair of Italian loafers, and a white starched shirt. He left his jacket in the car. His entire outfit was custom fitted and shipped direct from the Dolce and Gabanna store in Paris.

Loot was fresh out of the urban wear store, with a pair of classic tims, an oversized white tee shirt, a large pair of Rock-a-wear jeans, with a coordinating belt hugging his exposed boxer shorts near his body. Life was about to join the two men in their mission.

* * * * * *

John's first mixed cargo trip was for a shipment of a dozen kilos. Although Poppie said that no payment was needed, John made sure that he wire transferred fifty thousand. He had his accountant create a back-up invoice to cover the transaction. He would worry about the tax liability and other factors later. John was a businessman and knew that any type of credit was not a good idea. Poppie wanted to give John an extra dozen on consignment because there was so much dope to be moved, but John was not having it.

"Let me see how this moves first," he said.

Ecuador had over a hundred farmers who cultivated the product, and did not have an outlet. Whenever an outlet was discovered, the families that cultivated the rich commodity scurried around to try to be the supplier or get in on the action. There were no secrets on the drug front. The dealers treated an outlet like finding the holy grail. It was their ticket out of poverty. Two thousand American dollars converted to twenty thousand pesos per kilo. Twenty thousand pesos could feed a family of six, and assist them in living comfortably. That is why credit was given. It was better to have a bird in hand than plenty of product stuck in the bush with no outlet. If a farmer successfully completed supplying a few trips, he could comfortably retire.

The cost of living was a lot lower for Ecuadorians. The economic gap between the rich and the poor was wide. Poppie's daughter Maria Linda worked as a librarian. In primary school, her profession was decided by her teacher. Librarians were paid two hundred to three hundred pesos per month. That was considered a good job. Like most jobs, there was not a big turnover of employees in Ecuador. People seldom got fired or willingly moved on. Only sickness, death, or immigrating to America freed up job positions. The reason why Ecuadorians migrated to America was because of the workforce. Poppie's cousin went to America to work as a waitress and a housekeeper. With two full-time jobs she was able to send home four hundred dollars a month to her family. In Ecuador, that translated to four thousand pesos. Her family was able to live comfortably off the money that was nothing in America. There were not enough jobs to go around in Ecuador. In America, there was always a waitress, housekeeping, or dishwasher's job available if you were a hard worker.

Most of the farmers were barely surviving. Families shared homes. Before Poppie became employed as a manager, he lived with his parents, brother, sister-in-law, and his wife. The custom warranted that sons support their parents. The house was forty-five hundred square feet with four bedrooms. There was no formal sleeping place. It was not uncommon for Poppie and his wife to sleep in the living room on pallets. His brother had four children, and he had two. There was never less than a dozen people living in the house. His parents' relatives that were down on their luck due to poor crops commonly lived with them in intervals. Eventually he was able to move out of the house with his family and have his own. He still contributed financially to his parents' financial expenses. People in Ecuador did not understand the concept of nursing homes for the elderly. The family structure and expectations were very different from the States.

Everything went smooth. John and Loot both had their own agendas. The two men pretended to split the six thousand obvious profit from each kilo. John pretended to purchase them at twelve thousand, while Loot stated the selling price of eighteen thousand instead of twenty-four thousand. Both men gained an extra profit. It was still a very lucrative partnership.

Chapter 7

Harry loved his nights on the street. Fox and him ruled the beat with iron fists, and a pair of brass knuckles to boot.

There was a problem in their district with a few of the drug dealers, but Fox and him were about to clean up their streets.

The east side of Cleveland posed a challenge for them. A lot of the young dealers began hustling while still in high school. Most of them dropped out and took to the streets. The flat foot hustler was nothing but a pawn for the bigger fish. Harry learned that what happened when these potential dealers failed in class, they were recruited to the corner. Where school was a mystery for many of them, all of them understood the bling and code of the streets. A young guy would borrow a hundred dollars from a friend or relative and buy a dub. A dub was street terminology for a double up of crack cocaine. If the dub was served to them proper, they could make two hundred off of a hundred dollar investment. Many young men saw the drug game as their way out of poverty. Harry saw it as a shot to lock them up for life and get them off the streets.

Harry knew from experience to start

from the bottom and move up to the top. One day he almost got his break.

"Five-O!" the young boy screamed, alerting all of his partners. He had been standing on the corner of 135th and Kinsman when he noticed an unmarked car slowing down. His instinct told him to unload and run.

"Oh, shit!" one of the other young ones said, quickly pivoting the opposite direction. Harry and Fox were out of the car and on the trail of the first dealer. It was Lil P, for Pete. P grabbed the back of his belt to hold up his pants, while reaching in inside his jeans with his right hand, and maintaining his stride. Running gap legged, he picked up speed when he saw the two vice jump out of the car. His heart was racing. His parole officer would not give him another break. He served thirty days in county for a dirty urine from smoking a blunt, but he would not be that lucky with getting caught with crack. He hauled ass, running for his life.

He touched the package that was securely tucked up under his balls, balling it up in his hands. He dropped it near a garbage can, as he rounded in the alley behind the main street. His adrenalin was coursing through his veins. He could not go back to prison. He ran faster.

Harry was on the boy's trail. He started to shoot him in the back.

"Freeze bastard!" Harry yelled.

The man had to be crazy, P thought. He would not go out the game without a fight. P saw a four-foot fence in front of him. He decided to jump it and hit the other side of the street. He knew the area like the back of his hand. He stuck his left foot inside the grilling of the fence while using his body to throw his right leg over.

Pow!

A shot from a gun blasted. The noise made P jump but he pushed harder.

When he landed on the other side of the fence on both feet, he felt a sudden burn in the back of his left leg. His leg felt like it was on fire. *Was he shot?* He didn't know, but he didn't stop.

"Freeze you little bastard!" Fox yelled.

P knew that he was shot. For a brief second, he thought about going out the game like a soldier because he knew that if he kept running, the two grimy detectives would kill him. Only the thought of his mother's pain stopped him from making them kill him. He froze in his tracks. Before he could exhale, they were on him, throwing him face down on the ground. Harry kicked him hard in his side.

"That's for making us chase you, you worthless piece of shit," Harry said.

P grimaced from the kick but decided not to give the creeps the pleasure of knowing he was in pain. While P was face down with his dick in the dirt, Fox kicked him in the head while Harry stomped his gunshot wound. P passed out from the pain.

When he woke up, he stared at two uniformed police officers and the drab scenery of a hospital room. He was handcuffed to the bed by his arms but his legs were free. P anxiously attempted to move his legs. Although it hurt like hell to move his left leg, he was grateful to be alive. P was released from the hospital into the custody of Harry and Fox. He had not been charged. He was under investigation. There were no drugs found on him, but by law they were able to hold him under investigation without a bond for up to seventy-two hours.

"We know who you work for. You can get a long time in prison. You know we found the drugs you tossed, so do not try to play games with us. We busted you red-handed," Fox said.

"Man, who do y'all think you talking to, Willie Wanker or something?" P said.

"Your ass is on parole, fresh out of the joint, caught with dope, and on your way back to prison, that is who we are talking to," Harry said.

P looked at both of them like they were aliens.

"Tell us about where you buy your drugs from. If you help us, we trade up. You can walk free, today," Harry bargained.

"Man, I don't know what y'all is talking about. I don't know nothin' 'bout no drugs," P said.

"This is your last chance, nigger," Harry threatened.

"Man, get a life," P told them calmly.

He was escorted back to his cell to await charges and bond. *How did they get that dope? He knew he should have thrown it harder*, P thought.

"Mr. Thomas, you have been released," the guard said as he unlocked the cell.

"What? My bond has been paid already? I was ready to wait on that worldwide check stuff that usually takes all day," P told the officer.

"No bond. You were under investigation. There were no charges. The detectives dropped the investigation," the C.O. said.

What was going on? Those two dirty cops would never drop any charges. P thought. He knew then that they were lying about having found his package, and just trying to trip him up. He was glad he wasn't no sucker. He ran out of the Justice Center like a starving, thirsty, man would run to food and water.

Harry and Fox attacked the streets with a vengeance. They would not let a couple of young punks get the ups on them. Since most of the petty criminals knew that Thursday night was vice night, they switched it up. They made the pickup night Saturday. The district did not like to use Saturday as vice pickup night because that meant that for the rest of the weekend they would be responsible for the persons arrested. Also the weekend was always full of drunk drivers and people charged with disorderly conduct from bar brawls. The lieutenant would just have to get over it.

Although it was a few guys to choose from, Harry and Fox chose their prey well. They wanted guys that worked for a drug dealer named Marcus. He was the man in the streets. He was controlling everything that was bought on the block, ranging from a twenty piece to a quarter kilo. There was no order that was too big. Harry wanted him bad.

While drinking his coffee, Fox spotted their target.

"There's our boy!" he said, tossing his coffee and cup out of the window. The two men jumped out of the car and took off running.

"Vice!" the young lookout perched on the corner yelled before taking off. Their target was Marcus' main soldier. They sat and observed him making sell after sell. Marcus was his supplier.

"Freeze!" the two men yelled. In the hood, freeze meant haul ass if you were dirty, and that's exactly what the crowd of hustlers did. This time Harry was ready for them. He had uniforms blocking all exits of the street and the alley. Dre saw the flashing lights of the police car ahead, and knew that he could not get away. He did the next best thing. He tossed his package in the sewer as he hit the curb.

"He threw something in the sewer!" one of the uniformed officers yelled. Dre slowed down. He did not have any dope on him, and his name was clean. He allowed the two detectives to catch up with him to make the arrest. Instead of harassing him, they stuck him in the back of the police car.

"Call sanitation. I want this sewer dug up. I don't care if it takes all night,"

Harry ordered.

It did take most of the night. At 4 a.m., one of the sanitation workers got everyone's attention.

"Found it!" he yelled, like he'd struck gold.

Harry ran over to snatch the package out of his hand.

"Yep. That's it. It's rocks," he announced. Dre watched in amazement as the dirty cop held his package up in the light in order to view the quantity better.

"Pull your crew in. We are finished here," Harry told the foreman of sanitation.

As Dre watched the two detectives talking and eyeing the package, he saw himself on his way back to prison, again. He had just re-upped, and the baggie was fat with over an ounce of dope. It was also hard instead of soft. Unlike P, Dre did not have a soldier street mentality. When the two vice officers began to interrogate him, he had already decided that if they offered him a deal, he would roll on Marcus. He and Marcus started out on the same level, but when the money started piling up, Marcus treated him like a servant or something. Marcus did not know that Dre knew, but Dre found out that Marcus was even banging his baby momma on the sly. Dre wanted to step to him, but did not want to be cut off. Now that the opportunity existed, Dre was about to show Marcus who was boss. Him. He was.

"We know who you work for. We don't want you. We want him. He is the bigger fish. Tell us what you know, Andre," Harry said.

Dre looked around. He was not in one of the standard interrogation rooms that he always watched on TV. He was sitting in a padded chair that swiveled, at the side of the desk of vice detective Harry Treason. The detective's name was displayed in large gold letters on a plaque in the center of his desk.

"Get us all some coffee, Fox," Harry requested. He was about to go into his good cop routine, while Fox played bad cop. Dre knew the roles well. He loved to watch and study *CSI, CSI Miami, Cold Case, Law and Order*, and all other investigative crime shows. He considered himself an expert on figuring out who did it. He guessed right ninety-nine percent of the time.

While Fox got the coffee, Harry sat at his desk clicking the keyboard. Dre could not see the screen. If he could have, he would have seen a large colored mug shot of himself plastered on the monitor. Harry was searching his criminal record to see how to stack the deck in his favor. He wanted Marcus off the streets and he knew that Dre was the key to bust Marcus.

"Coffee, girls," Fox said.

As the men sipped their coffee, they got down to business.

"Dre, I see you really don't have a bad rap sheet. How did you get into dealing drugs?" Harry asked. He really did not care to hear the sob stories, but it was important that Andre felt comfortable with him. If he could lock all of the black males into a large concentration camp and torture them for the rest of their lives, he would be in eternal bliss. He hated niggers, and he hated dope dealers. In his neighborhood, they were one and the same.

"Cause he's a worthless piece of shit," Fox hollered into Dre's face, close enough for Dre to feel the heat of his breath.

Seeing good cop-bad cop on TV did not prepare Dre for the mental anguish he felt while trying to ignore the small specks of Detective Fox's spittle on his face. Dre could not take the pressure. He decided at that moment that he would tell them whatever they wanted to know to speed up the process of getting out of there.

Dre felt no shame about telling. He had been in prison before. He served a six-month sentence at Lorain Correctional Institution for Drug Abuse. During a routine Thursday night vice shakedown, he had six rocks in his pocket. He told the uniformed officer that assisted in the arrest that he was a clucker. The officer passed on the information to the charging detective. He was released on a personal bond and later sentenced to six months.

While serving his six months at the reformatory, he was raped during shower time by a group of dudes from Dayton, Ohio that wanted his tennis shoes. They weren't even new or special. Just an old, outdated pair of last year's Jordans. When they surrounded him in the shower, Dre tried to put up a fight, but he'd never been good with his hands. He tried to talk them out of it.

"Come on naw y'all, y'all ain't got to act like this," he pleaded.

"Shut up, you sucka ass nigga. We asked you for the shoes, and gave you a chance. Now we get the shoes and your ass," the leader said.

The leader of the group demanded to go first. The biggest two guys grabbed one of his arms and held them to the side.

"Step back from the wall and bend over, nigga," the leader said.

Dre did as he was told. He sized them up. It was six of them, including the leader, and one of him. He fixed in his mind to try to make it out of the shower alive. Many men did not.

The leader plunged his dick in him hard with no Vaseline.

"Uggghhhh!" Dre screamed, but there was no one to hear him. He felt the invasion throughout his body. His back and stomach screamed with pain, and his legs felt weak. He tried to drop his arms down.

"Be still, young'un. If you act right, we won't have to fuck you up," one of the men said.

These men were crazy, Dre thought. *What the fuck did he mean that me might not have to fuck me up? I am already messed up for life!* Lucky for Dre, only three out of the six was in the mood.

"I don't want to go behind y'all's asses, and you fucking raw. I am scared of AIDS. I ain't doing life," one of the bigger guys said that held Dre's hands.

"I'm straight too," his other side

partner said.

It took Dre's body two days to heal, but the psychological damage would never heal. Dre knew he had to carry his secret to his grave, so any man that appeared to be stronger than him became his secret enemy. He transferred his anger from the men that raped him to any man that had strong qualities. Marcus was included in the bunch that he envied and hated at the same time. Dre was damaged for life. Sitting in the chair of the detective bureau, it was the rape that he recalled vividly. No, he could never go back to prison. It would kill him.

"I got in cause my dude Marcus asked me to roll with him to knock off the dough," Dre sang.

This is going to be a lot easier than I thought, Harry mused.

During the following hour, Marcus unraveled the organization that employed him, and that was affiliated with Marcus. If left up to Dre, the fat lady had definitely sang her last song for his crew. It was about to be game over. He left no information untold. At the conclusion of the interview, both of the detectives were pleased with the outcome.

"Anything else?" Harry asked Fox. He led the investigation, but did not want to forget anything. He took good notes while Fox recorded their conversation on a mini-recorder. Harry wanted them to have both hard copy and cassette as hard evidence. He also had Dre sign a Miranda form, stating that he had been read his rights, and that he refused to have an attorney present during questioning. He did not want a clever defense attorney disqualifying Dre's statement, or the impact of his evidence.

"Yeah, one more thing. Where does Marcus get his dope from?" Fox asked.

"His name is Loot. He is Marcus' cousin on his Ma's side," Dre said.

"What is Loot's real name?" Harry asked. He had never heard of anyone named Loot before. He had a crew of informants who kept him up on the street activity. He wondered if Dre was making up names to get some of the heat off of Marcus, or having second thoughts about working for him. Snitches did it all the time. They put their life in danger, and then when it dawned on them, they tried to either retract the statement, or tell more lies to try to confuse the investigation.

"How does this Loot look?" Harry asked.

"Pssstt. I ain't never seen him. He only deals with Marcus," Dre said.

"Well, how do you know where Marcus gets his dope from, or that he gets it from him specifically?" Fox threw in.

In Dre's mind, the two detectives were acting slow. Loot was out of reach for dealers like him. He realized that a detective would not understand the street hierarchy.

"We are not going to arrest you. We are going to book you in, fingerprint you, have you sign some papers, and then release you. Your assignment is going to be to gather everything you can on Marcus and his cousin.

You will not be officially charged or indicted, and we are going to give you full immunity for assisting us with an indictment," Harry said.

"So, I still continue to sell dope on the block?" Dre asked.

"That's right. Act like it's business as usual, but report to me a few times a week by phone," Harry said.

Harry handed Dre a business card with his direct extension on it. When Dre called the detective's direct number, it was arranged that the call would automatically be forwarded to his cell phone.

Dre walked out of the police precinct on cloud nine. Without having to pay them off, the police and detectives were now on his team. Dre had no qualms about snitching. His motto was get the next man before they got you. Also, he wasn't really a criminal. He was really a good person. Now, he could sell his dope openly, playing both ends from the middle. The near arrest was definitely about to change his life.

Chapter 8

The streets took to the quality of drugs that John offered quickly. It was the best. Street hustlers were able to add a full cut on each package and still have the best cocaine available at a street level. Each time that Loot tested a shipment, it was ninety-two to ninety-eight percent pure cocaine, with the remainder of the product being oil from the coca leaf. It was in its purest form. John was not involved in the day-to-day, however, he was interested in how the product was moving. The first shipment took the longest to get rid of, but when the dealers discovered the quality and the quantity, it was on. Within ninety days' time, John was moving more than a hundred kilos a week, and having to increase his trips to weekly instead of twice a month. He did not trust anyone to handle the shipments. The only two people that were allowed on La Fenetre were Mary and Loot.

It became harder and harder for John to focus on the legal cargo. For the first time, he understood how a criminal could get caught up in the drug game. Each week he tried to convince himself that the shipments should cease, and that he should return to legitimate cargo, but greed convinced him otherwise.

The streets were begging for his product. The dealers were all trying to switch to dealing with Loot due to the quality. John was becoming one of the top five suppliers without even trying to. He had no idea because he stayed out of the day-to-day operations.

Marcus was happy for once in his life. He was rewarded what every hustler prays for—a break in the game. It was finally his turn. His cousin Loot had the juice. Things were jumping off on all levels.

Marcus was not a player. He had a wifey that he adored. They had been together since high school. She birthed him two sons and a daughter over the last few years. Lee-Lee knew the game cause her father was a hustler, and she had been raised in it. Her grandfather earned his wealth as a policy runner, that took and played numbers for inner city clients before the lottery was established. Most of the black families in Cleveland were able to establish wealth and businesses off of the income from the numbers game. Like all other organized crime, the numbers business was run from the top down by the Gotti lieutenants that ran the policy businesses in Cleveland. It was one of the only ways for black families to come up during the 50s and 60s after the northern migration turned out to be nothing more than subtle prejudice in the north. The numbers were one of three ways for blacks to come up. There was only real estate, death through insurance money, or running numbers, and the last choice was the most realistic.

Marcus benefited indirectly from the fruits of his woman's family's labor. The house that they lived in was passed down from Lee-Lee's grandfather, who owned over four hundred properties throughout the city and surrounding communities. When her grandfather died, all of his estate was divided among his two children and four grandchildren. That was another plus of having a woman like Lee-Lee. When Marcus was down on his luck, Lee-Lee had property and bank that could assist him in his illegal business ventures. She was able to put her hands on large sums of capital whenever Marcus needed it. Although she did not have to work, she chose to run a daycare facility and do property management for her family, which kept her busy. Because the family owned so many properties that included apartment buildings, whenever one of Marcus' spots got hot, he simply shut it down and moved his operation to another spot. There were always tenants being evicted all over town. Whenever a tenant was evicted and a spot became empty, he would take over the spot for no more than ninety days. He would then rehab it, and put it back on the market to be rented out. Whenever he took over a spot, he always factored in the rent payments so that Lee-Lee or her family members did not lose money, so it was a win-win situation. If he did not immediately take over, some units would have remained vacant indefinitely.

Lee-Lee was also fine. She was pure eye

candy, with a behind that looked like it was bought from Fredericks of Hollywood instead of gained from thousands of sessions with her personal trainer. She religiously did sets of lunges, Stairmasters, and Pilates. Her body was tight. She did not look like she had given birth to three healthy children. Marcus felt blessed to have her as his boo. Although he was not perfect, he never strayed far from home.

Since he had mobbed up with Loot, there were only good times. Most of the time either a supplier ran out of product temporarily, or the quality was garbage a few times. Not with Loot. Each package was raw dope that could take a full cut. Most of Marcus' customers were smokers, so he put manitol, B-12, and a portion of Come-back whenever he rocked up his product, to double the amount he purchased. Even stepped on, the streets loved the product.

He had a few soldiers, but it was one in particular who caught his eye. His name was Dre. From the beginning, Dre and him had a history. Although they had not been running buddies, they came through the ranks together. Marcus felt that he could trust Dre with his back.

"Can I ride with you?" Dre asked him on more than one occasion. After watching him from a distance, Marcus finally gave in.

Dre played his cards right. He did not ask questions, nor did he pretend to be interested in Marcus' activities. That is how he accidentally ended up meeting Loot.

Marcus and him had been riding around

all day, and about 4 p.m., they decided to stop at *New Orleans* on Kinsman to get some seafood. The Tucker brothers owned a few restaurants, and a bar called Tucker's Casino. They were well known in the city, and their seafood was good.

"Orange roughy for me. What you want man? It's on me," Marcus said.

"Give me a scampi dinner with a piece of that sweet potato pie," Dre said. The food was tight. As they sat and ate, Marcus shared with Dre that he wanted to get out of the game.

"Yo, the money is good, but I want to spend more time with my family. I am in these streets two and three days at a time, go home and crash, and then right back at it. It's getting old," he said.

"Well, if you do, who is going to take over for you?" Dre asked.

"That's why I have been checking you out. My cat usually stops in here this time of the evening cause he loves their frog legs. He stops either here or Lancers. If he stops in here, I am going to make an introduction just to see how it goes," Marcus said.

Dre could not believe it. It was his lucky day. He was about to meet Loot, and did not have to plot or scheme to do it. He was falling right in his lap.

That night, Loot did not frequent *New Orleans*. Marcus decided to run it past Loot.

"Hey, Cuz, I really need to talk to you," he said.

They arranged a meeting at the Lancer.

They both loved Lancer seafood and the atmosphere. George and his sister, Georgia, were two ole-Gs that treated them well and fed them good. They ordered two perch dinners with a bottle of Henny. Georgia was right on time with the bread and drinks, and then the hot food to follow.

"Loot, I hate to say this, cause things are going so well, but I want to retire," Marcus said.

"Shit. You don't want to say it, then don't. That's not a good look right now," Loot explained.

"Why not? We both are banked up, and have had a good safe run. If we get out now, we can retire without having to do a bid. Man, our name is ringing everywhere. Even squares know that we are handling big things," Marcus explained.

"What brought this on? Has there been an incident?" Loot asked.

"Naw. Everything is cool. I have over ten million put up free and clear, plus play money, and money to cover my bills and living expenses for the next year that is separate from my retirement stash. I miss my kids, man, and they are growing up on me," Marcus said.

"The game was not designed to quit at our level. We are not civilians, Marc," Loot said, with a very serious look on his face.

Marcus did not like the tone he was using with him. *Was Loot threatening him?* he had to ask himself. He hoped that it never came to that. He knew Loot. Loot was a killer. Marcus knew that he did not stand a chance if Loot ever decided to turn on him. They lived by the same code. There would be no police. They cared for their own, fed their own, and buried their own when the need arose.

"What exactly do you propose? I know you have something in mind, since it seems that you've thought this thing out," Loot demanded.

"Yeah. I have a soldier that I would like for you to meet that I feel would be a good look. I've known him from a kid. We grew up together in the same neighborhood, but never really hung out. He's solid," Marcus said.

"I trust you. I don't know about the next man. I still don't understand how you just walk away from being a commander," Loot said.

Marcus decided that it was time to go hard on Loot.

"Listen, like you, I have been in the game and around the game all of my life, Loot, but how a lot of us get it twisted is it wasn't designed for a lifelong profession! It was designed for a means to an end, and to take dope money and flip it to something legit to sit back and retire off of. Don't get it twisted!" Marcus said.

Marcus and Loot were cousins through their mothers. They came up together. Marcus' dream was to have enough money to live legitimately, and be able to support his family, running legitimate businesses. He and Lee-Lee had already mapped out the business plan for his car washes and detailing shops. He had priced two closed auto garages that were in excellent shape for what he was trying to do. Lee-Lee had the credit and the buying power to purchase them immediately. Marcus had served time in prison. Lee-Lee rode with him. He did not plan on going back. His decision was made. He wanted out.

Marcus set up a meeting so that he could introduce Dre to Loot the following night at the Lancer Lounge on Carnegie.

After Marcus made the introductions, Loot quietly observed the two men's interaction. Loot could not place why, but he did not like Dre. The man came across as solid, but it was something about him that was in his body language that Loot did not trust. Maybe it was in Dre's eyes. The eyes did not smile when his face did. Loot had learned to follow his first mind. In the game, you only had one time to mess up. The one mistake in not following your intuition could cause you your life.

He decided that he would check out Dre's background and see if he had any skeletons in his closet. The street and prison grapevine were much more thorough than all of the federal databases in the country. If National Security would have cut loose a street team of gossipers from the corners and the projects overseas, Bin Laden would have been found. The streets held no secrets.

Marcus decided to take a vacation from the streets to celebrate his twenty-seventh birthday. After he adamantly refused to have a large, banging birthday party, Lee-Lee planned a quiet event. She rented a honeymoon suite at the *Americana Suites* at Niagara Falls, on the Canadian side. The room was equipped with everything. It also had a large Jacuzzi, sitting in the middle of a mirrored off area, with a stripper pole to the right of the Jacuzzi. Marcus was in for a treat, and did not realize it yet. While playing his favorite video game and listening to some classic Ohio Players' *Heaven Must Be Like This*, "It must be just like you, girl." The music crooned. There was a loud knock at the door.

"Lee, did you order something?"

She was in the bathroom doing something. The woman was always spending hours in the bathroom. He did not know what all she did in there. Even on occasions when they showered together, he was in and out. She was always in there for an additional hour or more. Maybe it was the shaving thing—he didn't know.

"I'll get it!" Lee-Lee yelled.

Lee-Lee floated past him looking and smelling good enough to eat. She had on some ole sexy, partially sheer, chiffon joint that was pastel pink and white with the matching pink and white mules. The outfit was sheer in all the right places.

"Damn, come here," Marcus ordered. The door could wait.

"Don't get that. Get this," he added, grabbing a handful of his crouch.

Lee-Lee and Marcus had been together since the age of fifteen. As far as he knew

Lee-Lee had never strayed. He took her virginity and her heart in the same year. Their oldest son was born shortly after. Twelve years later, Lee-Lee still knew how to drive him crazy.

"Come on in," she said to the person at the door.

A tall dark brown complexioned stallion walked into their suite, followed by a shorter blonde, blue-eyed Barbie-looking woman. The women wore trench coats, but from being at enough bachelor parties, Marcus knew that there wasn't much underneath. *Was Lee-Lee going to give him an orgy for his birthday?* She always said that she wasn't down with that kind of thing. What was this? Marcus noticed the stripper pole, but he knew that Lee-Lee did not have any rhythm and was born with two left feet.

Just as he suspected, when the two honeys dropped the trenches to the floor, they were semi-naked.

"Hi, we're Ebony and Ivory. We're here for you tonight," the tall one said, as she extended her hand out. He shook her hand, but was otherwise speechless. Lee-Lee was full of surprises, but never anything like this. Ebony had on a tight, white pair of partially sheer booty shorts, with a matching push-up bra and white heels. The white accentuated her pretty, even black skin.

Marcus was glad he had on loose sweatpants. He already had an erection from the lingering smell of his wife's cologne mixed with the smell of the dancer's body juices. Marcus knew the smell well. He was a connoisseur of strippers throughout the state. Each time he strayed from his wife's bed, it was usually with a stripper. Lee-Lee knew it. Unlike all of his dudes, he spent a set amount of money, called his leisure money or play money. He had a hundred dollar limit per night. He got turned on and then went home and gave his whole load that he built up to his wife. Lee-Lee always knew when he'd been to the strip clubs because he would come home horny, frisky, and rock-hard ready. She liked how the strippers made her work at home easier. She suspected that whenever Marcus was out of town, he sampled the wares of strippers, but she didn't trip. She knew that he would practice safe sex, and he never brought any drama home.

Ivory had on a black sequined thong, with nothing but black tassels on her nipples. She looked like she was ready for Broadway. Marcus watched intently. The girls got the party started by Ebony giving Ivory a full tongue kiss. The hip gyrating, popping, locking, and dropping began at the same time. The girls could dance. It was more like a performance. They were a team. While Ivory worked the pole, Ebony walked up to Marcus, climbed on his lap, and gave him a lap dance. He knew not to touch her from receiving lap dances at the club. Lee-Lee was studying Ebony's double-jointed moves like she was a student at Stripper 101 class. Ebony knew she had her attention, and while holding eye contact, she gave a good show. Lee-Lee wasn't into girls, but she was turned on by Ebony's seductive performance. Also, Lee-Lee understood better why her man could not keep his hands off her whenever he left the strip club.

Marcus was being entertained, but locked eyes on Lee-Lee.

"Thank you, ladies, for coming, but it's time to go. I have some business to take care of," Marcus told them.

His love and lust for Lee-Lee had him heated. Her innocence along with the fact that she was all his made him anxious to go up in her. They were kids when he first claimed her. He had molded her, scolded her when she needed it, and watched her mature from a young girl into a woman. He wanted his wife bad, and couldn't wait another second. The girls had performed three records and a lap dance. That was enough. Lee-Lee knew what was up. She'd bought her outfit for her man. She knew what he liked, and how to work him just right.

The strippers had been prepaid. She gave them both a fifty dollar tip as she rushed them to the door. It was time for the grown up and sexy party to begin, and they were not invited.

They never made it to the bed. Before she could latch the door, he had already snatched her up. He lifted her up, pinning her to the wall near the door. He grabbed two handfuls of her firm big butt, and spread her cheeks for easy access. Pressing her back against the wall while guiding himself inside her, he slid her body down on his hard dick. Lee-Lee groaned with pleasure. After making sure she got hers first, he filled her body up with his seed.

Their vacation was a two-fold celebration. It was for his birthday, and also his retirement party from the game.

He decided that if Loot did not want to deal with Dre, he would have to find his own replacement. Dre would also have to go elsewhere to cop. He was not going to allow Loot to drag him along for the ride when he wanted out. He was determined to follow his own agenda, not the next man's. Marcus felt that Loot was stalling him, and that no replacement would make him feel comfortable. Marcus was thinking of his family first, for once in his life.

Lee-Lee filled out all of the papers to purchase both of the commercial properties outright. He did not want a landlord or a mortgage. In the beginning, Marcus planned on putting in as many hours as he did in the game working for himself, in order to build his clientele. He was determined to succeed as a legitimate businessman, and never look back on crime.

Although they chose only three hours away from Cleveland to take their vacation, the Niagara Falls resort worked wonders for his mind and body. Marcus felt rejuvenated and sore from so much banging. He and Lee-Lee took advantage of every spot in the small cozy suite. He needed the time off badly to get his mind right, and to be able to switch gears smoothly.

* * * * * *

Dre kept in constant contact with

Harry.

"I don't think Loot likes me," he told the detective.

"Did you get us a license plate number?" Harry asked.

"Yeah. It's personalized. It's t-h-e-l-o-o-t," Dre spelled out.

The plates came back to a William Gray, Jr. They had stumbled up on Loot's birth name.

Harry and Fox decided not to wait to see if Dre could win Loot over. They knew from experience that seasoned hustlers like Loot were not easily swayed by strangers. Dre informed them that Marcus called a meeting with him at the *Rascal House* pizza parlor. The restaurant was across the street from Cleveland State University, and less than a mile away from downtown. At Harry's request, Dre wore a wire, in order to build a better case against Marcus.

Although it was still broad daylight, Marcus set up the meeting at 3 p.m. The lunch crowd had departed, and the dinner crowd had not yet appeared, so there were plenty of empty tables and booths.

The first thing that Marcus discussed was his departure from the business. Dre knew that it was coming, but he did not expect it so suddenly.

"So, the main thing I wanted you to know is that I have nothing to do with you and Loot getting along. You are on your own with that," Marcus said.

"It's like that? You are just going to abandon ship, and say fuck me?" Dre asked.

Harry and Fox listened and recorded, hanging onto every word.

"Man, this thing is dead for me," Marcus replied.

"So, you got mad dough put up, huh?" Dre baited Marcus. He was fishing to see where the money was. He wanted Marcus stripped naked of everything. Dre was broke. He took no responsibility for tricking off every extra penny he had in the strip joints and with the chicken heads. Dre was a pure sucka when it came to the ladies. His boo was breaking him off and his whole crew, including Marcus, whenever he turned his back. The rumors were correct. Marcus had hit her off a few times, but he never allowed any other woman but Lee-Lee to be a part of his life. He was not looking for anything serious and treated all women outside of Lee-Lee like jump-offs, no matter how classy they seemed to be. He knew that if he did not have the juice from the dope sack and the paper, they would not be interested. Lee-Lee loved him when he had nothing. She had given him a bank to do his business on more than one occasion, and held him down during his bid. If he saw a jump-off or stripper he liked and she came on to him, he would do her if he felt up to it. Most of the time, Lee-Lee had him spent. He didn't have a lot for the streets unless he was traveling, because she believed in waking him up first thing in the morning with the best head in the world.

Sometimes Marcus wondered if Dre knew that his baby momma was a ho. It wasn't his place to tell him, but he had no desire to continue to contribute to her scandalous behavior, so he cut her off.

Marcus agreed to give Dre all of his customers, and permission to book his soldiers with work. He even offered to loan him bird money when Dre told him he was broke. Marcus did not realize that he had said too much, and solidified his fate. He also gave Dre permission to cut into his soldiers, but explained to him that he would have to establish his own connect.

Harry was excited. Thanks to Dre, he had established money laundering, conspiracy, drug trafficking, drug distribution, and kingpin charges.

Marcus hated leaving Dre without a connect, but he had given him a big head start with an extended loan to cop. He gave everyone advance notice. It wasn't his fault that none of his crew took him seriously. He decided that he could not be responsible for the next man and still be loyal to his family. He chose his family, walked away from the table, out the building, across the street, and to his car that was parked on the corner.

Dre was furious.

"How that nigga think he gone carry me like that?" he said into the mic.

What Dre did not know was that Harry and Fox had other extensive plans for Marcus following the meeting.

Marcus got into his car without checking his surroundings. He was not leery of Dre, nor was he aware of doing anything wrong. He proceeded up Euclid Avenue, then decided to cut over to Chester Avenue to avoid some of the Euclid lights and traffic.

As he cruised eastbound up Chester Avenue, he noticed lights from a siren behind him as he approached the Cleveland Clinic area. He check his speed. He wasn't speeding. He made sure he had on his seat belt also. He was also traveling incognito. He had Lee-Lee's drop top black Mustang. Her car was conservatively blinged out with the sound system, televisions, Play Station Three, and other small gadgets, but looked normal from the outside. He slowed down to let whoever was following him know that he intended on stopping when he was able to pull over. He did. The two plain clothed detectives that had thrown a siren on the top of their cars signaled for him to round the corner out of the traffic. He parked on East 101st. The street was empty except for a few parked cars on the opposite side. The younger of the two officers came to his window, and motioned for him to let down his window. He did.

"What's up?" Marcus asked. It was not common for detectives to pull over a routine traffic stop, so he knew that the stop was not about traffic.

"We need you to pull your car into that parking lot right there and come ride with us for a few minutes," Harry requested.

"Why? Am I under arrest or something?" Marcus asked.

"Of course not. We heard a few things, and we just wanted to run them past you,"

Harry explained.

"Like what things, and who are you?" Marcus questioned.

"I am detective Harry Treason, Marcus," Harry said, handing Marcus his business card, and then showing him his badge.

"This will not take a long time. We just need to clear the air about a few things here," Harry said.

"I don't know what this is about, but let me pull this car in here. I will be with you in a second," Marcus said.

From experience, he knew it was better to act like you were cooperating when your head was in the lion's mouth. There was nothing to be gained from being a smart ass with two detectives, but a good ass whooping and a hard way to go. Still, his mind was racing. *What the hell could they want with me, and even more, who had got arrested that I didn't know about*? He wondered. He was about to find out.

When Marcus got in the car, Harry was in the front passenger seat, and Fox was driving. They were headed back down Chester, toward downtown. Harry pressed play. He did not bother with formalities.

"I will turn over all of my customers to you also." Marcus heard his voice convey clearly. He continued to listen to the rest of his conversation on the recording in silence. He knew he was fucked. Dre was a snitch, and he had just worn a wire. Marcus knew he was good as dead because he had mentioned Loot's name over and over again. That kind of slip of the tongue was unacceptable. Loot said that he did not trust Dre, and Marcus should have listened. Marcus was angry enough to kill someone with his bare hands.

"Look, we don't want you. We want the bigger fish. We know you work for someone else, and we would like to trade up" Harry said.

Marcus had been in a raged daze. He snapped out of it.

"What?"

"We said we want you to work with us to bust Loot. We have enough on you to assure a minimum of ten years, and if we let the feds get a peek at you, we can double that ten" Harry said.

Marcus was not in a talking or listening mood. *How did he get himself in such a fucked up position?* he thought. He was full of rage.

"This is a one-time offer. I mean it. You will not get this chance again. We want Loot" Harry said.

Marcus was about to kirk out on them. He felt no fear. In his heart and soul he had already mourned his family, cause he knew that he would not succumb to their program, and snitching was really out of the question.

"You two bitches can suck my dick," Marcus said boldly.

Harry turned all the way around in his seat to get full eye contact with Marcus. After staring at each other indefinitely, Harry made a decision.

"He's no good," Harry said.

"Speak up, I couldn't hear you," Fox said.

"I said that this nigger is no good." Harry's voice trembled with hate and anger. Marcus had ruined his plans to bust Loot. He had to be dealt with. Harry also had to protect Dre. He could not let this fool pull the cover off of Dre.

"Pull onto Twelve and Lakeside. You know the spot," Harry demanded.

Fox did know the spot. They usually took hookers there to get free blow jobs. The spot was a small empty lot that was secluded and blocked in by two small factories without windows on both sides. The north side of the lot was Lake Erie. There was never anyone around due to the secluded, spooky location.

When they arrived at the spot, Harry got out and opened the door for Marcus.

"Get out," he ordered. Marcus did as he was told.

"Face the water," Harry said, as he reached in his holster, and cocked his 38 special.

"It's over for you, stupid bastard," Harry said, and shot Marcus at point blank range in the back of the head. Blood splattered on Harry's shirt and a few drops on his shoe. He didn't flinch. As he watched the life drain out of the victim, he felt relieved. He could not allow Marcus to live. No sooner had he got to jail, he would have been calling collect to put the word out about Dre. He had no loyalty to Dre. He did not like him at all. He did have loyalty to his mission and agenda, and that was to bring down Loot, and gain control back of his streets from the drug dealers.

* * * * * *

Marcus knew he had been shot instantly. His body was hit with a solid force that knocked him face down in the dirt. He felt his body sinking, and plunging deeper. He was falling at enormous speed, toward a bright light that tunneled into nothingness. He did not feel fear. His last vision of this life was Lee-Lee's warm smile. If half of his head wasn't missing, he may have formed a smile, but instead Marcus was dead almost instantly.

* * * * * *

Lee-Lee sat on the couch in front of the television watching Oprah. The billionaire superstar had opened up a school in Africa for girls. Lee-Lee embraced the idea. All African-Americans were of African descent, so she did not understand why it was black people who were criticizing Oprah most for doing something for her heritage. Out of nowhere, the temperature in the room became unbearably cold. Simultaneously, her palms began to sweat, and she experienced a funny, bad feeling all over. *Something bad was happening to Marcus*, she thought. She tried to convince herself that she was being paranoid. What could possibly be happening to him? He was no longer in the drug game. Still, she could not shake the feeling. The last time she had similar feelings, Marcus had been arrested. She dialed his cell phone. There was no answer. It went straight to voicemail.

"Daddy, I need you to call me. I am missing you," she said, after the beep.

She attempted to carry on like normal, and pay attention to Oprah, yet she could not shake her fear. Yeah, she had named it, it was fear. Fear of what? Had Marcus been picked up? Lee-Lee could not resist. She dialed his cell again. And again. And again. Despite the unknown, she began to cry. Marcus never missed her calls on his cell. He was adamant about that because of the children. By 4 a.m., which was more than twelve hours since she last talked to him, she became physically ill. She kept throwing up over the toilet until there was nothing else left on her stomach.

By the next morning, she called all of the precincts and the hospitals. There was not a record of a black male being brought in under any circumstances that fit Marcus' description. Lee-Lee exhaled. Although she was not an early morning person, by 6 a.m., she was fully dressed, with shoes on and cash in her pocket. At the last minute she decided to also add her MasterCard and their joint American Express. If she had to pay an attorney or a bondsman, she did not want to waste any time on having to go to the bank.

After filling up Marcus' voice mail where it would not accept any more messages, she got comfortable on the couch to await her future. She dosed in and out of a restless sleep.

At 10 p.m., the telephone rang, snapping her awake. She almost dropped the phone from being discombobulated.

"May we speak to the head of the household, Ma'am?" an unknown caller said.

"This is she," she replied, with more confidence than she felt.

"What is your name?" the caller asked.

"No, what is your name?" Lee-Lee reversed.

"Oh, excuse me for having bad manners. My name is Dr. Lisbon. I am the assistant mortician for County General. Ma'am, do you know or are you related to a Marcus Thomas?" the stranger asked.

"Yes, I am."

"We need you to come down to the station. Do you have someone that can drive you?" he asked.

"No, I don't. I will be right down."

Because of the eerie feeling that she'd been experiencing, a part of her knew that she was going to identify Marcus' body, but yet a part of her refused to fully accept it.

It was her husband. Her beautiful Marcus. She was not allowed to view his entire body. The engraved wedding ring, his wallet, car keys and clothing were all in a large plastic bag for display. She was allowed to view his covered up form, after she kept insisting. She wanted them to pull the sheet back, so that she could see his face.

"We can't do that, Ma'am. He has had considerable damage done. It is against policy. We assure you, before we called you in we checked fingerprints and dental records, and it is your husband," the examiner said.

Lee-Lee walked out into the parking lot and collapsed at the side of her car. She did not know how long that she'd been out—it may have been a moment, or a day. She picked herself off the ground, got in her car, and drove away in a daze.

Chapter 9

John graduated to bigger things, and more money, if that was possible. His company was internationally known for its assistance to Third World countries. The world was his playground. He plugged entire cities into generators and the Internet. John raised the standard of the rulers to be able to compete with America's technology. He was the hook-up for many unadvanced countries. His mixed cargo was still going strong.

Loot had decided to expand geographically in all directions. He added Pittsburgh, Pennsylvania, Syracuse, New York, Buffalo, New York, Covington, Kentucky and most of the state of Indiana to their territory that they provided dope to.

Ohio was also on lock-down. All dope in Ohio originated directly or indirectly from Loot.

John was definitely on top of his game.

Loot was also doing big things. Unlike Marcus, he vowed to himself that he would never leave the streets. He loved the power, drugs and money, and even more so the level of respect. He was a boss. It had taken a lot of discipline and violence to earn his label, but he had arrived. The chaos of the streets kept the fiends running back and forth for their drugs. The same streets he ruled paid him like a slot machine.

Loot's life was not without problems. Marcus recently had come up dead. Although he had been aggravated with his decision to leave the game, his cousin's death crushed him. He was off sync. What bothered him most was that he had no idea what had happened to Marcus. The streets gave no clues. Marcus did not have any known enemies. There were haters everywhere, but they would not kill a person execution style. Loot made it his business to have one of his lieutenants backtrack to every woman that Marcus had been intimate with. Everyone, including Lee-Lee was just as puzzled by Marcus' death as Loot. He would have to check it. That is just how the streets were. If he did not, niggas would begin to check him. He knew how it went.

"Loot, please find out who took my baby's life," his aunt, and Marcus' mother, said, with a face full of tears.

"I will, Auntie. I promise," Loot said, taking her into his arms and embracing her tightly. His mom was also stressed out because Marcus was the son of her baby sister.

Things were about to get hectic. Loot started things off by offering through the media and the streets a fifty thousand cash reward for any information leading up to the perpetrator of the murder of his cousin. He used Lee-Lee's legitimate name and reputation on the TV newscasts, and his power in the streets to attempt to muscle the truth into the open. Loot was determined to find his cousin's murderer, and avenge his death.

The breakthrough came three weeks later. It was Dre's baby momma that solved the mystery for him.

"I need to meet with you. I think I have some information that you might want," Chante told Loot over the phone.

When he met Chante, he felt like he knew her. *Had he banged her before?* he thought. She sure looked familiar.

"What's up, Ma?"

"I wanted to let you know what's up with my boyfriend," she said.

"Who's your boyfriend?" Loot asked. He hoped that this chicken head wasn't wasting his time. She had tried to dress for success, but instead looked like she came straight out of the projects. Her form-fitting dress was supposed to be a Versace, but was a Bersace. Her large sunglasses were supposed to be Dolce and Gabanna, but were Dole and "G." She was a knock off queen. Everything about her was fake and cheap.

"Andre. They call him Dre."

That got Lott's attention. He tuned all the way into her. The reason why Chante called Loot was because she hoped to gain his favor. She was sick of Dre, and ready to move on to a bigger prize. She saw on TV that there was a reward of fifty thousand dollars, and had already begun to spend it. She knew she had the information that Loot needed to avenge his cousin's death. She also held the information to free herself from Dre. Dre never had money anymore. He told her that he was working on acquiring a new connect since Marcus' death. That was a month ago! In the meantime, he was laying up and eating off of her. That was unacceptable. Dre was broke. The last straw was when he asked her for some money! She was ready to move on.

A few days ago, when she and Dre were at home together, she picked up the extension of their bedroom to listen to his phone call. She did it all the time to see what he was up to. She hoped that it was the drug hookup that he kept talking about. She was tired of hearing about it, and wanted to see some action.

"Detective Treason, please," Dre announced in proper voice that was different from his regular jargon.

Detective Treason? What was this fool up to on her home phone? she thought. There were about three minutes of silence, and then the sound of electricity cackling. Finally a voice penetrated the silence on the phone line.

"Andre. I'm on. Shoot," Harry said. He wanted to hear what Dre had to say. He knew that Dre had found out about Marcus' murder by then.

"Man, don't try to play me. What happened to Marcus?" Dre asked.

"What kind of question is that?"

"What do it sound like? I was the last one seen with him, wearing a wire from y'all's office, and then POOF—in thin air he disappeared and then came up dead two days later," Dre said.

"Look, I don't have time for this kind of conversation over the phone. Meet me outside the station in fifteen minutes," Harry said.

He was furious. How dare this young punk call his job and talk reckless like that. He would teach him. He was about to lay his ass down too.

"Give me thirty minutes. Peace out," Dre said.

Chante hung up the phone softly to make sure that Dre would not hear her.

"Boo, I have to make a run. Let me hold a few dollars for gas," Dre said.

Chante looked at him without answering. He had the game twisted. He was not about to keep asking *her* for her money. When he saw that she wasn't going to answer, he went to her fake Coach bag that was hanging on the door knob and removed a twenty dollar bill.

"I'll give it back," he said, as he walked toward the door.

Chante wondered what happened to Marcus. The streets had it that Lee-Lee had to be hospitalized for fear of a nervous breakdown. The street news also said that Marcus had big dough, and had left Lee-Lee and their children well off.

Chante sat on the side of the bed shaking her head back and forth at her own dilemma. She was broke. Her baby daddy was broke and a snitch. He also may have been a conspirator to murder. She did not want to be with Dre any longer. That is what led her to her meeting with Loot.

Loot listened to Chante repeat the entire conversation that Dre had with the detective. Chante even knew the detective's name. She told him that Dre had gone to meet with the detective.

"Come back at this time tomorrow at this same place, Shorty, and one of my lieutenants will hand you your ends. Just say you are here for me, and he will hand you a paper bag with the cash in it," he told her as he got up from the table. He read people well. He did not feel a double-cross from this woman, or he would have made arrangements for her to be dealt with, as well as her man at the same time.

Loot called two of his lynchmen. He called the most trusted, dangerous, and expensive. This had to be a professional job, because he had left the girl living. He had to also make sure that he had an alibi. He knew how the tables could turn. The chicken head was there for the money, but once the money was gone, she could easily start to grieve her dead boyfriend and send the police on him. He had to cover all angles.

The hitmen charged him one hundred thousand dollars each. They demanded half up front and the other half upon completion. Loot needed to round up one hundred and fifty thousand dollars in cash. He had to make sure that he had fifty thousand for Dre's girlfriend also. He told the men to meet him at a specific location the following day, high noon.

What Chante didn't know is that it was a double hit ordered. Loot wanted Detective Treason also. He knew how it went. Although Dre wore a wire and set his cousin up, Dre was not a killer. Detective Harry Treason was. He knew his rep. The man was crazy. Loot was surprised that he did not have a lot more bodies to his jacket, and that he hadn't killed a few of the hookers he tricked with. Street women feared him. He was nothing nice. Loot hoped that he would get lucky, and score a two-for-one. Maybe he would catch Dre snitching, and be able to do them both at the same time. What he knew is it would happen. The two soldiers he sent had an undisputed record—all successes. No mistakes and no misses. They were trained by the CIA, and the federal government had not missed a trick. When they retired and resigned, they continued to kill for hire. The clients were simply non-government.

Although John did not like to hear about the business end of things in the street, he knew that there was a lot going on. Whenever he talked to Loot over the past week, he could hear it in his voice. When Loot came to pick up the shipment and transfer it to the safe spot that he used, John asked him.

"Cuz, you are under a lot of stress. What's going down?" John asked.

"It is really out of your league, but I will tell you that a few clowns killed my first cousin on my mom's side," Loot shared.

"Word?" John said.

"Yeah. And you know I can't let that go

unchecked. If I do, I'll be treated like a bitch in no time," Loot said.

"Well, if you need me man, I'm here. We grew up together. I can't imagine losing you, so I feel your pain," John said. It was real. He loved his cousin, although he did not understand him sometimes. He had propositioned Loot to get out of the game and retire more than once, but his answer was always the same. He would not get out. Instead of John pressing the issue, or pulling out himself, he continued to supply Loot with the best dope in the country, and plenty of it.

Chapter 10

Harry paced the floor of the precinct basement. He was trying to decide how and where he wanted to do Dre. He knew that he would have to take him for a ride, because the force did not condone his ruthless behavior. He decided to invite Dre to lunch with him. That way he was sure to eliminate Fox. Although Fox was his partner, he did not believe in letting his left hand know everything his right hand was doing. That was not a good policy.

"How about some Sammy's corned beef?" he asked.

Dre was hungry. Sammy's sounded good. In fact, Chante hadn't cooked him anything in a month. Anything sounded good, including Mickey Dee's. Sammy's had the best and the biggest corned beef sandwiches in the city. It was clean, cozy, and out of the way. Being on the corner of St. Clair, near downtown, the busiest time was the lunch traffic. Lunch was over, and it was too early for the dinner crowd. Harry ordered two jumbo corned beef for both of them.

He listened impatiently as Dre whined about the Marcus killing, and kept continuously blaming it on him, despite the fact that he'd asked him repeatedly to hold that down. The man was a fool.

After lunch was finished, Harry suggested that they visit the pier. At first

Dre hesitated, but only for a split second. Harry would not harm him. He needed him to try to gather information about Loot, and the streets that Loot controlled. That is what was driving the two men. Both Loot and Harry wanted to control the streets.

Once the two men arrived at the pier, they parked at the end of the parking lot. The timing was perfect. A light drizzle was falling. People hated the rain, and so if anyone was thinking about coming to the lake, they would change their mind when they saw the rain.

Harry did not bother with formalities. He pulled out his gatt, and shot Dre point blank in the temple of his head as he tried to light a cigarette. Harry cursed at the mess on the passenger's side of his car. He opened the door, and kicked him out of the car by his hip. Before Dre's body hit the pavement, Harry was already pulling off. It was his lucky day. There wasn't a car in sight that he could see. The cars that passed on the nearby shoreway were looking straight ahead, not sightseeing at the pier.

He took his car home, pulled it into the garage, and began to detail it well with soap and the water hose. He didn't spare water. The insides would dry.

The following day, Loot gave Chante her money through one of his workers, and paid both hitmen. They asked for seven business days. Loot said that was fine.

The men knew how to get a reading on Treason. They talked to the hookers. It was already well known that Detective Treason had a fetish for free pussy. He would not pay, but could not stay off the ho-stroll. The women eagerly gave the messenger sent a clear description, and one of the women even had the license plate of his personal car. She told the men that he preferred to drive his personal car during pickups.

The license plates were registered to Treason's home, which would have been an easy lick, but the two men decided to hit him in the streets to make it occur as a random robbery or accidental killing.

Friday night, Harry cruised the strip. He was looking for the blonde stripper that turned tricks on the side. He liked her because of her lack of personality. She did not smile, talk, or ask questions. She didn't even complain about him wanting free sex. Her attitude about everything was nonchalant.

He watched her get out of a red pickup truck. His body responded to her in a way that he did not know possible. He got an erection from watching her enter the bar that she worked out of. Before she could venture back inside, he blew his horn and flashed his lights. From a distance she could not tell it was him, but she knew it was a date, so she ran toward the car. Her street name was Brittany, because she was a Brittany Spears look-alike, but her real name was Sarah. Harry chose to call her Sarah. She hated that, and got an instant attitude.

"Hey, how about coming back later. Let me make a few dollars first," Sarah said.

Harry did the unthinkable. He threw a one hundred dollar bill across the seat. She glanced down at the money, hesitated for only a second, and then got in the passenger's seat of the car. Harry had never paid her anything before. Maybe he wasn't such a bad guy after all. Also, the good thing about him was that he had a small member, and he came quick, so it was easy money. The inconvenience was that he did not like the inner city. He always wanted to go somewhere remote. She liked to stay near the strip and the action. Harry hit the freeway. Where they went was not her decision. If he would not have been looking at her long, gorgeous bare legs spread throughout the passenger seat of his car, he may have noticed that he was being followed.

Although Harry had never thought about being committed, he wondered if Sarah was tamable. He reasoned that a wife and a child may not be the end of the world.

* * * * * *

Chante went home after collecting her money to plan how she would spend it. She felt no remorse for setting Dre up, and felt no loyalty to him. As quiet as it was kept, Chante did not know if he was the father of her son. She considered going on the *Maury Povich Show* to establish paternity, but her mother said she would disown her if she brought embarrassment to her family in that way. Her son did not even resemble Dre. He never suspected her of cheating, or the paternity of her son. He was such a buster. The sooner she was able to discard him, the better. She wanted to come up with a real baller, not a wanna-be like Dre.

The first thing she did was go to the mall and buy herself some clothes. She also bought her son new clothing and a coat, and gave her mother five hundred dollars. She did not want to give her too much, because she did not want her mother to know what kind of money she had. By the following day, she began to suspect that Dre may be dead. He always came home at night, and not only did he not show, but also no calls. She did not want to get too happy prematurely. She waited three days before she called his sister, and also filed a missing person's report with the authorities. Of course, they had no interest, and their investigation into Dre missing ended before it started.

* * * * * *

The word of Dre's death traveled through the hood fast. His body was found by two factory workers that went out to the side of the building to take a cigarette break, and noticed a funny shaped object sprawled in the empty adjoining lot next to their worksite. The smell let them know that it was a dead body long before they got close enough to see. They called the police instantly. The man had been dead a few days.

Loot knew that the hit would be carried out successfully. He was surprised that they had completed everything within the first forty-eight hours of getting paid. With Dre done, he knew that the detective would be their main focus. He also knew that the detective would not be as easy a mark as

Dre. You get what you pay for, and he'd hired professionals.

* * * * * *

Harry arrived home in the wee hours of the night. He thought that he'd left his front porch light on, but the bulb was always going out. He didn't understand why they didn't last as long as the light bulbs inside the house. He reasoned that it must have been some type of interference with the elements to make them burn out quicker.

When he entered his front room, he froze suddenly. He could not pinpoint it, but something was not right. He did not turn on the light. He allowed his eyes to adjust to the darkness. Everything appeared to be normal on the surface, but every instinct he had let him know that things were not right. Someone was in his house with him. He felt the presence, but did not know what was going on. He quickly pulled his gun out of the shoulder holster for good measure, and decided to also arm himself with the small revolver from his leg holster.

He walked through the house, concentrating on his surroundings with each step. As he approached each door, he loudly kicked it open, assuming the position in case of gunplay. Just as he was beginning to believe that he was paranoid, he became face to face with his assailant.

"Drop the gun," his perpetrator whispered. Harry knew that this was the point of no return. He took a chance on saving his own life. He dropped the gun that was obvious from his right hand, and shot from the other one using his left hand, out of sight of his intruder.

It was no good.

"This is from Loot. You killed his cousin, Marcus," the hitman said quietly, before squeezing off four rounds from a 9 millimeter, semi-automatic with a silencer.

Harry Treason did not stand a chance. He did not fear death, nor did he feel fear. He felt violated, and very angry. He made himself focus on his murders during the last few minutes of his life. He left this world with a clear picture of Marcus and Loot in his mind. If there was an afterlife, he was determined on getting revenge. His last prayer was not to God, but to Satan, saying, "Please help me to avenge those animals. I will be your servant," he whispered to the king of evil, and the one who governed the afterworld.

BOOK TWO

Chapter 11

The man was dead.

Whenever life disappeared from the earth, the Ruler of the other world was able to seek power from the dying. The Ruler used His powerful forces to snatch the soul of the man in transition.

How it worked was simple. Once a person reached their last six seconds of life, their fate was up for grabs. The enemy, who possessed as much power as Him, needed only to hesitate a nanosecond. If the enemy hesitated, that meant that the deeds of the person while among the living were questionable. The Ruler loved when there was hesitation, because that was His only chance. When the enemy paused, the Ruler of the earth and purgatory made his move. The enemy did hesitate with the fate of Harry Treason the day of his death. Because of that, Harry Treason belonged to Him. He placed Treason's soul in his vast collection, called the living dead.

He did not need any more disciples or followers. He had conquered millions throughout time. When He became tired of them, he simply turned their bodies to dust, and their souls to nothingness. There was a big turnover in his world.

The Ruler did not possess the power to give life to the living, or to the dead. That was one of his main limitations that he despised. Because of that obvious shortcoming, the Giver of Life truly held the key to eternity, and was more powerful than Him. The Giver of Life was his enemy. There was no question about it.

When the Ruler of earth encouraged Eve in the Garden of Eden to partake in the corrupting of Adam, the enemy ousted the Ruler's powers. Thousands of years later, the incident was still a sore spot between the two.

The Ruler reigned throughout the earth, and the enemy ruled the heavens. The final showdown for them was Judgment Day, but until then, the Ruler planned to play His position, and play it well.

So, the enemy's hesitation is how the Ruler came across Harry Treason. There were many Harry Treasons that crossed the Ruler's path.

The Ruler sat still and waited for the next slip through to happen, while he mentally began to create Treason's treatment plan.

Chapter 12

Harry Treason did not see a bright light, nor did he see a vision of a tunnel. The instant that his body died and exhaled its last breathe, his soul separated from his body. He did not feel this, nor was he aware that it happened. He knew that something strange was happening because his body went from feeling excruciating pain to no pain at all. He knew that he'd been shot. He felt the bullets, and then after a few seconds in time, nothing. Nothingness. Everything was dark and cold.

The darkness lasted for a few seconds, and then he found himself standing outside of his physical self, studying his own body. He watched one of his murderers make sure that no prints existed. It was like watching a movie with yourself in the star role. It felt more than weird. As he watched his assailants methodically move around, he felt like time stood still.

The men wore gloves, but even then were still being overly cautious. The second intruder carefully rummaged through Harry's personal belongings. Everything he found of value, he dropped in a knapsack. Harry closely studied the faces of the two men that murdered him. He had never seen either man before in his life. Reality had not set in with him that his life was over. Seeing the two men, he knew who killed him, and because of the death message he received, he also knew who was responsible for his death. Loot had left him a message that would prove to be helpful later.

Harry would not have to search for his killers to avenge his own death. Although the two men in front of him had to be dealt with, they were not his main focus. Their time would ultimately come, but it was Loot who he felt an urgency to kill.

Being new to death was strange. Where was his welcoming committee? Would anyone be giving him a smash course on the proper etiquette of the dead? He had many questions. Would he ever be hungry again, and have to perform regular daily duties like other living human beings? What were his limitations, and did he have special powers? So many questions, and no answers. He would just have to try things out.

* * * * * *

The newspaper article that listed the death of Detective Harry Treason was barely noticeable. It labeled his death as a burglary of his home. There were no witnesses or suspects. Because he was a member of the force, Fox insisted that the case be left open. It was not standard policy, but Fox was determined to interview every robber and burglar within a one hundred mile radius. He had also offered a small reward for information that led to the arrest of anyone connected to his partner's death. The force saw it as a random crime. The rate of daytime burglaries was increasing annually. Sooner or later one of the force members was bound to get hit.

Harry Treason had no living relatives, and no steady girlfriend. His mother and his grandmother were the only two persons that he had ever mentioned, and they both were deceased. Fox knew that he did not date anyone regularly, and that he bought his affection from the cathouse. Although Fox did not believe in sleeping with hookers on a regular basis, he was grateful that his partner was not deviant in his quest for sex. Fox knew many cops that secretly preferred girls over women, and even boys over girls. That was something that he could not tolerate, and he was thankful that Harry Treason was a man that had been married to his job. There was not a thing wrong with that.

Fox ended up being the one that had to clean out Harry's drawer space at work. He decided that it was no rush. He did not want another partner anytime soon, and had decided to spend more time in the office than on the beat, and to take it easy. The streets were beginning to create severe mental wear and tear on him.

Harry began to figure out his new arrangement of existence. He no longer had to pee or eat, nor was sleep a requirement. He also noticed that there were hundreds of his kind around. There was never a conversation, and a few times he got the living confused with the walking dead. Harry saw everyone. He was able to observe people moving along day to day, without them having a clue that he was observing them. He was shocked to see his girlfriend Patty! Patty looked, well, she looked different, he decided. The confusing part was being able to tell whether or not he was looking at a living person or a dead one. A few of the specimens he encountered his first few days left him unsure. The give-away was the direct eye contact. The dead were able to see him, yet they never communicated verbally.

Another discovery helped Harry put a plan of action together. Harry learned that if he found a living vessel that was on the verge of death, he could take over their physical self.

His first test run was with the body of a dog that had gotten hit by a car. The dog's limp body lay on the side of the road, barely breathing.

"He is not going to make it." A large, round, barrel shaped woman said to the circle of three people standing around waiting for the dog to reach his fate. Harry bent down to examine the dog. His breathing was shallow, and it appeared that it was also painful for the dog to inhale air. When Harry placed his hand on the dog's chest, he felt a surge of a current. It felt similar to the shock you feel when your body touches an object full of electricity. Harry snatched his hand off the dog's chest, releasing the current of energy. As he did, the dog began to whimper softly. It was at that second that Harry realized the connection. The dog was a few seconds from dying. He was able to see Harry clearly and knew that Harry did not belong to this world. The dog whimpered from fear.

As the three onlookers stood by without seeing Harry, he placed his hands on the dog's chest again. This time he focused on the dying state of the dog. Harry felt himself swiftly being sucked into a state of nothingness that he was not able to control. His world turned black. He tried to open his eyes and see light, but could not focus. Nothingness. Then he felt motion around him again.

When he focused his eyes, he was no longer touching the dog. Harry was the dog. He had taken over the dog's body. When the dog entered into the corridor of death, Harry was able to switch sides while in the corridor. The feeling resembled a ride inside a dark tunnel where you switch lanes.

Harry decided to test his power and will. He focused on standing up on all four legs. Although wobbly from being hit hard by the car, he stood.

"Oh my God! He's alive!" the lady onlooker yelled. The lady made him want to yell at her. People were so gullible at times, and that aggravated him.

Harry walked over to the lady and purposely peed on her black, low, square-heeled shoes. *That should shut her up*, he thought. It did. The woman was appalled. The three onlookers quickly dispersed. They did not want to be bothered with a temperamental, injured dog.

Nobody informed Harry that he had a time limit to use his new vessel, but somehow he knew. He did not know how much time he had, but he did know that technically, the dog's body he was in was a few seconds from being as dead as he was. Harry entered his body just in time, before the dog entered into the state of the afterlife.

He was only ten blocks from his beat. He wanted to see what was going on with the circle of things that poisoned his streets and worked for Loot.

Harry discovered that he possessed a sixth sense. Without anyone giving him a clue, he found Loot within minutes of reaching the block. Loot was parked in the parking lot of the Shrimp Boat, on the corner of East 131st and Kinsman. He was on the driver's side of a late model, pearl colored Lexus truck, sitting in the driver's seat, talking to a very conservatively dressed black man that looked to be around the same age as Loot. There was also a slight physical resemblance. The man that sat on the passenger's side showed signs of being in deep thought.

Harry moved closer to the truck. His body easily was hidden by the height of the truck. He was glad that both men had the windows of the truck partially rolled down. It would have been impossible to hear their conversation with the windows up.

"Cuz, we moving things so fast, now before you been coming in all them things are already sold," Loot said.

"I know you making it rain for real, but I've been telling you that I really need to cut down on trips, and I eventually want to phase the illegal business out," John said.

"Cuz, if you could just roll with me for six more months, then I will be able to retire," Loot lied. He had no intention of ever retiring from the game.

"Loot, I'm not committing to that. I know you rich. Why not quit now?" Why six months?" John asked his cousin.

"John, you've always had a job. This life ain't for you. You've lived on the other side of the fence and did well. This is all I know man," Loot said.

He was being honest with his cousin. Loot had never been employed for anyone. The streets were his educator and employer. He had fulfilled every hustler's dream. He started out with nothing, selling dubs on the street corner and barely eating. Now all of his crew were on swoll. Loot was a very handsome man. When he was able to check money like he was bringing in, looks were not important to the ladies. Hustling was all he knew, and all he cared to know. For once in his life he was finally The Man. He had no intention of giving up his power and control of the drug game and the streets.

As Harry ear hustled while the two men conversed, he was able to put things together. The man in the truck with Loot was named John. He was Loot's connect and possibly his cousin. The rest of their conversation did not interest him. Harry pretended to be smelling for food around the truck the two men were in. They did not notice him. Harry walked across the Shrimp Boat parking lot, exiting on 131st Street. He needed to gather all of the information that he could on the new suspect. The problem was how.

He was a dead dog. He could not talk, and he surely was not able to get near anyone's computer to complete his research. Being dead had its limitations.

Chapter 13

Loot felt good about the hits. They were clean, and even with the cop, there was no heat. The rumor was that his death was the result of a house robbery, and that it was random. Dre's death was ruled the result of a drug deal gone bad, like most execution style deaths that occur with young black males. The hit men made it seem like a robbery by stealing everything that was small and valuable. The men knew that it was important to set it up so that it didn't look like murder.

With the replacement of Marcus and the national expansion of the drug game, Loot felt on top of the world. He was definitely at the top of his game. The money, women, and more recruits followed his trail like bees on honey.

John was counting so much money, he had to hire an additional accountant to keep up with his finances. His international business account was one of the most lucrative at the law firm of Hansen and Smith. The firm assigned John a team of his own that was comprised of an attorney, an accountant that managed his local affairs, and a second accountant for international affairs. Each accountant had an assistant.

All of them received a healthy salary after the firm billed John for all billable expenses.

John was excited about getting out of the drug game. He understood the law of averages. A person could not continue to keep breaking the law and not run upon a snag. He had a good run, but it was time to quit. Even further, his son and wife needed him at home more.

He worked sixteen hours a day, seven days a week. He traveled on the average of twenty-three days out of a month. Seven days a month were not sufficient to raise a family and keep a wife happy. Mary was a good woman. John had been blessed.

John's last ninety days of importing drugs was a time of challenges. Poppie expected him to find at least one replacement. John did not like the idea of that. As much as he did not want to, he had to consider Loot. John was not a hater in any form or fashion. Loot needed a strong, consistent connect, and Poppie needed an American exporter.

What made John hesitate was fate. He knew that if he put the two overly zealous, greedy men together, his cousin would end up either dead or serving a life sentence in federal prison. John did not want that on his conscience. There were no other alternatives for Loot or Poppie. What John did not understand is that Loot understood his fate, and would not bend. He operated from an inner primal fear of being broke and common. Loot was a career hustler. He felt that to give up the power of the streets would be equivalent to death. He was already caught up deep into the game, with no turning back. Like a perfectly harmonized marriage, the union was 'till death do us part.'

John decided to meet with Loot and discuss the possibility of meeting up with Poppie in Ecuador, and break down for him what could and could not happen.

Loot drove eastbound up Chagrin, preoccupied with a few of the small details of his life. John had asked him to met him at Bravos, which was a suburban ritzy Italian restaurant located in a suburb of Cleveland. Loot would have preferred the inner city. The Lancer bar and grill was where he conducted most of his meetings during the lunch hour. John preferred to be away from the city. His cousin ordered Italian dishes that he could not even pronounce. If he wasn't raised with the man, he would have thought that he was putting on airs, but his cousin was just like that. The man was the only black person in the world he knew, that sipped on martinis. Before Loot got there, he knew that his cousin would order one of Bravo's chocolate martinis. Apple was his second favorite. Give Loot some Henny or Patron and he was straight.

Chagrin Boulevard traffic was always congested in the afternoon, due to all of the corporations surrounding the area, and the large street being a throughway for interstates 271 and 480.

As Loot approached the Central Cadillac display lot, he glanced in his rear view mirror to make sure that there weren't any cars tailing him. He did not want to cause an accident as he slowed down to check out the new selections of Caddies in the window. They also displayed Rolls Royces, which was going to be his next buy. As he glanced, he saw something that almost made him have an accident. His car swerved over to the opposite lane, dangerously crossing the yellow line that separated oncoming traffic from his lane.

"What the hell?" he said aloud. Loot was shook. He quickly snapped the car over to the curb lane in front of Central Cadillac, almost causing a multi-car collision by changing lanes and stopping abruptly. Loot grabbed the door handle to exit the car. As he did, he glanced again in his rear view mirror to keep an eye on his intruder. Loot's mind was playing tricks on him! There was nothing in the back seat of the car, or no sign of what he had seen a second ago in his rear view mirror. The image was of a white man, conservatively dressed in a gray suit jacket, appearing to be small framed, and—he could not allow his mind to travel to the end, and yet he could not get it out of his mind. The man appeared to be fading, as a bright, billowy heap, with a dark foundation resembling the man's shape, like a cumulus cloud.

Loot was not sure what had resided on his back seat, but what he did know is that it did not belong to this world. He tried to think logically. He was not the type of man that spooked easily, yet he was upset enough to pee on himself. His stomach was also full of knots. He had not examined his true beliefs on things and objects that were not of this world. If you would have asked him before this very incident, he would have had to say that he did not believe in ghosts. Now he was being forced to examine his belief quickly. Sure, he'd read every book that Stephen King ever wrote. Stephen King was one of his favorite authors. Although he did not take time to read novels now, in prison it was his favorite pastime. He also watched movies that portrayed *things* that were not clear, but he simply attributed it to Hollywood theatrical effects. What he saw in his back seat was Steven Spielberg quality effects on steroids.

Loot was still slightly shaken when he pulled into the parking lot of the mini strip that contained shared parking for Bravos Restaurant, Barnes-n-Noble, Cold Stone ice cream, and a houseware place.

"Hey, Cuz!" John greeted him with a firm family hug.

After all of the small talk, ordering food and drinks, and dismissing the waiter, the two men got down to business.

"Loot, I need you to take a trip with me," John said.

Loot's palms became instantly sweaty. He was able to temporarily put the apparition he saw earlier out of his mind. This was the moment he had been waiting for. He silently sulked about John not hooking him up with his connect in the past. It did not make sense to him. He felt that John did not trust him a hundred percent. Loot was old school, and lived by old school principles. When he was turned out to the game decades ago, to snitch or talk with the police about anything other than *"How those coffee and donuts taste?"* was the lowest level that a man could go. Loot did not carry his strict standards to women snitching. He believed that women should not ever be placed in the game. Women acted on maternal instincts and emotion. They were created to protect their children. This extended to animals. They were not logically thinking creatures. Loot adopted the exact same philosophy as the mafia dons that brought organized crime to America. A woman's place was in the home, and in the bed. They were born to be supported, spoiled, and protected. Their emotional makeup made them bad candidates for the game. Loot expected women to protect the home front if put in that situation. Anytime he heard of a woman cooperating with the police for a lesser sentence, he blamed it on her man. Men were supposed to be the head of household. If a man did involve his woman in any aspect of the business where she faced arrest, he was supposed to risk his life to attempt to set her free. Only a weak man would allow his woman to fall with him or for him. Loot kept his business as far away from his family as he possibly could. His children's college tuition was already paid, and had been adjusted for inflation.

Also because the world was at the edge of an international bout of recession, he put away twice as much money. Each of his two children had two hundred thousand dollars buried in a trail of paperwork, originating from the Cayman Islands, to avoid high tax liabilities.

They also had ten million each being invested in hidden accounts in Cape Town, with twenty percent of that being invested regularly in hedge funds. The hedge fund business was Loot's favorite investment. With the guidance of John, Loot had increased his fortune ten-fold. John introduced him to the investment and savings wizard. His name was Presti Ouwega. Ouwega laundered his money across the continents. Loot insisted on having a man manage his savings and investments. Ouwega was the best. He was an African, with a strong dislike for Loot's wastefulness of money. He spent and invested every penny as if it was his own.

John insisted years ago that Loot begin investing. John set up a meeting with Ouwega and Loot. It was one of the best things his cousin could have done for him. There was no greater gift. Loot was able to secure his future and his family's future. Ouwega was a master at eluding the feds. His skills were undefeated. If Ouwega hid your money, only what he announced could be discovered was accessible. He was a financial strategist. Switzerland was always the first country that the feds investigated to uncover laundered money. It did not used to be like that. Switzerland had to ask for financial help by way of a loan from the United States. The trade off for the loan was to allow full disclosure of all accounts. That included all American originated accounts. A few numbered Swiss accounts are what Ouwega allowed to be uncovered if an investigation of any of his clients occurred. Even the amounts were strategically placed in accounts that would not proffer a lengthy federal sentence.

For his gracious services, Ouwega charged a *mere* ten million dollars and a two percent compounded commission on all investments. Loot was one of the only clients that also paid him large bonuses. That made him give Loot extra time and attention. Ouwega also liked that Loot did not question his expertise.

"Spare me all the details. That's what I pay you for, man. What's my bottom line?" Loot said regularly.

Ouwega had the freedom to invest openly, as if the money was his own. By participating in a few of the more risky stocks, he made a very, very rich man out of Loot. Ouwega was also extremely wealthy. However, he lived frugally. He was not as flamboyant in his spending as the Americans or the Europeans that he served. Ouwega did purchase the village in Africa that he was born in, and was able to urbanize it. He built wells for water supplies, furnished lots of large generators for electrical appliances, and began his own school and hospital. His money was used to further his heritage. American people were not into a collective plan for the group as a whole. Ouwega saw that as the main problem with African Americans. In his country, everything was done collectively. If a person belonged to a village, it was the responsibility of the entire village to make sure that the citizen had everything that was required in order to be successful in life. Tribal homogeny was mandatory in Ouwega's world. It was unheard of in the United States. Although it bothered him, he could not change the world, so he focused on making his own surroundings better.

Before they departed, Loot asked John a deep question.

"Cuz, what is your take on ghosts?"

"What kind of question is that?" John asked.

"I don't know. I think I may need a vacation," Loot said.

Maybe he did. As soon as he asked John, he felt stupid and wished that he could take back his words.

"We should be ready to leave within the next week or so. I am setting everything up now," John said.

The trip to Ecuador went well. Loot and Poppie clicked immediately. They acted like they were born to work together.

John took the time to show Loot where his hidden compartment was located on the boat. When he built La Fenetre, he had designed a waterproof, air proof, steel chamber in the bottom of the boat that was accessible from his bedroom. No one was allowed to ever enter his bedroom on the boat but Mary. Mary knew about the hidden compartment. John gave her a tour the first time they went sailing. The compartment was empty.

"What is this used for? It is separate from the other cargo containers," Mary said.

"Special cargo," John said. Mary was smart enough not to question the details. She really did not want to know. She learned years ago that if she did not wish to know something about her husband, she shouldn't ask. She loved her husband, and would do anything for him. What Mary did not realize is that she would be put to the test concerning her loyalty to her husband very soon.

Chapter 14

Harry was ready to make his move. He had been following Loot. He knew where he lived, where he spent his time, and where all of his stash houses were. He was also getting more advanced in his powers. He knew how to teleport to different locations, saving hours of time. He also knew that when he took over a body, the length of time that he had to maneuver using their physical self depended on how damaged the body was. The dog that he had inhabited was torn apart. He lasted only thirty-six hours. Since that first incident, he had been a dying woman, a man that had overdosed on heroin, and three cats. There was no manual or instructor to teach one how to take over another's body, or the proper etiquette of the dead. Harry was learning how to maximize his powers by trial and error. Once he mastered teleporting, Loot became an easy target. He bided his time.

Loot's favorite time was an hour before sunrise. He checked his traps regularly during this time, but was always cautious about following the same route more than twice. He understood the law of the streets that said, *a moving target is hard to hit.* It was not impossible, but it eliminated the amateurs, cowards, and riff-raff from stepping to him.

The Lakeview Terrace projects was a fort for him and his soldiers up under him. They were able to supply the entire west side of Cleveland from Lakeview Terrace as headquarters. The projects had only two entrances or exits. You either had to enter on West 25th and drop down the hill, or the front side of the housing complex, on West 28th. The West 28th entrance also began with a hill. Both entrances dead-ended at the mouth of the Ohio River that ran into Lake Erie within a quarter mile away. In view were piles of salt, waiting for distribution by the city sanitation department, and a large body of water. That was it. There was no way to surround the estate, or trap anyone in, because from both entrances there was zero visibility of the rest of the compound.

Loot strategically placed lookouts equipped with walkie-talkies at both exits.

The area was raid tight. There had never been a successful raid on his area.

When he got ready to leave, he spotted a dope fiend named Sunshine waving him down. Sunshine grew up with him. She'd given him her virginity, and despite the cruel hand that life had dealt her, Loot still cared for her.

"What's up, Shine?" he said.

The woman standing before him had on a pair of Apple Bottom jeans that fit her like a glove, and a pair of nice Nine West black high heeled boots, with a coordinating black lather jacket. The only thing that gave away the fact that she was a junkie was her ashen-colored skin, and the slight tic of her left jaw and left corner of her mouth. When Loot looked at her, the corner of her mouth was twitching like crazy. Also, he noticed that her hair and clothes were dirty, which meant she was ending up a binge. When Loot stared into her face, he always noticed the naïve little girl that he had turned out. Chasing dope had aged and hardened Sunshine. She had served time at the Ohio Reformatory for Women twice, was sent to rehab many times, and was almost murdered by angry tricks that she'd robbed for their money.

Despite all that, Sunshine was still his girl.

"I was hoping to catch you. I know dis your hours. I need you to drop me at the lake—it's the East 72nd exit."

"Get in," he said.

"I knew it was on your way home," she said.

Sunshine walked around to the passenger's side. She appeared to be moving a lot slower than normal, and was almost dragging her right leg along. When she got ready to get inside the car, Loot noticed that her upper right thigh was soaked with blood, saturating the upper leg of her jeans.

"Hold up, let me grab this towel and plastic out of the trunk." Loot kept all kinds of bandages, towels, first aid kits, and plastic to protect his soft leather sets. Someone from his crew was always getting shot or hurt. The dope game was grimy and territorial.

"Do you need a doctor? I have a private one I can take you to now."

"Naw. I'm good. I am having you drop me to one of my regulars, who will patch me up, and then nurse me back to health," Sunshine said.

"I hope you know what you're doing. You look like you're dying, girl," Loot said.

Sunshine's usual caramel colored smooth skin was pale. She seemed to be losing color by the second. At first impression, Loot thought it was the look of being on a binge, but now he saw it was more. Sunshine was in bad shape.

Loot attempted to make small talk, but she seemed to be preoccupied with whatever was happening to her. Loot was worried about her, but knew not to pry too much. They both always respected each other's privacy, and never put each other on the spot about anything.

When Loot exited into the East 72nd marginal road exit, he pulled into the lot. There was nothing in front of him but the lake.

"Pull over to the corner. He is probably running a few minutes late," Sunshine said.

Loot hesitated for a few seconds. It seemed he was forgetting something, and that the entire scene playing out with Sunshine was déjà vu. *Was it?* He tried to grasp if it was, but lost the thought as quickly as it occurred.

As Loot headed toward the corner of the embankment that separated the asphalt parking area from the large span of water, Sunshine quickly reached into her jacket pocket and removed a small can of pepper spray. The container was not bigger than a cigarette lighter. She used the small vial during her long nights on the streets to fend off stray dogs. It worked on both two and four legged dogs, allowing her the necessary time she needed to get out of the path of danger if it presented itself. The item was inconspicuously brown colored. Loot was unsuspecting of her and would not have noticed her actions because he would never suspect Sunshine. She was the closest thing that he had in the world as far as a female friend would go. Like all others, at one time or another, he had slept with them. That seemed to solidify their loyalty to him.

When Sunshine reached over and sprayed him in the face swiftly with the vial of pepper spray, he did not flinch at her movement until it was too late. His eyes, nose and mouth were instantly contaminated with the strong aroma of the spray, making him gag. His first impulse was to release the steering wheel and grab his eyes. That is the move that Sunshine had anticipated.

"Argggggh! What the fuck! Bitch, I am going to kill you!" he screamed. The agony was apparent on his face. She had to move quickly. She threw her left leg over to his side of the car, positioning it under the steering wheel. She placed her body as close to his as she humanly dared. Sunshine gunned the accelerator, sending the car with both of them roughly jerking over the embankment, and into the dark, engulfing, chilling water. The vehicle made a large splash, but there was no one to hear the noise in the middle of the night. Loot did not have a chance to analyze what had happened with him and Sunshine because he was too busy fighting for his life. He tried to gain control of the car, even though they were already in the water, but his face and eyes burning kept him from being able to focus correctly. Loot was thrown off. Sunshine had premeditated the entire attack on Loot, so her window on the passenger's side was already rolled partially down to allow the water to gush in. The car was beginning to fill up with water quickly. Sunshine only had a second more to act. She awkwardly reached in her right jacket pocket, removed a small, full hypodermic needle full of quality heroin, and jammed the needle into Loot's right thigh. Loot tried to grab her hand, but missed his grip. Within seconds of feeling the impact of the heavy car hitting the water, he felt the cold water begin to soak his clothing.

"This is revenge from killing Harry Treason. The detective you murdered. See you in hell." The voice of Harry Treason boomed out of the mouth of the body of Sunshine Ramos. Loot heard the voice.

"See you in hell" were the last words that Loot heard before his respiratory system gave out on him as a result of a drug overdose. If the overdose would not have killed him, drowning would have.

Harry swiftly teleported out of the woman's body, landing on the black. He was very pleased with his accomplishment. The woman was a known prostitute and heroin user who had been bleeding to death from a deep cut from a trick that she had attempted to rob. Harry was able to enter her body within seconds of her death.

Loot's autopsy would label his cause of death as a heroin overdose and their two bodies would be found together. Harry visualized the news report, if there was one to be made. It would read that two drug addicts got too high and accidentally pressed the accelerator instead of the brakes. As a detective, Harry often gave the newspaper reporters the context of their articles that involved crimes from his beat.

He was anxious to continue revenge on the men that had taken over his beat, which was his life and career, and then literally robbed him of his life. With each death, Harry Treason became more powerful in his newfound role as one of the living dead. He had never fit into mainstream society among the living, but he was able to shine in his new position. Harry had finally found his niche, and comfort zone.

Chapter 15

Mary's life could not have been better. John and J.R. were her world, and both were staying very close to her nest she had woven for them to fit snugly into. For a few years she was worried about her marriage. John was never home. He was always traveling. He had missed both her's and J.R.'s birthday, their anniversaries, and all other special days. The only time that he was home was for Christmas. In her weariness, she sought counsel from her pastor. Reverend McKnight was known for pulling together the rockiest of marriages.

"Do you feel that he's fornicating?" Reverend McKnight asked.

Mary gave the question serious consideration. She answered honestly. "No, I don't."

"Has he neglected any of his duties as a husband and father in any way?"

"He is not physically at home like he should be."

"Have you spoken to him about how you feel?"

"No," she answered.

Reverend McKnight stared hard at the large statue of Jesus Christ's handsome brown face before him on his wall. He spread his fingers, arching his hands, touching them at the fingertips. His congregation had seen him assume the pose hundreds of times. He did it when he was in complete thought. Mary joined him, staring at the portrait also. She was trying to feel what the pastor was feeling, but felt nothing but anxiety in the pit of her stomach.

She began to doubt her intentions. *Was she being selfish? Should she have talked to Reverend McKnight without talking to her husband first?* she asked herself. She stared at Reverend McKnight. He gave no sign that he acknowledged her presence in the room.

After what seemed like an hour, Reverend McKnight tuned back in and looked at her.

"Mary, you are one of the wealthiest families in the congregation. Young couples are inspired to do better when they see the solid foundation that you and John have. Everything in life has a trade off, Mary. The trade off for your wealth is your husband's absence. Do you agree with that?"

"Yes. Um, I do," she said softly.

"You've heard many sermons of mine about the 80/20 rule, do you remember that concept?" Reverend McKnight quizzed.

"Yes. When we have eighty percent, we should be grateful," she answered.

"It's more than that. No two people are exactly alike. No human will meet a hundred percent of another person's expectations. Realistically, only eighty percent of those expectations will be met. If you are not careful, what a person will do is start to focus on the shortcomings of their mate. It is easy to do. Many relationships and marriages end, only to find out that the twenty percent they didn't have was a lot less than what they had. It's that old cliché surfacing that says that the grass always looks greener on the other side, until you cross to the other side, and see its full of holes, and up close has a vast amount of weeds and crabgrass. Are you with me?" he asked.

"Yes."

"So what I would like for you to do is focus on the eighty percent you have, Mary. John is a good man. If it's unbearable, then speak to him. Other than that, try to focus on what he is instead of what he isn't. Also, I would like you to consider joining at least one of our committees. We have the Youth Mentoring Program, the elderly care program, prison fellowship, and our international teen project that is taking fifteen of our teens to Africa for two weeks on a retreat this summer. Think about how you feel about it, and what you would like to do, and stop in to see me next Sunday before or after service. Deal?" he asked.

"Deal," she answered.

"Now, let's pray together, and remember that He does answer prayers, Mary. You just have to be patient."

They prayed in depth together, and she left, feeling better.

Mary did believe in the power of prayer. Within weeks, John began to be home most of the month. He had always had an office at home, but until recently, never utilized it, except to check his e-mail.

It was standard procedure now for him to wake up at his usual un-Godly hour of 5 a.m., wake her up with a full stiff hard-on, and wear her out. He also did the unheard of. John Gray would go back to sleep until 7 a.m. He enjoyed a light breakfast with his son, walked him to school, then got a morning jog in on his way home. He got dressed in semi-office attire that eliminated the suit jacket, but did include dress slacks, comfortable loafers, and dress shirt, without a tie. He still went into the office all day Friday, half a day on Saturday, and sporadically during the week for appointments and meetings that required his presence, but his office was officially at home.

"Let's go half on a little girl," he breathed passionately while kissing on her neck. His kisses were soft and wet. They had discussed new additions. John always concluded that it was not the right time due top his hectic schedule. The only schedule that was hectic and urgent while he worked at home was convincing Mary to skip work and stay at home with him. All of the nasty things he did to her while they were alone in their house should have been a felony. John did everything from secretly sprinkling pure powder cocaine on her nipples and clit, making it numb, then licking her body back to life, to persuading her to straddle him while butt-naked on the porch swing on their back porch. John tried to pound her back out. He laughed heartily when she refused to be totally nude in broad daylight. Although their yard was shielded from public view by six-foot shrubbery, Mary vowed not to comply. John had to settle for her wearing a thin, short robe that kept getting in his way, but not enough to stop the intense pounding he had for her. The cool breeze carrying the afternoon air felt good on his bare skin. Mary's sweet scent of her cologne mixed with her juices of open and willing sex excited him. He had no mercy on her body. It was his punishment for her refusal to succumb to pure nakedness with him. In the beginning, Mary thought that she had control, because she was straddling him. John showed her who was the boss. He gripped her waist with one hand, and her hips with the other, and gave her full, long strokes. By the time Mary climbed off him, she was sore and pound drunk.

"Whewww!" she said aloud. *Be careful what you pray for. I hope I can handle this man's high sex drive,* she thought.

John signed up for the Father and Son's events at J.R.'s school. He and his son enlisted for the basketball, baseball and football tournaments. John was a good athlete. He was a patient teacher and partner to his son. J.R. reveled in the newfound attention and dedication from his once absent father.

For the first time in Mary's life, she felt whole. As a mother, wife, director, and child of God. Mary had begun to self-actualize.

She found herself getting a little jealous of the closeness that her son and husband were developing, because she was not a part of it.

"Can I go with you guys? I am all caught up on my work here," she asked on more than one occasion. Instead of answering her, the two of them exchanged smirks, then laughter.

"It's boys night out, girl," John told her.

"Well when is family night?" Mary asked, trying to hide her attitude.

"Not tonight," John said, giving his son a high five.

Mary felt betrayed. She had nursed J.R., never missed a PTA meeting or school event, was at his beck and call every evening for a dozen years. *Where was his loyalty?* she thought.

The only comfort she had left was Judy E. Judy E. was an old white mutt. She'd been in the family since J.R. was two years old. J.R. spotted the stray bum dog one day when they were out for an afternoon walk. The dog was so dirty, it looked gray. J.R. refused to settle down in his stroller until the dog was following him home.

Mary tried to give the dog a canine name, but from the beginning J.R. called the dog Judy E. He pronounced it Joo-Dee-Ee.

Usually Mary was indifferent to the dog, but today she allowed her to lie at her feet. Unlike the males in the house, Mary was not a pet lover, but she obliged them by adding pet food to her shopping list, and incurring the cost of the quarterly rug shampooing.

* * * * * *

John took Loot's death hard. He couldn't help but blame himself. He did not understand why Loot had heroin in his system on the autopsy. Loot no more used smack than crack. He was old school, and lived by the "never get high off your own supply" rule.

John hired the best private investigator in the city to find out all he could. He did not rely on the police. They were disinterested in the case, and anything they uncovered would be publicized. He did not want to cause his aunt any further grief than she already had to bear.

The investigator was a retired cop with a street edge.

"Did you know that your cousin was a very large drug dealer, with an organization of over four hundred workers, spanning seven states?"

"No. I didn't know that," John said.

"That's a full confidential report in front of you. Mr. Williams was no more a dope fiend than I am," the investigator said.

"I felt something foul happened. Do you know what?" John's voice was laced with sadness and grief.

"The lady with him was Sunshine Ramos. She had a long rap sheet and history of drug addiction. Her file is enclosed."

"Sunshine Ramos! I remember her! We grew up together. That was one of my cousin's first girlfriends. She really looked bad when I saw the pictures. I didn't even recognize her. She used to be a ten," John said.

"Drugs do that to you," the investigator said.

Their business concluded. When he read the report, he did not know any more about his cousin's death than he did before hiring the investigator.

Chapter 16

J.R. had not entered high school, but he was ready. He was too old to be tucked in by his mother, but too young to drive a car. Being twelve was a difficult age. He wanted to be grown, and couldn't wait.

J.R.'s grades were fair. The problem was he did not apply himself. His father wanted him to be smart and focused. J.R. was heir to a small fortune. His father tried to explain the concept of business to him over the last two years, but his problem was that he wasn't interested. He wanted to be a rapper, or a producer of rap albums. He had no interest in the import-export business his father built.

John was concerned about his son's attitude toward the business, but he was still hopeful that he would catch on. He witnessed young adults squandering away their family fortunes on ridiculous things, like diamond cell phone carrying cases, and even an old potato chip that was rumored to be Elvis Presley's. He tried to prepare his son for the world, but the truth was J.R. was not focused.

Junior would have rather been home in his room, playing with his Play Station 3. School was so boring. Because going to school meant a lot to his parents, he could not cut school in peace. He cut a few classes, and did not get caught, but came very close. He lied to his mother, telling her that he had gone to the bathroom when the teacher took attendance, and explained that the attendance monitor was computerized, and that was why they didn't notice that he was there. His mother bought it. The few other times he cut, he had his friend's oldest sister call in as his mother. The office clerk was immediately suspicious. The girl did not sound as much like his mother as they originally thought she did when they practiced.

"Ma'am, give me your number. I am going to have to call you back," the secretary said.

Junior hauled butt to school, and by the time the clerk came in his class to check on him, Junior was sitting at his desk in the middle of science class, staring her in the face. She concluded that it must have been some teenagers making random prank calls. It was a game that she played often when she was their age. She dismissed the incident out of her mind, but because of the close call, Junior did not attempt to cut class anymore. He did not want to disappoint his mother. Feigning an illness turned out to be much easier than having to leave home, and with being ill he was able to remain in his room, playing with his video games. Although he was not allowed to go outdoors on days he did not attend school, he did not care. He enjoyed being indoors. Being an only child, he was used to being alone and playing alone. His room was a small fortress of electronics and gadgets. His father was good to him. Junior had every video game ever made, software, and other electronic helpers that had been made for his age range. His father did not spare expenses on toys for him. Sometimes he wished that he was not the only child, and other times he reveled in receiving all of his parents' attention. His dog, Judy E., provided complete company.

He did not worry about having to clean his room much like his friends at school, because his father provided a maid named Selma. He did not particularly like Selma, due to her nosiness. Selma always asked him questions that he felt grownups would be better at answering than him. She especially liked to ask him about his father.

"Has your father been home this week?" Selma asked often.

"No."

"Has he called?"

"Yes."

"What did he say?"

"He didn't say anything about you," Junior replied. That type of statement always made her back up the questions. He did not understand why she questioned him and not his mother. His mother loved to talk, and his father was her favorite subject.

Junior did notice that whenever his mother was around, Selma's behavior was different. Also, she never said more than two words in his mother's presence. He came to the conclusion that Selma was displaying another one of the weird grownup behaviors.

What aggravated Junior more than Selma's prying was the pale looking man that was always appearing in his room. He used to have an imaginary friend named Joe. He used to talk to Joe often and shared everything with him. Although he knew that Joe was not a real person, Joe was fun to have around. The only time his mother would get angry about Joe is when he blamed things he had done on Joe. It wasn't a lie, he just did not want his mother mad at him. When he brought the homeless mutt that he named Judy E. home, Joe disappeared. This was different. Joe was nice. Although his mother did not like Judy E., the dog was his companion. Junior had a gut feeling that the intruder was not anything good or safe. He thought about telling someone, but who? His family or friends would not understand. Junior did not understand grownups, and he was sure that some things in his world were too elementary for adults.

The man did not talk. If he did, Junior would be able to determine his authenticity. Junior believed in ghosts, goblins, aliens, and Star Trek. He was a first generation Trekie. His mom did not get it. His dad thought the show was corny. Junior was not afraid of the man. The stranger always had on the same attire. He wore a gray suit, with a dark shirt, and dark shoes. His hair was unkempt and light colored, to match his skin. It was the eyes on the man that seemed to belong to someone else. They were Freddie Kruger and Jason Worthy. That was a mark against the intruder. The man did not have B.O. That was a plus. If he would have smelled bad, Junior may have been blamed by his mother or Selma, and that was torture. Junior had been accused of having B.O. on more than a few occasions. The insult did not bother him. He did bathe semi-regularly to assure that he would be left alone.

"Did you bathe today?"

"Yes," he lied regularly.

Junior read in a book that Jesus Christ did not bathe everyday, or even once a month. Jesus Christ was a superstar. His picture was everywhere, and his mother prayed in His name, at least once a day. *If people accepted Jesus Christ without bathing regularly, why couldn't he be left alone?* Junior tried to school his mother about Jesus Christ's hygiene.

"Little boy! If you don't get your behind in that bathtub, you are going to make me loose my religion!" Mary yelled loudly.

* * * * * *

Harry did not plan on hurting the boy. He enjoyed watching him. Because he never had any kids of his own or been around any, the boy was intriguing. Sometimes the boy stared at him as if he could see him. He would sit in the chair for hours and watch the boy play on his computer, or challenge himself in a video game. Harry wondered how his life may have turned out if his parents would have given him the type of attention and love that John's son received. Would he have chosen a different profession? Would he have taken a wife? Would he have allowed himself to have children, and participate in the American dream? He did not know. It was much too late. What he did understand was that there was no heaven after purgatory. He wasn't sure if he would be judged on judgment day. He knew that one day purgatory would end, and that his wondering soul would be laid to rest.

He also knew that he would be destroyed along with his ruler, Satan the devil. He simply did not know when and where. God still had the power to decide. Harry Treason had no fear or trepidation about his future. He was pleased to be a servant of the ruler of the current world—Satan. Harry was determined to bide his time. He wanted to study John's life, get to know the ways of his family, and then make him suffer a slow, tortuous death. John had ended his life, and soon he would take his, but not before he destroyed everything around him that he cared about.

* * * * * *

Junior decided to ask Selma about the intruder, instead of his mother or father. Selma was easiest to talk to. His mother would turn the question into a moral interrogation. His father might think that he was losing it. Junior did not care what Selma thought.

Since his mother had caught him looking at the screen with women that were topless on it, his computer was full of all kinds of parental blocks. He could not visit the adult sites, or the casinos, and most games were blocked. He had learned how to go around a few of the blocks by going into the site the back way, but he was still restricted. His friend Shawn's computer was wide open. He was being raised by his mom. His dad left his mom when he was a baby, and never returned. Shawn's mom was not computer literate, so she didn't have a clue of what a parental block was. He and Shawn spent hours visiting the porn websites, and entering the adult chat rooms. He used the code name of Junior 12-inch, and Shawn used Freaky Shawn. If their parents were to ever find out, they would be grounded for eternity. Both of the boys were receiving a full array of sexual education from the Internet. They even watched the short videos of couples having sex. The advertisements were meant to lure customers into buying the full movie, but for two pre-teenage boys, the thirty-and sixty-second videos were perfect. They played the same ones over and over again.

Selma always came in to clean his room on Saturday morning, at 8 a.m. She breezed through it every other day during the week with the rest of her chores, but on Saturday, she collected his dirty laundry, changed his linens, straightened out his drawers, and organized his closets if time permitted. His mom designated Saturday for those chores so that he would be there with Selma if needed.

When Selma walked into the room, she

gazed over at the boy sitting at his computer looking at her.

"What is on your mind today?" she asked.

"Can I ask you something?"

"Sure. Anything."

"Do you believe in ghosts?" he asked.

"Why do you ask that?" she said.

"I just wanted to know. I saw a program on TV," he explained.

"Yes. I do. But there are good spirits and bad spirits. Sometimes it's hard to distinguish which are good and which are bad."

"How can you then?" he asked.

"Sometimes you can tell by their actions, but that is also tricky."

"Have you ever seen a ghost?" he asked.

"Yeah. Both good and bad. I lived in a house that was full of bad spirits when I was growing up, and the ghosts roamed the house openly and freely until we ended up moving out. The house was haunted. On the other hand, when my grandfather died, who I was very close to, he came to visit me in the form of an angel many times for years. He was my guardian angel. Whenever I was stressing about something or someone, he would show up, and then I would ask myself, *what would he have done?* and the answer would come to me," she explained.

"Why do bad spirits come?"

"Usually when they are stuck in purgatory, they come to haunt, scare, or stalk their victim. Most of the time their soul is not at rest," she explained.

"Once they avenge or do whatever they are here for, do they go away then?" he said, feeling hopeful.

"Yes, often, but the best thing to do is pray to God, and ask for peace. It will be granted, and if they are bad spirits, they will eventually disappear. God is King," Selma said.

Junior noted everything that she said in his mind. He would begin praying immediately. He wanted to get started as soon as she left his bedroom. He did not like the increasing visits that he received regularly from the ashy pale man with the bad hairdo.

Chapter 17

A few decades ago, Peru seized a large area of the Amazon Basin that belonged to Ecuador. Back then, the leaders met in Rio de Janeiro, where the decision makers decided that Peru could have the disputed territory. Now the president and the people wanted the land back.

Unfortunate for Poppie, he belonged to the political administration that had been ousted. It was all a result of bad decision making, and hogging the wealth. Only ten percent of Ecuadorians lived above the poverty level, and people were tired of getting robbed blind by the government.

The new political party that ruled called themselves the Ecuadosista Party. They were eleven million strong. Within four months, Poppie found himself stripped of his wealth, position and power. They took everything from him. There was no reprieve. Poppie and all of the members of the previous administration were told that they were free to live elsewhere. Live elsewhere? That was absurd! Poppie had lived in Ecuador with his family for many generations. Moving was not an option.

Poppie tried to change sides. The Ecuadosista Party was a very well organized, liberal party that was for the people of Ecuador as a whole. Their main mission was to spread the wealth of the country more equally. They wanted all people to be able to at least have food. It was not a vast request, but would take strong organizational skills, and a few territorial fights. Poppie was willing to fight along with the Party. He was not a stranger to war, nor was he a coward. As a matter of fact, Poppie decided that he would enjoy the spoils of war. He had been sitting on his fat behind, enjoying the wealth of the country for many years without so much as a paper cut. He needed to experience some action in his life.

The Ecuadosista did allow him and his family to keep their home, but they legally stripped him of his savings. It was close to a million dollars that exchanged to more than twenty times the dollar amount in pesos. The only money that he did not lose was the small amounts that he had buried all over his home and backyard. John had begged him to move his money to other sources, and to start several financial projects such as an account and some investing in the United States. The problem was that Poppie did not like the idea of being so far from his money, and also he did not like the fact that he was not a citizen, and if robbed, could not protest.

John's money was heaps more than his because of the difference in the prices. In his country, a kilo had close to no value. In the United States it was a high commodity, and sometimes more valuable than gold. Where John was a rich man, Poppie was labeled a well-to-do-farmer. Now even that title had been stripped from him. He was not a young man anymore. He wondered if he would be able to make a comeback.

Ecuadosista did not want Poppie inside their organization. They felt that he was a part of the problem instead of the solution, and they were solution oriented. Poppie was the type of man that they protested about. He hoarded the wealth, and protected the administration that the Party was able to overthrow. Although they tried to obtain indictments for the politicians that were involved, that was practically unheard of. They were lucky to get them to step down.

What Poppie did have was product. That was one thing that was always readily available in his country, and it was legal. The problem was going to be what it had always been. He did not have a source in the United States to carry it over. John was not interested, and before he was able to do any real business, John's cousin Loot had died. It was an untimely death. Poppie liked Loot. He felt that they were about to do big things. Many people in America thought that finding an outlet for the large packages would be easy. It was not. It was as complicated and intricate as locating a needle in a haystack. Poppie knew that he had to contact John and request his help. It was his only chance to get back on his feet.

* * * * * *

"John, the phone is for you!" Mary

yelled from the back yard. She was on the phone with one of the church sisters who had just found out that she was expecting her first child.

"Marr! Who is it? I am in the middle of writing this stuff up for the tax guy and I need to concentrate," John yelled back.

"May I ask who is calling?" she asked.

"Just tell him a friend in need," Poppie said. He did not trust any land lines that were unsecure.

"Darn it. Who is playing games?" John said, aggravated openly.

"Yeah?" John answered.

"Oh, so you don't have time for old friends anymore?"

"AWWHHHH! It's my dude! Dude, how you doing, partna?" John asked happily. He had not expected to hear his friend's voice, but he was glad to hear from him.

"I would like to talk to you. Can you call me back on a secure line?"

"Oh, yeah. Give me about twenty minutes. I am in motion now," John answered. He grabbed his car keys and wallet and hit the door.

"Where you going?" Mary asked.

"To the store. You want something?"

"No, only you," she said, blowing him a kiss.

"Alright, you gone get faded, keep playing," he laughed out the door.

The store was about ten miles away, but John decided that it would be better to drive to the nearest strip mall that was an extra five minutes away. The mall had more phones, and lots of traffic, so that his phone call would blend in smoothly.

He called the same number that had appeared on his caller ID. Most things did not have to be said or explained between him and Poppie.

Poppie answered on the second ring. After the small talk, and catching up on family, they got right to business.

"How long will it take you to get everything together?" John asked.

"This will be the biggest yet. We will try to make it a one-time thing. I will call you back within a week to give you a tentative time," Poppie said.

"Can I shoot you some money or anything in the meantime?" John asked.

"I did not say I was butt naked, I said I was broke. There is a big difference," Poppie joked. The two men laughed heartily before ending their conversation. John decided that he would not tell Mary of his plans until more of the details had been worked out. He knew that she would not be happy, but he also knew that she would understand, and allow him to be a man and make his own decisions. Poppie was the staple that had made him rich. He would never turn his back on him. Loyalty was everything in this life.

The call came in exactly seven days.

"Can you be here in exactly two weeks from today?" Poppie asked.

"I sure can. I have already been rearranging my schedule to be ready to move when necessary."

"Thanks again partner, I will never forget this. My ass is out here," Poppie said.

"It ain't nothing among real soldiers," John replied. They bid farewell and John prepared for his trip.

Chapter 18

Although John was not interested in going back into the game full blast, he couldn't help but to tally up his profit. This was a very big move. He did not need the money like Poppie. He was set for life legally. Today it was the challenge and the thrill of making it rain in the states. Like the rapper Jay-Z said, *"It sparks a thrill indescribable when watching product make it across the water."* Of course, Jay-Z used his own words and John used his own, but the feeling was exquisite. The dollar signs adding up were physically visible.

John had reached out to the streets. It was not as hard as he thought. He went back to the hood and asked questions. He talked to Loot's baby momma, and she told him who was closest to Loot. The young man's name was Pookie. He was a cousin on Loot's mother's side, where John and Loot were cousins on his father's side.

Pookie and he hit it off smoothly. He got good vibes from the dude. Pookie looked a lot like John. Where Loot looked more like his mother, Pookie could have easily passed for John's brother. It was ironic when he looked at the young man, because he looked like a younger version of himself. Same height, same skin tone, and same facial features.

John also liked the way Pookie handled himself. He did not talk a lot, nor was he easy to read.

"Since you are still out there, how fast do you think you can dump some weight?"

"If the quality is the same as it has been, I can move it quick," Pookie said.

"This is a one-time shot. I need you to know that, so try to make it work for you," John told him.

"It's all good," the young man replied. It was on.

Poppie was elated that things came back together so easily. He was expecting a delay in being able to move the product. He knew that John did not frequent the streets. Once again he had underestimated his partner. John was able to maneuver on a street level as well as a business level.

Poppie tried to get as close to one thousand kilos as he could on short notice. He had to round up the small families throughout Ecuador, literally. They did not have an outlet for their crop, and were anxious to have an opportunity to work with the infamous Poppie. Although he had lost his clout with the government, Poppie still was a boss in the underworld. The farmers knew that a chance to work with Poppie meant cash, and a break in poverty. Poppie was an enigma.

What John did not know about Pookie would change his entire life. Pookie had been arrested by the feds two weeks after the death of Loot. The arrest was accidental.

"We are going to move in on the Jamaican. We have had him under our surveillance for eleven months. I think we have enough on him to convict him now," Agent Frisco, the senior agent in the investigation, instructed.

The agents were from the financial crimes unit of the FBI. They had received a tip that an employee at the Ohio Driver's License Bureau was making and issuing valid driver's licenses to Jamaican immigrant drug dealers. The driver's license had the identifying information of legitimate citizens. The names that were welched from the complex license system did not have a clue that their names and information was being used. How the FBI got involved was when a "Mark Thomas" was pulled over on a routine traffic violation, and found that he was wanted in two cities in Ohio for drug and gun possession. The man did not have a clue what the arresting police officers were talking about. Another major problem with the arrest was that the real Mark Thomas was a white man with blond colored hair and blue eyes. When the officer pulled up the driver's license on the screen from the DMV site, the information was correct, but the picture that filled up the screen was of a dark-skinned black man. The agents had to laugh when the picture covered the screen.

"Well, this gentleman certainly does not have blond hair and blue eyes!" Agent Frisco said.

They placed the entire agency under federal surveillance, after tracing the exact location that the license originated from by the encoding device used. It did not take long to see that the creator of the caper was busy. She was a young black woman that had been recently employed by the license bureau. She was making and giving away illegal licenses like McDonalds serves customers during the lunch rush hour. The immigrants lined up regularly, and usually came in packs. The young woman did not have a clue that she was being watched. She freely deleted out the license holder's original picture, and replaced their picture with one of the immigrants without hesitation. They watched the immigrants pass her an envelope on camera, over and over again. They found out later that she charged five hundred to one thousand dollars each license. The girl had a good hustle going while it lasted, but it was about to come to an end.

One day while monitoring the license worker, the agents watched one of the Jamaican men meet outside the license bureau with another young man. They ran the plates of the visitor and saw that the car belonged to a Demond Braxton, aka Pookie. He had a detailed rap sheet for drugs, although he was only twenty-four years old.

"Where the hell did he come from?" Agent Frisco said out loud.

Agent Frisco called in his accomplice from the federal drug enforcement agency.

"I think you might want to take a look

at two guys I have under surveillance. I have a gut feeling that both of them are drug dealers. Come on down."

The two agencies got an earful, and an eyeful, after placing Pookie and the Jamaican under watch. Pookie was moving drugs throughout three states with more finagling, stashing, slamming and dunking than LeBron James' court moves for the Cavaliers.

The Jamaican had his hand in everything. His business ranged from lining up illegal immigrants to pose as American citizens, to gun dealing. Dope was also part of his large array of criminal activities.

He and Pookie had established a good partnership. Sometimes Pookie supplied him with drugs, and other times the Jamaican would set up robberies and split the profit off the stolen drugs with Pookie in exchange for Pookie dumping the drugs throughout the city. The Jamaican's motto was simple: *Trust no one, and be loyal only to yourself.* From a small boy, he lived his life having to fend for himself. He had no expectations of people, therefore he was never disappointed when they showed their true colors.

The afternoon that the agents decided to move on the Jamaican, Pookie showed up.

"I have a quarter key for ya. Can you down it?" Pookie asked the Jamaican.

Both of the men were grimy. The Jamaican did not know where the dope came from, and he did not ask. When Pookie sat the package in his lap, he quickly began calculating a profit.

"Both of you raise your hands above your head!" the DEA agents screamed. They were already charging the two men with bullet proof vests, and tactical outfits. Before the men could react, the agents stormed them.

"What do you want? I have nothing," the Jamaican said calmly.

Pookie looked at him like he was an alien. *What did he mean he didn't have nothing? I just passed him nine ounces of yao,* Pookie thought. Pookie didn't have any money or dope on him, so he knew that he would at least be able to make bond.

"Look what we have here," one of the DEA agents that was searching Pookie said. The man pulled out a medium sized plastic bag that was triple folded over a nice bundle of powder cocaine.

"I'll be damned," Pookie said out loud.

"Yep. You sure will," the agent said cheerfully.

The dirty gully Jamaican had somehow managed to put the package of dope <u>back</u> on the person of Pookie when the bust went down. Pookie did not even feel him do it. If looks could kill, the Jamaican would have died nine times, slowly. Pookie was fired up.

"You have the right to remain silent...anything you say can and will be used against you...." The agent read the Miranda out loud. Pookie knew the drill, and he also knew that he was back to jail again.

When he got to the federal building, instead of taking him to the basement booking area, the agents escorted him through a long corridor of halls that were lined with offices on both sides.

"Where do you want him, Frisco?" the tall, black, Michael Jordan looking DEA agent asked the other agent that was bringing up the rear of the four agents.

"Put him in the large conference room. I am going to grab a cup of coffee, and then I will be right in. You want some coffee, Pookie?" Agent Frisco asked.

Pookie simply stared at the man. He knew how the good cop-bad cop routine worked. He knew that Frisco was setting him up for the good cop treatment. He wasn't feeling it. He was not a snitch, and did not think that he would be able to make bond, so he was getting saltier by the minute. He was on parole, and his parole officer had warned him of his shady business associates. He was worried that he would not be able to separate himself from the Jamaican, and even if he did, *he* was the one who was caught with the dope, not the Jamaican, so it really did not matter in the big picture.

Once the men got situated, two of the agents left, leaving Frisco and the other agent to do the bidding.

"My name is Williams. I am a Drug Enforcement Officer. Here is my card," the tall black dude said. Pookie refused to reach for the card, so the DEA agent placed the card on the table in front of him. Pookie could see how Williams would be a good agent. He did not look like a federal agent. His attire was all street. He had on a pair of Rock-a-Wear jeans, sweater and matching leather bomber jacket. The outfit had a gold colored trim that matched his traditional colored Tims. His pants sagged, barely covering his waistband on his drawers. His Tims were half laced, giving him a thugged out look. Pookie did not believe in complimenting guys, but he had to admit that the agent looked snazzy. He would not have questioned him or given him a second glance on the streets, and would have certified him as a G. That worried Pookie. If he made it back to the streets, he wanted to remember how Agent Williams looked so that he could wire up the ballers. The agent was like a chameleon. He could easily blend in and out of the game. That fact had Pookie shook.

"How well do you know Annotto?" Agent Frisco asked.

"Who the hell is Annotto?" Pookie asked.

"He probably knows him only by his street name, which is Ant," Williams said.

"Yeah, in the streets we don't use our government names," Pookie said.

"So, how well do you know him?" Frisco asked again.

"I don't," Pookie replied.

"Well, let's cut through the chase. We have you on several recordings, and a few videos making drug deals, and your voice talking about other things that are illegal with this man. We know that he doesn't trust many people, so we know that you two were mobbed up," Williams said.

"Well, it seems like you already know quite a bit, so what you want from me?" Pookie asked.

"We want your help. I am not going to play games with you. We have evidence, but we need your testimony to lock Ant away. Juries want to hear what happened in person, not read papers," Williams said.

"So now you want me to be a snitch? What makes you think I want to help y'all?" Pookie asked.

Instead of answering verbally, Williams pulled out a thick file with all kinds of evidence in it. Pookie watched his face smile as he made several drug transactions, and exchanged money in the large photos. He glanced at the transcripts from the phone calls, and also at the arrest warrants of the man he knew as Ant.

"Ant's been busy," was all he said, and handed the file back across the table to Williams.

"I am going to ask again, what do you want from me?"

"We want your testimony. You are knee deep in this shit. You are a category six, and if convicted of even a small component of the evidence we have on you, you could receive a minimum ten-year sentence. I am talking ten years for the guns you helped him to negotiate alone, Pookie," Williams said.

"I need to talk to an attorney. I didn't waive my right to no attorney, and I want one," Pookie said. He knew that getting an attorney would delay him getting a bond, but he was not about to get himself caught up in a cross with the feds. He had never dealt with the feds, but he'd heard plenty of stories. Not only did they not play fair, but also they made you offers that you couldn't refuse. By the time they finished stacking up cases and time on your butt, you were lucky to come out with a football number if you had a record like his. Pookie knew the drill.

The agents called for him to be transferred to a federal detention facility in Trumbull county, to await bond or their next meeting. Whichever one came first.

After a fitful sleep, the following day an attorney came to see him. His name was Mr. Goldberg.

"They have you booked solid. I reviewed the evidence against you. They really want this Jamaican guy, not you, do you know that already?" Goldberg said.

"Of course I do. But what exactly am I facing time wise?" Pookie asked.

"Well, it's kind of early to tell, but the gun transaction alone carries a minimum of ten years because you are a convicted felon. In federal court it's under statute 922, and you can also receive enhancements because each time you made a gun transaction, there were also drugs involved. We don't even want to think about what the maximum sentence could be," Goldberg said.

Ten years minimum. That is the same number that Williams put in his head. It was the number that kept him awake through wee hours of the night, and robbed him of sleep the night before. Pookie was not a punk. He could do time, but ten years minimum? That was a stretch.

"What kind of deal are they talking?" he asked.

"Both agents said that they would be willing to give you total immunity from the upcoming indictment if you would be willing to cooperate fully," Goldberg advised.

"Do that mean I might be able to get a bond?" Pookie asked.

"I am sure it does. These trials can go on for a few years, and they haven't even completed the entire indictment yet, so it's safe to say that you will get a bond at the least," Goldberg said.

"Let me think this out, man. I know how this snitching thing goes, but I have always manned up and did my time. Snitching on this boy is a lot, and then they expect me to testify. He ain't no friend, but he ain't no enemy either. I will get back with you," Pookie said.

"Make sure you don't take too long. They have enough evidence to move on both of you and present a good case. With the feds, it's whoever gets to the table to make a deal first. I will be waiting to hear from you so that I know exactly what you and I are preparing for," Goldberg said.

When Pookie got back to Trumbull, he decided to talk to a few of the old heads that were bunking around him. There was an old black guy, a white guy, and a Mexican man in his immediate cubicle.

"If y'all could walk, would you

cooperate and testify against one of your associates?" Pookie asked. Pookie was amazed at the response he got.

"Of course I would. I am not going to sit in a cell for anyone," the white man answered.

"I would and I did!" the black guy answered.

"Sheet. I told on my mother. I was facing a life sentence. My mother is the one who introduced me to my connect," the Mexican said.

"But you all knew that you were doing wrong when you stepped into the game, right?" Pookie asked.

"The feds is going to win. They have a winning rate of ninety-eight percent of their cases. It is the government. Who wants to really take on the government?" the white man asked them all. He looked like one of the guys that had been involved in the Enron scandal, once Pookie took a closer look at him. "So, all of you are snitching?" Pookie asked.

The black man cringed at the use of the word, but the other two men ignored the question.

Pookie spent time quizzing the men to see what kinds of cases they had, and what kinds of deals the feds had made with them. All of them had received more than a twenty year reduction on their sentence for cooperating with the feds. The Mexican and the black man had avoided life sentences. The Mexican man was facing seven once he testified, and the black man was facing a similar fate in exchange for his testimony during a large drug ring, where a few of his codefendants were getting life for obtaining kingpin status.

Pookie did not want to take the stand against Ant, but if that was the only way that he could avoid going to federal prison for a lengthy sentence, then so be it. He had always heard that the feds made you an offer that you could not refuse. If he refused to testify as one of their witnesses, he would receive a thirty year sentence as part of a plea bargain. If he cooperated, he would receive forty-one months in a federal prison camp, with regular home furloughs where he could go home for the holidays and live like a king. Although he was always against snitching, the government held the purse strings and kept sweetening the deal until he honestly would be suicidal to refuse their final offer.

With the final offer, he would go into the drug program called the RDTP or residential drug treatment program. It was a five hundred hour program that would give him a year off his forty-one month sentence. Pookie would end up doing around two years tops instead of doing thirty years in a hard core federal prison. Yeah, the feds did make you an offer that you could not refuse.

"I have a written proffer for you to sign. The agents detailed what they expect from you, and what they will give you in exchange. I believe in getting every single detail in writing from experience of dealing with the government. Their saying is, if it is not in writing, it did not happen," Goldberg said.

Pookie took time to read the proffer, and then signed it the following day. It was detailed. There was a clause that read that if at any time he refused to testify, he would forfeit all deals. There was no turning back, once he signed the proffer.

Many of the guys that he came in contact with while in federal custody were working for the government regularly as informants and committing crimes at alarming rates. Pookie decided that he would not play that game. When he broke all principles and decided to cooperate with the government, as far as he was concerned, he had officially switched sides. He no longer considered himself a hustler, but instead a person on the right side of the law. However difficult things got, he would have to make it as a square. That was the promise he made to himself for being able to negotiate his life back from the feds. They wanted to retire a brother for real, or reduce them to a yellow-bellied, low-life snitch, and he wanted neither. He was fully aware of his actions, and they were well thought out.

What threw a wrench in everything was John Gray. Pookie was not looking for work. He was keeping a low profile, and he was not in the streets. John approached him out of nowhere, not knowing that the feds had him under surveillance, and in a full headlock. They followed him, his cell phone was tapped, and everyone that he was closely affiliated with, such as his family was also under watch, and being electronically monitored as well in some instances. The case that he was to testify in was about to go down, and the stakes were high. Agents Frisco and Williams knew that they were at the crucial stage, and anything could go wrong. They proceeded with more caution than ever. Pookie was not their only witness to testify for the government, but he was the most credible, and had gotten closest to their target than anyone. Both agents felt that the jury would eat up Pookie's testimony.

"We see that you've been offered a boss position by John Gray," Agent Williams voiced.

"He ain't got nothing to do with the guy Ant's trial. 'Cause y'all listening to all my calls, you know he approached me."

"Right. But after doing a background on him and his South American connection, we found he's almost as big a fish as the Jamaican. We want him," Agent Williams said.

"What that got to do with me? He wasn't part of my deal with y'all."

"You need to read your proffer again more closely; here's a copy." Agent Williams slid the piece of paper in front of him. "Read the third paragraph."

> *This proffer also includes the potential defendant to assist the government in any local, state, or federal investigations that may be unrelated to each other. Refusal of any form of*

cooperation can result in the forfeit of this proffer.

"What! What kind of shit is that?" Pookie said. "This is a cross. I want to talk to my lawyer."

Pookie did speak to Goldberg. The attorney explained to him that if he did not cooperate, the government could withdraw the original deal.

"You have to look at it like the government. Now you have access to two drug kingpins. They would never get an opportunity like this again in their careers."

"I should have never went against the grain. Now they really about to work me. I need you to see if I can stay free with no prison—this case is worth more than forty-one months jail time, man, and you know it," Pookie said.

"I'll see what I can do. The problem is the gun charge. It carries a mandatory minimum for convicted felons, and you are a convicted felon," Goldberg said.

"Just see what demonstration you can work out. I'm putting in too much work to go to prison too. That's crazy," Pookie said.

Goldberg was able to eliminate the chance of Pookie going to prison. In exchange, Pookie had to assist in bringing down John Gray and his organization. John was his cousin's cousin. He did not want to be uncovered as a snitch. He hoped that whenever they busted John, he would accept a plea, so that he wouldn't have to take the witness stand against him.

Pookie now understood how a person that was not intending to become a confidential informant could get caught up. Agents Williams and Frisco had assigned him a file number. It was 03-1981. It didn't take a rocket scientist to figure out that the last four digits were his birth year. Agent Williams asked him to refer to himself by his assigned C-I number if he ever had to call the office. *How did he get himself draped in cahoots with the law to need a number?* He was puzzled about how he'd got to the point of no return. He hoped that he would not ever need to utilize the agent's number. He preferred going through his attorney to communicate with the feds. He was learning that the feds could be as grimy and shiesty as the criminals they captured.

Pookie wished that he could turn back the hands of time. He would go back and erase the contact phone calls from John Gray to start. He admired the man. John was paid. He had built a multi-million dollar international business for himself, and that was a rare sight to behold in Pookie's neighborhood. Pookie decided that as soon as possible, he was relocate to a new state. He knew that as long as he remained in Ohio, the feds would worry him to death, and continue to monitor his life. He had no aspirations to remain a confidential informant for the federal government. It was a hectic position to put yourself in, and he wanted out. The game was dead and he wanted to get far away from it.

Chapter 19

The day that DEA Agent Williams was to run in on John Gray, Harry made sure that he remained close to the scene. The arrest of Gray would bring part of his plan for revenge together.

John notified Pookie on his cell phone that he would be arriving within the next twelve hours. That narrowed his arrival time down enough for Agent Williams to contact the coastguard and make sure that everyone was in place.

Harry studied his surroundings. He had to find something near death in order to be able to possess a physical form. He could have easily sat back and witnessed John being captured as a ghost, but having physical presence was much more intimate. When Harry was in the form of a ghost, it was as distant as watching something from a television. Harry wanted to be able to *feel* the anxiety and excitement of everyone involved. As a ghost, he could not feel anything. His natural state limited him to be an observer at most. Within a few moments of arriving on the scene, Harry spotted his prey. It was a beautiful, shiny black Raven. The Raven was surely dying. The bird was wounded. Someone had shot at him while in flight. Although still able to fly, the Raven's breathing became labored. Just as the bird's life began to slip away, Harry took over the physical body of the bird. It was moments like those that made Harry glad to be a ghost. He was flying! He always wanted to know how it felt to fly, and now he was soaring across the large body of water to join the coastguard. They were already in motion, heading toward John's yacht. Looking down at the shimmering water while the waves danced in the moonlight fascinated him. He would have to enter into the body of birds more often. They were also an easy target because dying birds were everywhere.

"Do not move. We are approaching," someone from the coastguard boat yelled out of a bullhorn. John heard himself say, "Ah, shit," out loud. His first impulse was to dart below the deck.

"Do not exit the deck!" yelled the same voice across the water, causing a slight echo in the darkness of the night.

Before he knew it, the coastguard boat was almost touching his. The passengers of the boat quickly attached their anchor to his yacht, and boarded in haste. It was at least twenty of them. Not all of the men were coastguard. He noticed that a few of the men had on dark blue jackets that read DEA in large letters in the center of the back of the coats. As he watched the intruders swarm the deck of his boat, his stomach began doing somersaults. One of the men dressed in a coastguard uniform walked swiftly to the stern. The man was dressed in a white shirt that was full of strips and awards.

"Good evening, Mr. Gray," the man said, without taking his eyes off of the panel at the stern.

While two officers frisked him, another ten ran below deck. John knew that he was dirty, but he could not comprehend that the coastguard knew that he was. He had taken many precautions to assure that he would be able to pass a random, routine search. To his amazement, he heard the locks being broken on his private container. There were three, along with a large combination chamber. None of the locks or chambers was in view. They were hidden by a series of hidden panels that was not visible by the naked eye.

"Bingo!" he heard a loud voice resonate. When the two officers that flanked him heard the officer below cry out, they immediately grabbed both his arms to contain him.

"Sir, you are under arrest. You have the right to remain silent...," the arresting officer proffered the Miranda. John did not pay attention to the words. None of the events happening to him was making any sense.

The two arresting officers escorted him to the deck of the coastguard boat in handcuffs.

"Sit down in this chair, Mr. Gray, until the captain boards the boat and we see exactly where he wants us to put you," one of his captors said.

John was livid. He listened to the sound of panels being ripped apart coming from his boat. One of the men had a sledgehammer in his hand. John cringed with each blow, as they ripped the boat apart, searching for additional contraband. He could not see what they were doing below deck, but the loud crashing noises let him know that they were trashing his property.

What was nagging at his mind was wondering who had set him up. He felt that the answer was there in his mind, but because of all the chaos that was unfolding around him, his mind refused to center on the matter, and that was even more frustrating.

"Radio into Miami Federal Detention Center and let them know that we will be bringing in a prisoner within the next hour," the captain ordered upon boarding the coastguard boat.

John's shoulders slumped over in defeat. He knew that it was game over. He had a lot of dope on that boat. His life as he knew it slowly began to play out in his head. He pictured his son, his sexy wife, his comfortable bedroom, and his nice plush office. As he sat in the chair under the custody of the FBI, DEA, coastguard, and no telling who else, John Gray wondered if he would ever get to see his home again in his lifetime.

Harry watched closely from the edge of the deck. He was posted up so that he would not miss one minute detail. Harry stared into the eyes of his target. He was disappointed when he could not connect with the soul of John gray. He also searched his eyes for fear. There was none. Harry wanted fear. He wanted to see defeat. John showed none of that, and Harry felt cheated. He was determined to make John Gray pay for being instrumental in taking his life.

John was booked into Miami Federal Detention Center at 2:30 a.m.

The detention center was located in the heart of downtown Miami. John thought that was a bad place to stick a large jail. The building stuck out like a giant among midgets. Unexpectedly, the staff had a laid-back attitude. They were not friendly, but also not rude. The majority of the men being checked in were immigrants. Many did not speak English. John noticed that the men did not seem to be stressed by the dirty environment. Many made pallets on the floor using each other's clothing. They slept fitfully. The noise, slamming doors, bright lights shining, or human traffic did not keep them awake. John envied them.

John made the dreaded call. He knew that Mary would be devastated.

"You have a collect call from an inmate in a federal prison," the operator said. Mary pressed five quickly without waiting for the prompt to finish speaking.

"John? What's wrong?" she asked anxiously.

"Bay, I don't want to talk too much over these phones because they are monitored. I was arrested a few hours ago. I am in Miami Federal Detention Center. I don't have a bond or anything," John said sadly. He heard Mary's voice break. He knew that she was trying to be strong, but the reality of the situation was taking its toll.

"John, are you alright? I am so scared for you," Mary said.

"Don't be. You watch too much TV, Mary." John teased to try to make light of the situation, and to keep her from crying. He knew that if she continued to cry, he would break down. The worse thing you could do in a holding cell with thirty men is to stand there and cry on the phone. That would be a kiss of death.

"I'm going to call you back in the morning. I need to locate the criminal attorney that I am going to use. I am going to call my assistant in the morning at my office, so let her know that I will be calling collect."

"John, I love you," Mary said weakly.

"I know you do. I love you too. Try to get some rest. I am going to need your strength, Mary. Good night," he said, hanging up to allow the next man waiting to use the phone.

John closed his eyes. He attempted to rest by propping against the cold hard wall. Men were lined shoulder to shoulder. There was no room to get comfortable on the steel slab. On each side of him were two black men, one older and one younger. Nobody complained that their skin had to touch. They all were consumed in their own fear. No one knew what their plight would be, but everyone knew that jail would be a part of their immediate future until court. John learned from the guard that processed him in that only a federal judge could set a bond at arraignment, or a bond hearing.

When John attended court, he was denied bond due to the amount of drugs that he was busted with. He was expecting as much. He hired two attorneys that were considered the best in the south. Donald Butler was a brown-complexioned black man that could have easily been his father, and Ralph Defranco. They were both a complete dream team.

It didn't take long for John to see that the rumors of what he heard about the federal sentencing guidelines were true. The reason why people said that you didn't need an attorney in the federal system was because the defense had no rights. The prosecutor carried and juggled the purse strings, and only the prosecutor could request any kind of downward departures or lesser sentences.

"I am not advising you to cooperate, but the government has offered you a deal if you are willing to bust your connect, and testify against them," Defranco said.

"That is not an option," John answered.

"Well, you know that with over eight hundred kilos, you are facing a life sentence?" Attorney Defranco said.

"I figured that. I looked at the sentencing guideline chart that they have available in the law library here. I am off the chart with the amount of weight that I had," John answered solemnly.

A week later, John was called to the visiting area to speak with both of his attorneys.

"The government has prepared a plea agreement for you that is around one hundred twenty to one hundred fifty months, not taking into account your criminal history. They want you to help them indict your connect and also all other players that are in the United States. They understand that unless you lure the foreign players to the States, it will be very difficult to get a conviction. Here it is. Look it over," Attorney Defranco said.

"We know that this whole thing is deep. It's your life. You have to make your own decision here," Attorney Butler added.

"I have thought it out. I will not play the snitch game with the feds. I am responsible for my own actions. I knew that it was a possibility that I could be locked down. I was hoping to get out the game before they caught up with me, but I didn't move fast enough."

"Well, just so you know, without the downward departure and substantial assistance, your plea agreement would carry a life sentence. We have to advise you of that," Attorney Butler said.

"I understand that life as I know it now is over. I have made up in my mind that I am going to sit down and write books, both fiction and non-fiction. As a man, if I don't stand for something, I will fall for anything. Like I said, when I was hustling,

I knew that it was against the law, and that there was always the possibility that I might be caught," John said.

John had looked at the statistics. He knew that over ninety percent of federal inmates chose to snitch in order to get lesser sentences. More than anything, he wanted to remain free or at least have a sentence that he could work with, but not at the expense of giving up his integrity and manhood. Mary did not agree. She felt that he should give up the entire nation in order to be home with her and their son. Mary was not in the game. The game of life had trade-offs. John had already begun to order writer's books and he subscribed to the *Writer's Digest Magazine*. He would not pity himself or lay around feeling sorry for himself. He would make his time work. He felt bad for his son. Fathers needed sons and sons needed fathers, but he would not become a rat under any circumstances, and would have to explain that to Mary and his son when the time came.

The prosecutors and agents were livid. They sat in the courtroom in a tense silence while John Gray was sentenced. They were not accustomed to defendants refusing to cooperate. The prosecutor decided that the best tactic would be not to make John Gray too upset with them in case they were able to convince him to cooperate under federal Rule 35. Rule 35 was when an inmate that was sentenced decided to cooperate after sentencing. Usually what would happen was an inmate would become tired of being incarcerated and then have their attorney or unit manager in the prison contact the prosecutor's office to make a deal. Federal court was the only area that a criminal could get out of prison after sentencing with a recommendation from the prosecutor.

The sentencing guidelines were mandatory and carved in stone by all federal judges. John received life in prison. He did not let Mary or anyone other than his two attorneys attend his sentencing. He did not want the drama. He just wanted to start his sentence.

John was transferred to Oklahoma Transfer Center, where he was designated to Beckley West Virginia. Transit was unlike anything he had ever witnesses in his life. John sat near the window on the large airplane and watched the vast trafficking of human cargo. The plane that he was on held one hundred twenty-four passengers. There were one hundred and twenty males, and four women. The women were placed in the front of the plane. Each passenger was shackled and handcuffed to a three-inch leather belt that was fastened in back of them around their waist. It was demeaning. The prisoners were forced to ride handcuffed and shackled for eight hours, with only one bathroom break. They were not uncuffed or unshackled when they used the bathroom. Each person had to wrestle to perform regular bodily functions. John had studied slavery. He'd seen movies, and he read books, but he never thought that he would experience the actual physical bondage of a slave in his lifetime. Coming off the plane in Oklahoma gave him a new respect for what his ancestors lived through. Many were in the awkward position that he was in for eight hours for many days. That thought helped him to endure the cutting pain of the shackles and the uncomfortable position of his arms being bound to his sides because of the handcuffs. John also noticed that the majority of the prisoners being rustled on and off of the airplane were minorities. Black and Hispanics comprised a large percentage of the prisoner population. Every now and then, a white face would appear. They looked almost out of place. He could tell that a lot of them were there for white-collar crimes. Many looked like nerds or computer geeks.

Before arriving at Oklahoma, the plane made several stops, picking up prisoners and dropping off. It was an assembly line. On the way to Oklahoma from Ohio, his plane stopped in Kentucky, Kansas City, and Tennessee to shuffle inmates around. When fifty would exit at one stop, fifty more prisoners would board. John watched in disgust out of the jet's window. After being designated to West Virginia, the plane stopped at Tampa, North Carolina, and then West Virginia, where he departed to an awaiting fifteen passenger van driven by U.S. Marshalls. A few of the men that had been in federal transit a few times called the ride "diesel therapy." They told John that the feds used transit as a way to break down a man's spirit. The ride had taken on a negative effect on John. He looked at the federal government in an entirely different light. He did not know that our country was into the mass warehousing of human beings. He had been caught up in running his businesses and living his life day to day, not knowing that people were suffering from modern slavery at an alarming rate. The thought was spine-chilling. He asked himself, *What has our country become? How has preying on the weak and poor become a business?* It was America's best-kept secret.

Once he got to prison, he had a lot of free time on his hands. He got a job in the law library. He decided to order his transcript, and to take a look at his case out of boredom. He found out that it was a confidential informant that had put the feds on him. It took him several months to find out that it was Loot's cousin Pookie. John didn't know that Pookie had been arrested and was working with the feds when he contacted Pookie through Loot's wife. Being in the system, John witnessed first hand how a weak person could get caught up in snitching. He was mad at himself for not getting out of the game when he had a chance.

His roommate was a homeless sort of guy. He wasn't a bad cellie. He was quiet, and reserved. The problem was he wanted to sleep in his coat and shoes, and have the window all the way open. The problem with that was the temperature fell drastically at night in the Allegheny Mountains, where the prison was located. The entire place was surrounded by the mountains. The man refused to remove his coat, hat or shoes at night. John tried to reason with him.

"Man, how about I buy you a brand new pair of long johns, so that you can be warm, and get you an extra blanket. I can't deal with this window being wide open at night like we're sleeping in a barn," John said.

His roommate outright refused.

The situation ended up with John Gray having his first fight in prison. His roomate's name was Jeff. He was a thin, muscular black man. His age was somewhere between thirty-five and fifty. John could not tell his age. From some of the things he mentioned, John felt that he may have been younger, and then he would sing the words to an old song that was old school. His lifestyle had been rough.

It started one night, when John attempted to shut the window. It was frost on the ground. Jeff got into the top bunk with all of his gear on.

"Man, I am about to close this window. I am not about to freeze tonight," John said.

"Naw. Leave it alone," Jeff said in his southern drawl. Jeff sat up on the top bunk. Was he about to try to flex on John? John hoped not. Although they were around the same height, John had him by at least forty pounds. Both men were six feet, but John weighed one hundred ninety pounds. Jeff was struggling to weigh in at a hundred and fifty pounds, plus he smoked roll-up cigarettes like they were the answer to eternal life.

"I said shut it, law boy," he said. Before he got down, John decided to get the upper hand on him, and cut the fight short. He quickly grabbed Jeff in a full Nelson headlock, and tried to pull his head off his body. Jeff could not get leverage from the top bunk. All he could do was try to hold on to the covers so that he would not tumble down on his head. John pulled him off the bed, after choking the life out of him. Jeff was weak when he tried to stand up. He tried to wager a strong swing at John. John did not give him a chance to get his bearings. He quickly drilled him to the body, until Jeff folded. John felt guilty. Jeff was no competition for him, and there was really no fight, but he had to get the window situation under control.

After the incident, John earned respect from the entire range. He bought Jeff a full set of long johns from the commissary, and gave him an extra blanket that he got from the clothing issue department. He wasn't trying to demean the man, he just wanted to be able to be warm. Both he and Jeff had long sentences, and the administration did not believe in changing rooms. Once they assigned you a roommate, you were stuck. John was determined to have peace of mind in his living area. Eventually, he and Jeff became alright. Jeff wasn't a talker, but both men were avid readers, so they shared and critiqued books.

It was when Jeff went for surgery outside the prison things started getting weird. One evening while John was about to doze off, he could have sworn that he saw the face of the man that he'd seen in the water. The face belonged to a white man that he'd never seen before. The man had blond colored hair and bluish gray eyes. Who was the man? Was it someone John was supposed to remember? And why was the vision coming to him, even in a prison cell? They are a few of the questions that John asked himself. He tried to recall if he'd ever met the man that belonged to the mysterious face. He could not recall. He graduated from college, and had a diverse group of associates while in school. Was the man part of his past? If so, what did he want from him? John ended up laying on his bed the remainder of the night, hoping that the vision would present some answers. The thing did not reappear. *Should he be afraid?* he asked himself. He was spooked.

Once Jeff returned to the room from his surgery, the vision did not return. However, John felt that someone was watching him at the most inopportune times. A few times when he was at work at the library, he felt a gush of cold air that made the hair on the back of his neck and arms stand up. He felt the presence of evil. He did not know if it was related to the incidents that he experienced with the gho...no. He could not bring himself to say the word. There were no such things as ghosts. This whole thing had to be some kind of psychic vision. There was no other logical explanation.

John received his final financial

update from his accountants. He was worth $144 million. The feds had stripped him of several assets, including his yacht, cars, and two vacation homes. Mary was allowed to keep the house that she and his son resided in because she worked a job with a decent income and John had made a reasonable amount of income from his business before he expanded into the illegal cargo. Also, he had made some smart investments. His portfolio was also all legal. He had started his investments while in college, so everything he had from that source of income they also could not confiscate. They were able to take close to $100 million in assets and money from him. He did not like that idea, but was glad that he had secured a chunk of what he had worked hard for. He was also happy that Mary would not have to work a day in her life if she chose not to, and that his son was well provided for. It made his time a lot easier.

John was surprised when he heard from Poppie. Poppie had been following his trial and his plight. He did not fear John giving him up, despite what he heard from his family members.

"The American will not do life for us. He will try to destroy us through our government," Poppie's cousins told him.

"I don't think that they will be able to expedite any of us. That's a large maybe. But I also do not think that John will rat," Poppie said. When the ordeal was behind them all, Poppie was glad to tell them all that he had told them so, and that John was a stand up man. It was time to put a plan into action. Poppie realized that John would have never received a life sentence if he had not tried to help Poppie recover after the change in the government.

He would not allow his friend to rot inside a U.S. federal prison. He also was not a coward, and lived by his integrity.

When John received Poppie's letter, he reread it ten times to make sure that he comprehended all of the hidden language in it:

Dear Amigo,

I sorry to hear that you not eating your favorite steak and lobster, but I see if I can help you to eat like you helped me in the past. The vending machines there have good honey buns. The vendors are just as sweet as the donuts. Say hi for me.

I will see you soon, my brother. Remember, nothing is as it seems, and the grass is greener on the other side of the water.

Your brother for life.

What in the world was Poppie talking about. John dared not think that he meant what he thought. He decided to wait it out, follow Poppie's advice in the letter, and let everything play out.

BOOK THREE

Chapter 20

Mary could not believe how her life had taken a turn for the worse. John was her life. He was her future and her past. She knew that some of his business deals were not kosher, but she never expected to be visiting him for the rest of their lives in federal prison. It was a very bitter pill to swallow, and she still had not accepted it as reality. Mary was a praying woman, and refused to give up hope. The only thing that was keeping her going was her son. When she looked at him, she saw his father in him. She didn't understand why John refused to cooperate with the authorities. She felt that he should have put his family first. She asked him more than once to cooperate in order to receive a lesser sentence, but each time he flatly refused. Deep inside she felt that her husband had abandoned his family. It was not a good feeling.

J.R. handled his father's departure in an age-appropriate way. He withdrew himself socially, and became closer to his dog, Judy E. The dog loved the additional attention. He talked to her, took her everywhere, spent many hours with her at the park playing Frisbee, and even cut school with her twice without being detected. The day that he skipped school, Judy E. and him roamed the streets. It was fun and adventurous. J.R. tried not to think about his father. He could not fathom that he would never be home again, so he blocked it out, and safely lived in his fantasy world.

Mary decided to quit her job and become a full-time mother to her son, since she was considered a single parent now. Her visits with John were frustrating most of the time. There was always a guard standing around assuring that they did not become too intimate with each other.

"You can only hug your visitor once coming in, and then once leaving," the guard explained during her first visit, where she hugged John and did not want to let him go. The guards even said something about John holding his son during the visit.

During the last few visits, John seemed more upbeat than usual. Mary wondered what was going on.

"Poppie contacted me," was all he was willing to share. She learned early in their marriage not to ask a lot of questions. Most of the time she did not want to hear the answers, so she didn't ask.

J.R. started to resent visiting his father. She didn't force him. He was at the age where he could decide whether or not he wanted to stand in a long line, be humiliated, and then be watched like a hostage. J.R. hated the visiting procedure. Mary did too, but a few hours with her husband was better than nothing at all. She missed his physical presence in the home terribly.

One afternoon while she was visiting John, J.R. decided to take a walk to the park. He was out of school on break. The day was warm, but the season was already changing. The leaves were turning from bright green to an array of fall colors.

At the park, they had a small pond. Children were not allowed to go in. It was forbidden because in some places the pond was more than ten feet deep. It was roped off. J.R. sat many days at the edge of the pond, throwing rocks in the water, watching them ripple. It was one of his favorite pastimes. Each time he held a contest, he tried to outdo his last throw. His arm was getting stronger, because he could toss the rocks clear to the other side of the pond. Judy E. always sat lazily while he tossed the rocks, seeming to be in a deep snooze. She was really getting up there in age. J.R. hoped that she would live forever. He had no friends. He didn't enjoy school, and he liked playing alone. Being an only child, he learned at a young age how to be self-sufficient.

Judy E. did something out of the ordinary. One afternoon, J.R. threw the rock in the water and Judy E. jumped in the pond after the rock. The dog's dash into the water was so unexpected, it alarmed J.R. initially, and caused him to be slow to react. It took a few seconds of watching Judy E. to see that she was drowning. Before Judy E. came up out of the water, J.R. quickly jumped in. The dog was moving further away from the edge of the pond. J.R. hoped that there was an adult watching. He was not a good swimmer, and had a phobia of deep water. Once he thought he had Judy E.'s collar, but it felt like the dog snatched away. He scrambled in the water. He had to save his dog. She was his best friend. He began to get frantic. He knew that he branched out too far, and the bottom of the pond was no longer up under him. Panic was beginning to set in, but not enough to desert his friend. Suddenly, Judy E. grabbed his pant leg between her teeth. The dog held on to his pant legs with a fierce grip, and pulled him down. J.R. needed to gasp a breath of fresh air. His chest was aching from not being able to breathe. He was frantic. He did not know what to do, and his reasoning was starting to fade. *Why was Judy E. holding on to his leg? Didn't she realize that she was killing them both?* He bent down, and tried to free his pant leg out of the dog's mouth. It seemed like an eternity, but was only a few seconds. Then it happened. J.R. sucked in water into his lungs and lost his breath. His chest burned like it was on fire. His last thoughts were of his mother and father, and how upset his mother would be when he didn't show up for dinner.

Chapter 21

Harry continued to put his plans into action, and it didn't take long before he got an opportunity to attack John Gray where it hurt most; his son. He worshiped the boy. It was his son that gave him hope and helped him to deal with the enormous sentence. Also he knew that J.R. and Mary were companions and they protected each other and brought comfort to one another in his absence. John expected J.R. to be the man that he wasn't. He also expected his son to steer away from crime. He'd left him a legacy. If J.R. chose not to, he would not have to work a day in his life. John's mission was to get his son primed for the world. Harry took full credit for removing the boy from John's life.

Judy E. was old. She'd been around the boy since he was a baby. The day that J.R. took her to the pond, Judy E. had already come close to dying in her sleep. She was perched by the door, and felt a sharp pain in her chest. She did not alert her owner. She simply lay still and let nature take its course. That is how Harry was able to take over. When they went to the pond, it was no longer Judy E., but Harry's ghost inside Judy E.'s canine body. Harry entered the dog's body just in time, and almost missed the opportunity by a half of a second. Harry was surprised that the boy did not suspect. He tried to walk slow, but found himself walking faster than a dog his age should. He also would not have entered the water if he was still Judy E. J.R. should have known. Judy E. also had a phobia of deep water, or any water. Even bathing the dog was a heavy chore. J.R. took her to the dog groomer, and Judy E. gave them their money's worth. She did not like water. Now the boy was dead. Harry was able to drown him. For a brief second, he thought about entering into the body of the boy. That would have been the ultimate vessel to commit complete chaos in John's life, but the boy was swiftly removed from his reach. J.R. went straight to heaven, bypassing purgatory at an alarming speed. Harry could not catch him if he wanted to. It was like that with some humans when they died, and also animals, but not many. Usually he had a few seconds to enter them before they crossed over to the next life.

The day that her son drowned, Mary had started to have an eerie feeling from the beginning of the day. She knew that something bad was going to happen, but she didn't know what it was going to be.

J.R. did not show up for dinner. Mary always allowed him a grace period after school to act like a child. She usually knew where he was at all times. Today she checked the usual spots, and he was not there. Although she knew that something wasn't right, her emotions were not prepared to digest the fact that her son may never come home again. She had not made a full adjustment from losing her husband to the prison system.

Mary called the police department and was told that it was too early to put in a missing person report, but that they would comb the neighborhood and look for anything they considered suspicious.

"He is traveling with a beige dog, that is old, and moves slow," Mary said. She described to the officers what her son was wearing last.

By 10 p.m. she still had not heard a word. She sat on the couch staring blankly at the television screen. The news came on and caught her attention.

"A young boy and his dog were found drowned at Metro Park. There was no sign of foul play that we know of. The name has not been released because the body has not been identified. Here are photos of the clothing items that the boy was wearing.... If you have any clues of who the boy is, please call..." The newscaster continued to recite the drowning, giving the telephone number to call to give information about the boy. Mary did not get the number. She was afraid to move, but also afraid not to move.

"It has to be some kind of mistake," she said aloud as she grabbed her sweater and headed for the front door with her car keys in tow. As she started the car, she realized that she didn't have a clue to where she was going. She called information on her cell phone.

"Could you give me the number of the morgue?" she asked unsteadily. She felt like she was going to pass out behind the wheel, but she made herself focus.

"County Morgue, may I help you?" the man said.

Mary told him that she had watched the news and that they showed a drowning and she needed to come to make sure that the person drowned was not her son.

"How long has your son been missing, Ma'am, and how old is he?" the attendant asked. Mary answered his questions. He was silent. The body that had come in was estimated to be the age of her missing son. He had worked the morgue too long to believe in coincidence, but he would not reveal his thoughts to the stranger. He knew that she was behind the wheel from the noises in the background, and he did not want to cause her to have an accident. He gave her instructions to get to their building, and told her to ask for him by name when she arrived.

Mary asked for the man by name. He came out quickly, leading her down a long sterile hallway to an elevator at the end of the hall. The building smelled like a mixture of formaldehyde and sulfur. It was a bad smell. Mary was anxious to get out of the building.

"Step this way," the man said softly. He led her to a room with a closed door. In the room there were two gurneys. Both of them were covered with white sheets, hiding their contents that protruded from under the sheets like a row of pillows hidden under a bedspread.

"Are you alright?" the attendant asked.

"No. I am not. I just need to get this over with," she said.

He walked to the gurney that was farthest from them and closest to the wall. He stood very close to her in order to steady her if he needed to. He pulled the sheet back. As she looked at the body of her dead son on the gurney, Mary's knees gave out on her simultaneously as she let out a piercing scream.

"Noooooooooo! Not my baby!" she cried. The attendant was not able to contain her. She buckled on the floor, holding her stomach while in a kneeling fetal position.

"Ma'am, I am so sorry. Let me help you up," the attendant said. He had dealt with many family members with the shocking news of their loved one's death. Still, he was not immune. He felt every bit of the lady's pain.

"Nooo! God please nooo! How can you take my baby from me! He is all I have!" she screamed.

When he tried to help her up, she slapped his hand away. He did not take it personal. He had seen the gentlest of creatures go haywire. At fifty years old, his grandson was the same age of the victim. He could not imagine losing his grandson and having to come and publicly identify his body. He hoped that his children and grandchildren preceded him in death.

"John Gray, please report to the chaplain's office," a loud voice bellowed from the paging system. John could not imagine what the chaplain's office wanted with him. He was not actively involved in any of the church services or religious groups. All prisoners knew that a page or visit from the prison chaplain was always bad news. They were the official bearer of bad news. They only came to inmates when a loved one listed on their visiting list had either died or was near death. Sickness was not considered serious enough to warrant a chaplain visit. The chaplain would intervene only for death notices and deathbed notifications. As John walked to the chaplain's office, his stomach began to flip. He was full of anxiety. He was afraid that something might have happened to Mary. His visiting list only had his closest relatives, and Mary was at the top of the list. As he neared the small single-story building that sat in the middle of the compound, he tried to brace himself for the news.

"Hi, Mr. Gray. Please sit down," the chaplain ordered. Chaplain Wallace had been employed as a chaplain for as long as she could remember. She received her training as soon as she completed high school, and started as a state prison chaplain. She was now one season from retirement, and had worked in three states and seven prisons throughout the lifetime of her career.

"I don't want to sit. This has made my nerves bad. What is it, Chaplain?" John asked.

"It's your son. He was involved in a

drowning accident. He didn't make it," the chaplain said softly.

John did not miss the clues. She had already referred to his son as "was," and past tense. His mind heard all the clues, but did not register them with his heart at that moment.

"My son? My son is gone?" he said to the air, as if attempting to figure out the most complex equation in the world.

"Mr. Gray, please have a seat. I would like for you to call your wife. She is waiting for your call."

John sat down roughly. He was not aware of his actions anymore. He was just going through the motions. Mary picked up the phone on the first ring.

"Mrs. Gray, just a moment, I have your husband here," the chaplain said, as she handed the phone to John. "I will be right outside the door if you need me, Mr. Gray. I am going to give you and your wife some privacy."

John did not hear a word the chaplain said.

"John! Our baby is gone! John, I don't know what to do! How can I live without him?" Mary cried. John had been alright before he heard Mary's desperation. He couldn't hold back anymore. He cried also. They both cried silently together, sharing only sniffling noises. At least twenty minutes later, John reached deep within to attempt to comfort Mary. There was nothing there. He could not talk. He could only cry, so they cried some more together.

Losing his son was the hardest thing John had ever had to endure. The prison did allow him to attend a personal viewing of his son's body. He was escorted in handcuffs and shackles, and guarded heavily by four officers, with two flanking his body at all times. John was required to pay for the officers' travel, and also all of their salaries and expenses. He did not even notice the money. He was grateful that he was allowed to say goodbye to his son and have some type of closure.

After the funeral, Mary was given a mild sedative, and John's sister June who had originally introduced them practically moved in with her. June was a big help. She cooked, cleaned, and talked to Mary, making sure she was never alone. John did not have that comfort. He endured his pain alone. A male prison was not the environment that one displayed any type of weakness. John cried softly alone in his pillow at night, but was always careful to allow anyone to see any traces of his tears or his pain. His weight dropped quickly, and often he was jerked awake by nightmares of an evil creature drowning his son, or the acute awareness of a physical presence in his room that was *not* sentenced there. He didn't have anyone to talk to about his feelings. He had to man-up. Although he felt like his heart had been torn out of his chest, he was forced to go on with his day-to-day life and activities in prison. Prison did not allow a person a mourning period, time to be alone, or any privacy. It was business as usual. Part of that was good, because John was able to pour himself into his work and not be able to hurt for the loss of his son during working hours. It was at night that he felt he couldn't breathe as he lay on his bunk.

He received a second letter from Poppie. It read:

Dear Amigo,

You have my deepest sympathy about the loss of your little man. He is in heaven with your parents, and they are glad to see him and take care of him until you get there. Know that he is surrounded by love if that makes you feel any better. I know you are in pain, but take a moment to try the vending system there. Also I talked to Mary. Call home more often, Amigo—she needs to grieve with you. Hope to touch down with you soon.

Your brother for life.

With everything that had happened to him so quickly, John had not followed up on Poppie's first message. He decided to take the time to see what his friend had up. He missed his friend and needed to talk to him because he did understand him. Poppie's culture was very different from how John was raised, but it was the different that intrigued John. Poppie believed in drama and visions. There was also a little voodoo and idolatry mixed into his beliefs. He was also very superstitious. Poppie believed that death came in threes, that a bird flying inside a building was as clear an omen of death to come as a terminal illness setting in. Poppie believed that the proper combination of a person's hair mixed with different feathers and particles could do damage to the target, and he believed in not cutting his hair except during a full moon, and all other kinds of religious preoccupations. John always found him entertaining, but could not commit to believe in it all. Now, at his weakest moment in life, he wished he had a stronger spiritual foundation or belief to fall back on.

He found the vender at one of the vending machines on the other side of the compound. He knew that they were refilling the machines because John saw his vending truck parked in front of the entrance of one of the units, full of cakes, honey buns, and other snacks.

When John approached the man, he was bent over a basket, filling up one section of the machine.

"Hey, how you doing?" John said.

The man turned to look at who might be addressing him. At first he thought he was another irate inmate complaining about money lost in the machine. He was prepared to give him the speech. They did not give refunds. Inmates had to write to their company office in Miami and wait for reimbursement. When he looked at the man's face, he realized that it could be the man that he'd been trying to make contact with. He got excited. It could only be God bringing the man to him!

"What is your name, sir?" the vendor asked, holding his breath.

"John Gray. And what is yours?"

"Ah! Julio! I am. I am excited to see you," Julio said anxiously. He looked around to make sure he was not in ear shot, and then he began to whisper.

"My uncle is help you. He sent you word. You do your end. He do his. Here is a note for you from him."

The small enveloped was sealed and taped. John noticed Poppie's handwriting and smiled. The man was always up to something.

"I will see you back here a week from today, same time. Nice meet you," Julio said, standing tall with a big smile, extending his hand.

John waited until he got off work to read the letter. He did not want to make the staff suspicious, and ask him to see what he was reading. Some of them were very nosy like that, but for the most part they left him alone.

Once he was alone in his room, lying on his bunk, he opened the letter. It read:

Dear Amigo:

If you are reading this, you have met my nephew, Julio. I have devised an escape route for you. What I do not know is the best way for you to buy yourself as much time as needed before you are missed. I have everything set up for you. The next letter you receive from me will be after you are out of there. It will have everything you need to get to me safely. I will see you soon, my friend.

Your brother for life.

Escape?

John had to ask himself, *Did he really want to be a fugitive from the law the rest of his life?* He did not take more than a minute to weigh out his options. Rot in prison, or age as a fugitive. He picked the second choice. Once he made up in his mind to escape, that was all he thought about. It dawned on him that within a month's time he could be a free man. He began daydreaming out of prison. The movie, *Shawshank Redemption*, that was always one of his favorites, came on television and he could not be still while watching it. He saw himself over and over again as Andy, and Poppie as Morgan Freeman. Each time he thought about it, he smiled openly. If anyone would have been paying attention to him, they would have thought that the death of his son had driven him mad. He went from sulking to smiling within days.

John was only able to buy himself six hours. He went to sick call and got an idle by complaining of flu-like symptoms. Because at least one hundred men were sick with the flu, it was not questionable. Instead of meeting Julio at the site where he met him the previous week, he had to meet him in a more open space. That would cause more eyes to see him, and he did not like that idea, but there was no other way. The spot that Julio suggested only gave him ninety minutes, and that was not enough time to get far away. John's Bunkie was at work. Work call was at 7:30 a.m., so most of the inmates were working. There were a few of them working on the compound in the yard. Because John was low key, no one really paid him any attention. At 9:45 a.m., he did not walk up to Julio, but instead got into his small truck on the passenger's side. It was very awkward. Inmates were not allowed in the trucks or vehicles of contractors or vendors. Inmates did drive around in government owned vehicles all day, and also ride as passengers to complete the tasks of the prison. Also the different work crews had white government trucks. Julio's was bright red, and full of snacks for the vending machines.

John was very nervous. He knew that it was a one-shot deal. If he screwed up, he knew that his custody level would be so high that he would never be able to walk a compound again. His sentence was too big for that. John knew that he would go crazy being locked down in a cell, but he had to take a chance. He had to try, although it was a one-shot deal.

Julio noticed him quickly. John liked

that in him already. He was not slow. But then, John knew Poppie. He would not send anyone to get John that was slow. It was a very dangerous task. The person sent to help him escape would ultimately end up in federal prison, behind bars with him. It was high risk for everyone.

Julio jumped inside the truck.

"Get in back. Go through the small window there, and then slide under the sodas. It is a hidden area for you. I will readjust the sodas after you in," Julio said.

John quickly climbed through the small square window that separated the front seat from the back of the truck and its cargo. The window could slide open or shut. John wished that it would open up just a few more inches, but he managed to squeeze through. It was awkward and tight. He also realized that he wasn't as young as he used to be. He literally fell on his face in the back of the truck. He moved fast, climbed inside the tight compartment and positioned himself. Before he could settle in, he heard Julio swiftly sliding the stacks of sodas over the compartment. The metal storage bin was tight, dark, and hard, but the thought of freedom made it all seem mild. John would endure the tight fit for days in order to see daylight.

The escape plan went smoothly. The small booth checked Julio's visitor's pass, looked at the merchandise, used a long pole with a mirror attached to look up under the truck, and then bid Julio a good day.

John waited for Julio to come back and uncover him to let him out. He was beginning to feel a cramp in his left thigh. He always received a cramp in his left thigh, especially when he was having sex in the same position for a long time. John Gray was no longer a spring chicken. His body made him realize that as it betrayed him regularly. Then to make matters worse, after a long period of time, he had to pee. It was all the bumps it was encountering. John did not have a watch on, but he knew that they had been riding awhile.

Chapter 22

It turned out that they had been riding for hours. Julio finally stopped the truck. John felt the truck come to a complete stop. He held his breath. He heard the sodas being slid over the metal lid.

"Come on up," Julio said.

"Sheeeessh. I thought you forgot me in here. How long have I been in here?"

"About five hours. We are in Akron, Ohio now," Julio said.

"Do you think I can call my wife since we're in Ohio?"

"No. I have strict instructions. One of them is to make sure that you do not make any phone calls."

"That's messed up," John said.

"Here, take these, and go inside the bathroom to change," Julio said.

He handed John a small workout duffle bag, with another small carry bag. John quickly exited into the men's room. Poppie thought of everything. He had a jherri curl wig attached to a pair of glasses, and a pair of clothing that was as square as square could get. The pants were bonded-polyester knit navy blue colored, with a stretch waist. His top was tight. The jacket was a plaid print, with a large wingtip collar. The shoes were comfortable Hush Puppies. John looked like he jumped off a picture from the 70s. There was also a billfold and a large wallet. Inside the wallet was a passport in the name of John Smith. It had his picture on it. John smiled. *Where did Poppie get such a recent picture of him from?* The man was a genius. The wallet also had his birth certificate, social security card, and a few credit cards in the name of John Smith.

The billfold had crisp one hundred dollar bills stuffed in it. There was also a one-way ticket to Peru inside in the name of John Smith. John discarded the clothing that he was wearing in the trashcan, and also the duffle bag. He wanted to travel as light as possible. When he stepped out in the open, he noticed a small newspaper stand with snacks and magazines. He purchased a book called *The Game Is Dead* by Tee Turpin, and the *USA TODAY* newspaper. When he checked the board for his flight, he saw that he had an hour before he departed. There was a layover in Atlanta, Georgia for an hour, and then he would be flown directly to Peru.

Julio had disappeared when he came out of the bathroom. He was back. He had also changed clothes.

"I won't be traveling with you, friend. I have to take business here. It has been real," Julio said, shaking John's hand aggressively. John dropped the handshake and gave him a manly hug.

"Thank you for my life back, man," John said.

"It was nothing. I am now a very rich man!" Julio said.

John watched him get into a small compact car and pull off quickly. He looked around the airport. *Should he be paranoid? How many people at the prison were involved in his escape?* He felt naked. He had so many questions that did not have immediate answers. He wanted to call his wife. *Who would know?* he thought. Then he decided against it. Her phone and home would most definitely be monitored. Most of the prisoners he saw captured were crazy enough to return to their homes. He longed for Mary, but it would have to wait.

The time seemed to be moving in slow motion, but he finally boarded. It was a cheap flight to Atlanta. Akron Airport used the flight to go to Atlanta daily. The flight was packed with college students, businessmen, and a few others. He blended right in.

In Atlanta it was much of the same. He waited in an inconspicuous corner of the airport. No one noticed him. He engrossed himself in his book until they announced the boarding of his flight. Because of the terrorist watch, his driver's license and passport had been scanned three times. Each time it went through with flying colors. Poppie was a magician.

The final check point came from the immigration officers as he exited the plane.

"What is your destination?"

"Touring Peru," John answered.

"How long will you be staying?"

"Three weeks."

"How much cash do you have?"

"About four thousand dollars," John answered.

"Do you have anything to declare?"

"No, sir."

The border patrol agent stepped aside to allow John to exit the airport. He was so excited about being officially free and away from the United States that he almost ran his ride over.

"Mr. John?" a short, brightly dressed, balding man said.

"Yeah."

"Come with me. I am your driver."

John hoped that the man wasn't a fed, but it was too late to worry about that. If he was a fed, John had no escape route planned and was busted anyway, so he followed him diligently. When the driver pulled up to a small one-story building that resembled a warehouse, Poppie dashed out of the door.

"Ahhh! My friend is here!" he yelled. He ran to embrace John.

John had never been so happy to see a familiar face. He knew that he was finally safe when he saw Poppie. Peru was Poppie's territory. John did not know anything about maneuvering around South America without Poppie. The two men caught up on business. It was very expensive to get John out of prison. Poppie had spent eleven million. He was about to retire with a sick wife and only his pension. He stated that if he got fired, at least he would be able to live out his life in dignity. Poppie's cousin, Julio, also charged one million. The owner of the vending company charged three million. He said that he would have to restructure and sell his company to one of the locals after John's escape. Poppie did not complain or voice it, but the eleven million put him in the poor house. He had to even borrow the last million from one of the drug lords in Peru. He would never leave a friend in prison, and he would never mention such a thing to John.

Poppie didn't have to. Because he tried hard to avoid the money part of the conversation, John knew that he was in financial trouble.

"How and where can I get a large chunk of my money transferred to, and how soon can I call Mary?" John asked after being in Peru for forty-eight hours.

"I need you to wait until the end of the week. We are establishing a phone that is good, and a secured line. The person you can send it to is my brother. He is in good with the new government, and any amount will not be questioned."

"Good."

John transferred by using a wire transfer service fifty million dollars to Poppie's brother's account. He issued a check to Poppie for ten million.

"I don't know what it cost to get me here, son, there's no price tag on freedom, but I wanted to hit you off," John said.

"You didn't have to do that. Friends step up when needed."

"Yeah, they do. That is why I am stepping up now," John said.

Poppie was always crazy about John, but he now understood why. John Gray was a good man. He was too valuable to leave rotting in a federal prison. Poppie was glad that he had broke hisself to bring his friend to South America with him. He did have an ulterior motive also. John was American. There was plenty of cocaine in Peru and Ecuador, but no outlet for his crop. Poppie knew that with time he could recruit John back into the business. He knew that John could never enter the United States again without being arrested, but he also knew that John knew a lot of Americans who might be willing to be a mule. John was a long shot, but his only shot. He did like the man, but it was also survival of the fittest. Poppie needed money. In Ecuador he had no other options.

John bought him a small house in Peru. His money went a long way because of the value being ten times more than the currency there. He was considered rich. Poppie sent his sister and his niece to live with John to care for him. At first John was very uncomfortable with having two women in the house with him, but after a few days, they learned each other's routine and managed to say out of each other's way.

John had talked to Mary in detail. He told her that he would not be allowed to enter the United States ever again. She cried, but said that she was happy that he was free. He wanted to see Mary bad. He had not had a chance to hold her since they lost their son. He also wanted to see if he could make her pregnant again. He needed Mary. He needed sex.

"I am getting my affairs in order here," Mary told him on more than one occasion.

"You are allowed to go back to the States. I just can't go with you, so come see me, and then go back. I need you," he pleaded.

"I can't just drop everything like that, John," Mary said.

He needed his wife. He needed her bad. He hadn't had sex in months, and he had a big present for her.

Chapter 23

Mary had mixed feelings about John being out. She was happy that he was out of prison, but she did not want to relocate to South America. Her family, her job and all of her friends were in Ohio. She did not want to go.

Then she also had another big problem. Mary was seeing another man. For the first time in her life, she was doing her. She felt guilty each time she went to visit John. She wondered, *Did he suspect? Did he feel anything different about her?* She felt that since their marriage John had been faithful. That made her feel more guilty. It wasn't anything that was planned. After John's arrest, two federal agents came to talk to Mary about the activities of her husband. She had seen the role of good cop-bad cop enough times to recognize it. She thought that Agent Frisco and Agent Williams were playing the role when Agent Williams began to act extremely nice to her, while Agent Frisco treated her rudely.

She never shared the visits from the agents with her husband because she did not want him to be stressed about it. He was stressed about the entire case.

Agent Williams insisted that she call him Tony. At first she was very uncomfortable with it, and ignored his request. She also corrected him each time that he called her Mary.

"We didn't go to high school together. We are not friends, Mr. Williams. Call me Mrs. Gray, please," she told him repeatedly. Each time he would laugh and call her Mary, as if he didn't hear what she said. At first it aggravated her, but after a while she began to find him amusing. He would be at her house when she pulled in the drive from work. He would often be at her job in the background watching her, and a few times he even appeared at her church! The man was crazy. He didn't talk most of the time. Many times he simply watched her intently. Even when she didn't see him, Mary knew that he was somewhere near. Once the aggravation wore off, she started to perform as if she were in front of an audience. Mary did not know that not only was she under physical surveillance, but also the feds had her phone tapped, and a hidden tracking device stuck up under her car, along with two small cameras in her bedroom and near the front door. Tony was the assigned monitor. There was a safe in the bedroom that was placed there by Mary's husband. The feds waited for her to enter the safe. It was no way that Mary could be innocent of federal conspiracy and open that safe. The safe was well hidden in the corner of the room behind a one hundred fifty pound bureau. Unless a person was looking for it, they would not notice the slight pocket in the wallpaper directly on the seam. When Mary was questioned, she told both of the agents that she was not aware of a safe of any kind in her home or anywhere else. Agent Frisco felt that Mary was a bold faced liar. Agent Williams had a gut feeling that she was telling the truth. Agent Frisco accused him of thinking with his second head instead of his first. Agent Williams was assigned to watch. They had the authority to add Mary to a superseding indictment even after John was sentenced for federal conspiracy.

Agent Williams did not start out early in life with aspirations of being a DEA agent. His life took a turn of events that almost landed him in jail. His only brother, Terry Williams, chose the other side of the fence early. Terry was willing to try anything and everything. The two boys were unsupervised. There was no father figure in the home, and their mother had to work three jobs to make ends meet. Terry was three years older than Tony and was his babysitter, confidant, disciplinarian, and his best friend. Tony looked up to Terry. Terry was the father that he had never met or had.

Terry decided one afternoon that the two of them would rob the neighborhood dope house. Terry was seventeen. Tony was only fourteen years old. Terry knew everyone in the neighborhood well. Although he had not entered into the dope game, the owner, Big Mike, paid him a few dollars to clean his yard, mow his lawn, and other odd jobs. Big Mike liked Terry. Terry did not like Big Mike, but he concealed his disgust. Big Mike was a fat, greedy, lazy, bugger-eating slouch. All he did was sit on the couch all day passing gas and giving orders. He had five runners that were allowed to enter the house, and then a lot of young street runners. He had attempted to recruit Terry and his brother, but Terry had other plans for him.

"Naw, I don't wanna be no runner. Imma help you out," Terry told Big Mike.

"Let me find out you a sissy or momma's boy. Every real nigga in the city wanna work for me, and you rather be the maintenance man?" Big Mike teased. He thought that the idea was hilarious. Terry was fuming but he didn't trip because he knew that he would get the last laugh.

He set up the robbery sweet. He knew where the money stash was and the dope stash. He already had a buyer on the Westside that would unload the dope off his hands. The Puerto Ricans were always looking for bargain prices, and would not betray him by telling anyone.

Terry geared up in a hoodie and a ski mask. He also covered his brother's face. He stole a pistol from his best friend's house that was not missed. When he pulled up on Big Mike, the fool was dead asleep. Terry tiptoed toward the door with his brother on the other side as the look out. He was two seconds from having close to two hundred thousand dollars and three kilos of dope. The duffle bag was heavy, but he was handling it with one hand. Just as he approached the door to exit, Big Mike sat up abruptly from the sleeping position on the front couch near the door.

"What the hell? What is this?" he yelled.

Terry darted toward the door, but was a half a second too late. Big Mike shot him in the back with a 358 magnum. He was dead before his body hit the ground. Quickly Big Mike grabbed the duffle bag and ran it back to his room. He threw the bag in the closet. Police sirens were already on their way. The noise was loud and close.

Big Mike assessed the situation. He was dirty. He had a house full of money and dope, and a body lying in front of his door. It was no way he could do anything with the body. After stashing the bag, he waited on the police.

"Hey! Where do you think you're going?" a police officer asked Tony.

"Home. It is past my curfew, so I am trying to beat my mother home," he said nervously. He was scared out of his wits. He had tried to talk his brother out of the robbery, but Terry's mind had been made up. He also heard the shot and the loud thump that followed the shot. He felt that something was terribly wrong with the whole thing. He prayed that Terry was alright and would follow him home soon.

"Yeah. You had better high tail it off the streets. You are way past curfew," the officer scolded.

Tony did high tail it home. He did not stop for breath or to look around for his brother. His mother was working third shift at a nursing home as a nurse's aide. She would not return home until 7 a.m. Her shift was 10 p.m. to 6 a.m. Tony climbed into his twin bed in the room he shared with his brother, shaking uncontrollably. While waiting on his brother, he dozed off more from fear than from being sleepy.

By the time his mother arrived home the next morning there was still no Terry.

"Where is your brother?" his mother asked, waking him up.

"I don't know, Ma," he lied.

"Get up, Sweetie. I need you to help me find him. I have already called off work today, and I really couldn't afford it, but your brother has never stayed out all night, and I want to find him," she said.

While they were out in the neighborhood checking with Terry's friends, they missed the first call from the police station. The call that changed Tony's life came later that evening. His mother had been pacing the floor since they returned. She could not sit down. Tony felt guilty because he knew that there was a problem and that he had last seen his brother.

The phone rang, making both of them jump.

"May I speak to a Mrs. Williams?" the voice said.

"This is she."

"Mrs. Williams, I am sending two officers to your house. We have a few questions for you, and we need to talk to you," the voice said.

"Alright. I will be here. You have my address?"

"Yes, we do. See you in about ten minutes."

Tony wanted to tell his mother what he knew, but he could not. He had waited too late, and she would be angry. She feared either of her sons being involved in crime. It was hard trying to raise two young men single-handedly with no help. She felt guilty often because she had to work three jobs to make ends meet. She hoped that Terry hadn't gone and gotten himself arrested.

"Mrs. Williams, we will get right to the point. Your son, Terry Williams, has been shot. He is dead. We also think that your youngest son was involved," the officer said. He gave her a moment to let it all sink in. She was speechless. The officer was not expecting her to react so calmly, but was glad that she did.

"How did he die?" Mrs. Williams asked.

"We have made an arrest. It appears that he was attempting to rob a well-known drug dealer. We also have information that your youngest son was posted outside the door as the lookout. We would like to speak to him also if possible," the officer explained.

"Tony, do you want to talk to the officers?" his mother asked.

"No, Ma. I don't know anything," Tony said between sobs. He could not believe that Big Mike had shot and killed his brother. It all seemed like a bad dream that he needed to wake up from.

"Well, we are going to leave and let you be, Ma'am, but if your son remembers anything else about the incident, give us a call. We have pretty much started to wrap up the case. We have the perpetrator in custody, and the weapon. He admitted to shooting your son, and that is how we knew who your son was. The case is pretty much closed, Ma'am. We will be sending your son's remains over to the morgue, where you can contact them and make further arrangements. Sorry about your loss," the officer said. He attempted to extend a smile, but Mrs. Williams appeared to be in a daze.

"Go to your room, Tony. I need to be alone," Mrs. Williams said to her only living child. Tony was glad to go to his room. He did not believe in lying to his mother, and also his heart felt like it was torn out of his chest. His brother was his life.

Everything died down, but not Tony's passion to bust drug dealers. Drug dealers were indirectly responsible for his brother's murder. When he saw the ad for DEA agents, he did not hesitate to apply. He made his mother very proud. Although she never got over the loss of Terry, she poured her attention and time into Tony, hoping that it would make a difference. It did. She even quit one of her jobs. Three jobs was too hard. She needed to invest time in her son before she lost him to the streets also. Tony was very successful in his career, and moved up the promotion ladder quickly. He was dedicated to his work. Although he was considered handsome, he did not get into girls except to fulfill his physical needs. He feared love. He felt that if he took on a wife and had a child, they would be eaten alive by the streets like his brother was. He was not able to share his intense fear of commitment with his mother or anyone. Anytime a woman tried to become too close, he ran like hell, ending the relationship without warning. He was terrified of commitment, and even more terrified of intimacy.

That is the state that he was in when he began to observe Mary. He followed the woman everywhere. He watched how she interacted at work with the public. He noticed how compassionate she was at church and with her friends. He listened to every single conversation she had with her husband and her friends. Tony did not know how it happened, but somewhere in his mind it clicked that Mary was safe. He determined that if he ever committed, h would want to find a woman like Mary. Tony decided to subtly lay his game down. From listening to all of her conversations with her friends and her pastor, Tony knew that John was the only man that Mary knew. That excited him more. That was unheard of also. Tony wanted to mold her. He wanted to give her another child after her loss. He wanted to make her smile, but didn't know how to tell her so he extended plenty of kindness. It was ridiculous. He told Mary that running to carry her bags, washing her car, and rushing to open doors for her when she was in reach was part of his job. She was naïve enough to believe him at first.

It was overhearing the phone sex that Mary had with her husband that caught him up. John was not the only one who was able to cum listening to Mary talk dirty. She looked extremely innocent. She was the perfect lady in public and in church, but was a true freak. Tony wanted her. Mary did not have a clue in the beginning.

Tony decided to go for broke. He asked her to attend a movie with him.

"Would you like to go view Tyler Perry's new movie, *Why Did I Get Married?* It has an awesome cast," he asked.

"I wanted to see that movie, but I did not want to go alone. Yes. I would love to go."

And that is how it started. A movie led to dinner, dinner led to dancing, where Mary taught him how to line dance, and he taught her how to dance to his tune in bed. She had not been to bed with many men. He was able to tell that. By the time he realized what was happening to them, they both were sprung. His investigation of her had been compromised long ago, and his fellow agent, Frisco, knew it. It was too late to turn back. Tony never considered marriage, but he wanted to wife Mary and he wanted her to be his baby's momma. It was some deep stuff.

Mary felt torn. She knew that she had violated all codes that John set for her, and God. She betrayed her husband in every way possible. From her first meetings with Tony, she was the one who gave him the intricate details of John's hidden compartment on his boat. She didn't know what the contents would be, but she knew, and she told Tony.

Now John had escaped. Tony asked her a few times a day if she had heard from John. She always answered that she did not want to talk about John, because she did not want to lie to Tony. She was in a very sticky situation, and did not know how to release herself. She could not leave the States, because she would not leave Tony. Mary also held a lot of resentment because John chose prison over their family, and abandoned her and their son. Mary felt that if John would have cooperated, he could have saved their son from dying, because he had always protected them. She did not understand his decision to go to prison, and she did not wish to. Her son was dead, and no one could bring him back.

To top it off, Mary had missed her cycle. Tony asked her not to use protection and assured her that he was not sleeping with anyone else. She believed him because every hour on the hour she either heard from him or saw him, unless they both were sleeping. He texted her, called her, visited her at her job, and made pop up calls everywhere. Neither one of them were able to stay away from each other.

John did not have a clue that his wife was cheating. Mary had changed after the death of their son. It was obvious, but also normal. He had changed also. John thought that Mary's hesitation to see him was from her not wanting to leave her family. She had always been close to her parents and the church members that she grew up with. Still, John felt that she should have been glad to come with him. He felt that their lives were growing in different directions since he escaped from prison. He wanted to see Mary, but she gave nothing but resistance. His patience was wearing thin.

Mary gave him an ultimatum. She wanted to meet John in Miami.

"Mary, you know I can't come back to the States. It would be suicide," John kept explaining to her. Finally, she wore down his resolve.

"I don't agree with it. You should never return to the States. You are a free man here. Why can't she come here?" Poppie asked.

John tried to explain that Mary did not want to leave the States yet, and that she could not break away from her job duties without raising suspicion.

"My friend, wait until she can take a

vacation. I do not feel good about you going back into the States. It's a bad feeling I have," Poppie said.

"I need you to help me. I need a new make. I don't want to use the name I am living under here. I will also need a disguise," John told him. Poppie was not happy, but he agreed to help his friend.

Despite Mary's insistence, John refused to give her an arrival time.

"I need you to reserve a room at the Marriott Suites for a week. I will be there within the week. I don't want to announce my time of arrival, Mary. I want to surprise you," John told her. Part of him wanted to surprise her, but also, he wanted to be able to elude the feds in case they were still monitoring her calls. He called her at work, and had her change her cell phone regularly, but one could never be too careful with the feds.

John was going to see his wife. He was horny and as desperate to see her as a hostage is for freedom. Only Mary would do, and he was going to be with his wife.

Chapter 24

John did not have to do a lot to prepare for his trip. The transfer of his money into Poppie's brother's account went smoothly, so money was not an issue. He packed a small bag. He did not plan on staying more than a couple of days because of the risk. He hoped that after spending time with Mary, he would be able to convince her to come back with him or join him soon. John was excited as if it was their first date. He had not been able to hold Mary since the death of their son. They needed to talk about it. Also, he wanted to know if Mary wanted more kids. He did. He would love to have a few more, and both of them were not getting any younger. More than anything, he wanted to work out the details of their future. John felt that he could resolve Mary's hesitation about moving to South America by talking to her face-to-face.

Before his trip, he talked to Mary regularly. He hoped that she was as excited to see him as he was her.

Mary was very nervous. Tony had convinced her to set her husband up. John could not be arrested in South America. The only way that they would be able to bring justice to his escape is by him entering on

United States grounds. Tony did not think that John would be stupid enough to return to the States, but he was glad that he was. Busting John would eliminate him from being competition for good. Maybe he would end up marrying Mary after all. Tony was determined to make sure that John knew that Mary was a part of his bust.

Mary rented the hotel room a block from the airport. She rented the honeymoon suite. It was a small apartment. She did not know if Tony would bust John at the airport, or wait until he entered the hotel room. Tony refused to share any of the details with her. He said that the information was classified and sensitive.

Mary had made a conscious choice. She wanted to be with Tony.

The same afternoon that she rented the suite, Tony came to her. They had confirmed her pregnancy. It was his baby. Tony was ecstatic. He was in love with Mary. There was no getting around it. She also loved him. If his supervisor found out that they were sleeping together, he would have removed him from the case immediately. Tony had compromised the entire operation. He was supposed to be gathering evidence in order to indict Mary. Instead he was trying to wife her in the very near future.

If Tony would not have been daydreaming about Mary, he would have seen the reckless young driver coming toward him a little too fast for comfort. By the time he noticed, the car was on him. The impact was forceful and knocked his body in the air. He came down with a loud thud. As his body hit the ground, his head smashed in the back. The impact would have killed him, except Harry Treason took the opportunity to take over his body before he was completely dead. Tony was no longer of this world. His physical self was dead, but Harry would use him as long as the vehicle lasted in order to accomplish his goal.

When Tony went to visit Mary one last time, Mary noticed that he had on a scully. She had seen him in a scully, but the weather did not call for it. He was also acting weird.

"What's wrong? Are you tired?" Mary asked.

"Yeah, I am. Let me give you a bath so that we both can unwind," Tony said.

"Are you getting in with me?"

"No. I just want to touch you and take care of you," Tony said. Mary smiled. Tony knew how to spoil her. She loved it when he was in that mind frame. She stripped naked in front of him, but he seemed to be preoccupied. She knew how to get his attention, so she hurried up in the bathroom to get ready for him. Also she needed to get him in bed one last time before John showed. She could not have him visiting anymore, and she had already had the room twenty-four hours. John was still in South America by the sounds in the background when they talked, but she could not take any chances. She did not want John to find out about Tony, although she wanted to talk to him about a legal separation or even divorce.

She had no intention of going to South America to live.

Harry waited until he was sure that Mary was comfortably situated. Then he entered the bathroom. She had already lit the candles around the tub with aromatherapy like they both liked it. The bathroom looked very cozy, and the lights were dim.

"Come here," she said, wanting to kiss him.

"I'm coming," he said. Mary did not notice the edge in his voice.

"Hurry up, boy."

Tony was fumbling with something by the sink, but she couldn't see what it was. When he turned around, he had the blow dryer in his hand.

"What are you going to do with that?" Mary asked.

"I saw something on TV that turned me on. I wanted to try it on you," he said.

"Alright. But be careful with that thing," she warned.

Tony turned on the hair dryer, and then walked toward the large bathtub. Mary lay back to close her eyes. Tony always did freaky stuff to her. She didn't know what he had up, but she knew that he would not disappoint her. Before she could open her eyes, he threw the dryer into the water, electrocuting her instantly. Harry smiled at his work.

"That's one more part of the puzzle gone," he said, as he exited the hotel room. He had thought about entering Mary's body, but decided he would have better leverage using Tony's corpse to bust John.

Chapter 25 — The Epilogue

Tony felt that John was on his way. The calls to Mary had ceased to come in. Tony had her cell phone and was monitoring her calls. He had waited for this moment from the day that he lost his life and left the world of the living to enter the world of the dead. John Gray owed him his life. He had planned on torturing him so that he lost his sanity while he served a life sentence in prison, but had been cheated out of that chance by the very thing he hated most. Drug dealers. Poppie had helped him escape. Now he would come face to face with the man that was everything he despised.

Tony set up shop. Although he appeared to be sluggish to his co-workers, everyone bought the idea that he had been up a few days without sleep. In order for everything to come together, he had to keep Mary's death low key. To do that, he made sure that he was the first one on the scene, since he had her under surveillance. He was also the one to report it to the hotel manager.

The hotel manager agreed to keep the incident quiet. The hotel was full of guests, and he did not want to damage business. They decided to keep it quiet for as long as possible. Harry did not want John to get wind of Mary's death and cancel.

Harry had already decided that he would take John Gray into custody, but he would not live to do the time. Harry would find a way to take his life this time before he was able to get away.

John got off the plane feeling good. He was going to finally get to see Mary! He was on a natural high. He was also very nervous. He was not dumb. If the feds caught him in the United States, he knew that his life would be over. The rest of his life would be spent in federal prison, in a maximum security cell, under the worse conditions. He had read about the building of super-max federal prisons. The inmates never saw daylight. They lived inside a cell never knowing if the sun was shining or not, or if it was day or night. John was an outdoor person, and did not know how he would survive that kind of agony. When he weighed it out, he decided that Mary was worth it. He would die for her. He realized that he just might be put to the test, but being able to see her face was worth the chance.

He decided to think out his strategy. He had to decide exactly how he was going to exit the States, and if he was able to convince Mary to go with him, he wanted to map out how he would proceed. He decided that he would buy a cup of coffee and a Danish and sit for ten minutes to gather his thoughts.

While sitting at the café, John surveyed his surroundings. It was at that moment he noticed a suspicious looking white man that looked like a fed. John tuned in. The man was focused on the board and the gate that the arriving flights came in. Although he tried to appear as if he was looking at the newspaper in front of him, John made him instantly. Because of his disguise, the agent did not notice him coming through. He had even changed the color of his skin. He had on a three hundred dollar makeup job from nothing but one of the best. His skin was a very light tan. He blended in with all of the other Latino men who worked at the airport. The makeup did not cover his skin under his clothing, but he knew that only Mary would see his real color. One of his concerns was how to get the skin tone back on once he showered or had to wash it off. He tried to bring the girl that made him up, but she refused. She was afraid to leave her country. In the United States she could have made a fortune, but in her country there was hardly any business so she worked at funeral homes to prepare the dead to look alive and peaceful at their final viewing. Three hundred dollars was equivalent to three thousand dollars in her country. John offered her ten thousand dollars to travel with him, plus all expenses. She outright refused. She had never spent a night away from home.

John brought the makeup kit along with him anyway.

He checked out his area closely. The airport was indeed under federal surveillance. Despite how hard the agents tried to appear incognito, they were all obvious. His name was also Juan Ramos on his passport and license. That helped also because they were looking for an African-American. Even his hair was Spanish. His mustache and slight accent also. All of the agents were tuned in to the departing passengers of the flight arriving at Miami. A gut instinct told John to clear the area. He exited the airport quickly, hailing a cab.

"Take me to a car rental place," he ordered. The cabbie took him about a mile to Avis Rent-a-Car.

John rented a small Chevy Cavalier. He wanted to be able to move around undetected. He drove to Fort Lauderdale, got a hotel room, and then drove back to Miami. During the twenty-minute drive he was trying to figure out how he would get into the hotel room to warn Mary. He got his chance. He ran smack into a worker that had the same build and everything as him.

"How much would you charge me for your outfit?" John asked.

"Why do you want it?" he asked.

"You don't need to know that. How much?"

"One hundred dollars. American only," he said.

John quickly peeled off a bill.

"Where can I change in peace at?" John asked the worker.

"In here." He took John to a small bathroom area for men. He gave John his clothes without hesitation. He had on boxer shorts and a T-shirt up under his outfit. In his bag, he had a pair of shorts and sneakers. It looked like he was on his way to the gym.

When John entered Mary's room with the master key, he saw that she was not there. It was weird. The room was spotless. He picked up the phone and made sure that he was in the right room. It was her room. He had verified that she rented the room for one week. It was only the third day. Something about the entire setup did not feel right. *Where the heck was Mary?* he thought. After waiting all this time, she was not available for him. John eased out of the room undetected.

He called her phone. There was no answer. He called her job. There was also no answer. He was not crazy enough to use his voice. He paid a stranger to ask for her. When her job asked what it was regarding, the woman told them her reservation. Something was definitely wrong. John drove back to Fort Lauderdale to figure out his next move. Poppie was right. It was stupid of him to come to the States. It was also very dangerous.

Things did not look good. John did not want to face what his gut was telling him. Mary had to have an explanation for everything. But the more he thought about it, pieces of the puzzle started coming together. Mary's insistence on him coming to Miami. Her demand for him to enter the States. Her outright refusal to come to South America, which didn't make sense at all, the more he thought about it.

The feds were intent on looking for their target. John was willing to bet his fortune that they were staking out him on that incoming flight. There was no other explanation.

John decided to give Mary the benefit of the doubt until he was able to talk to her. Still, the entire scene was foul. John smelled a rat, and once he stepped back to check out the situation, he knew that Mary had crossed him in some type of way.

Harry saw John when he exited, and he also attempted to follow him out of the airport. He did follow him to the hotel room. The body that he took over had lost a lot of blood, and could not make a physical arrest. Also, because half of his head was missing, he decided to put distance between him and the other federal agents. Besides, he wanted John for himself.

The worst thing happened. Before he was able to do anything, the body of Anthony Williams expired on him. Bodies only lasted a short time. The amount of time they lasted depended on the amount of damage that had been done while they were alive. The body of Agent Anthony Williams simply expired, and dropped to the ground with a loud thud. Harry quickly transformed back into a ghost. He saw John enter the hotel room looking for Mary. He watched him move, but could not do anything about it at the time. He was determined to keep a close eye on John. John would not get away from him again. He would have his life.

John could not get in touch with Mary. He decided to take a chance and call her father after one week of trying each day.

"You haven't heard?" Pastor Turpin asked.

"Heard what?"

"Mary died by accident in a hotel room in Miami. We are still trying to figure out why she was in Miami," the pastor said, grief stricken.

John was silent for a moment.

"I will get back with you, Reverend Turpin," he said, as he hung up. John cried in his hotel room openly. He was not able to attend the funeral or viewing of the body, due to his fugitive status. Mary was laid to rest at her church, with her father leading the ceremony.

With Mary gone, there was nothing else linking him to the States. John prepared for his exit. He also requested a copy of the autopsy and death certificate for his records. That was his only closure.

When he got the piece of certified mail, John was once again devastated. It said that Mary Gray was pregnant. The big problem with that was they had not had sex in many months. It was no way that it could have been his baby. John cried again, but the second time it was for the betrayal. He would never know who the mystery man was that Mary was seeing. He would never see Mary again. His son was gone. The life in America as he knew it was gone. It was nothing but bad memories and trouble for him in his birth country.

John exited the country as smoothly as he came in. Although his makeup job was not as professional as for his coming, he was undetected. He did not leave from Miami. He decided that he would take a flight from Fort Lauderdale, in order to stop any trials that might have been set up.

"I am sorry about your loss," Poppie's sister Maria Linda told him. John had temporarily forgot that he left two women in his house while he traveled. He had so much on his mind.

Before going to the States, Maria Linda had been openly flirting with him and trying to seduce him, but he had ignored her. His heart and mind were on seeing Mary, and making love to his wife. When he arrived back at the house, this time when Maria Linda attempted to seduce him, he let her. She came into his room wearing a short, sexy bathrobe. The silk material clung to her body, showing off her shapely curves. She was not built like Mary, but John was a man who had been deprived of a woman's touch for too long. His body became wide awake at the sight and smell of her. She came to the side of his bed.

"Is there anything I can get you?" she asked, staring him in his eyes. She was openly flirting.

"Yeah. Sleep with me tonight," he said.

He didn't have to ask her twice. Maria Linda climbed in the bed with him, snuggling close to him. John gave her what she came for.

Maria Linda did not crowd him. She allowed him to work through his grief. John had so many questions. *Who was the man that Mary was sleeping with before she died? Who was the baby by that she was carrying? How did the feds know when and where he was coming into the States?*

John would not be able to rest until he got answers.

He spent time to himself over the next few days, but did not sleep peacefully. The same face that he saw in the water, and the presence that had followed him even inside his prison cell had started to haunt him at night again. The only time John was able to rest was when he prayed hard.

He did not know where his life would take him, but what he did know was that THE GAME IS DEAD.

Note from the author

Although this story had a metaphorical meaning, the truth is that the game as we once knew it is dead.

Throughout the last century, hustling has changed drastically. The foundation was formed by a handful of crime families that were mafia affiliated. The term "soldier," "good fellow," and "family," were all created by the Godfathers of the century. Today, all of the real soldiers and bosses are in federal prison, serving real sentences. These men and women are standing alone. On the frontline, as soldiers in a pool of cutthroats. Back in the day, any hustler that was checking real money came in contact with the hierarchy of the boss or his families, and lived by the same creed.

There was respect for each other, understanding for the next man's struggle, even if you hated his guts, and snitching was rare or unheard of. To be a snitch when the game was alive was a public weakness and embarrassment. It was not accepted. The

Omerta prohibited snitches from eating and sometimes from living. The crime families ran the cities with iron fists.

Any young'un coming out in this mess today needs to understand that THE GAME IS DEAD. The power that the crime families held in the palm of their hands' is dissolved. The federal government broke up the mafia families and transferred the power to U.S. attorneys, aka U.S. prosecutors. Now they rule the game. National statistics state that ninety percent of inmates in prison are snitches. Also, three out of five minority males are in prison or on probation. Women are being sentenced at three hundred times higher than males. The feds make you an offer that you cannot refuse! They have Rule 35(b), substantial assistance departures, and outright immunity from a wide array of crimes if you are willing to cooperate fully with them.

The government took over where the mafia left off. They own the courts, banks, politicians, and the media. They hold the purse strings for your life. My advice to young people that may be disillusioned by the game is "Don't believe the hype!" Today that is all it is. The real way to outsmart the system as it stands is to do the opposite of statistics; go to school, educate yourself, and pull up your family and loved ones around you. Be too legit to quit. Prison has become the new modern slavery, with the Department of Justice becoming the plantation owners. The story is fiction, remember, THE GAME IS DEAD.

www.ingramcontent.com/pod-product-compliance
Lightning Source LLC
LaVergne TN
LVHW091021080826
845145LV00002B/323

* 9 7 8 0 9 8 2 1 7 4 9 3 7 *